LILAH'S GUIDE to HOYLE

13

13

ROBERT J. S. T. MCCARTNEY
ALBERT J. DEBUSSCHERE III

A.B.Normal
Publishing and Media Group
Anything but normal.

A.B.Normal Publishing and Media Group
PO Box 31311
Knoxville, TN 37930
www.abnormalpublishing.com

Publisher's note: The story, all names, characters, and incidents portrayed in this production are fictitious. No identification with actual persons (living or deceased), places, buildings, and products is intended or should be inferred.

Library of Congress Control Number: 2016919914

Hardcover ISBN: 978-0-9983930-7-0

Paperback ISBN: 978-0-9983930-1-8

Kindle ASIN: B01MRXTTLK

Edited by Rachel Small. Cover art and design by Chuck Regan.

Lilah's Guide to Hoyle / Robert J. McCartney & Albert J. Debusschere III — First Revision Print 2025. Published in Knoxville, TN.

CONTENTS

To my family.

Thanks to my friend, Joe Debusschere, for the opportunity to start something awesome and for helping me find my passion.

To Dad.

To whatever remainder of my sanity remains.

"You can be anything you want to be, despite what other people may say. My advice is this: be anything but normal."

Robert J. McCartney

A Note from the Author
Boop

When I first penned *Lilah's Guide to Hoyle, Requiem for Lilith,* and the original *Bob,* I carried a clear vision of how the pieces would fit together. Though it diverged from Al's original concept, countless late-night discussions eventually won him over.

Later, I sensed something far grander on the horizon and chose to expand beyond the original incarnation. Returning to these stories years later, I have reshaped them, refined the endgame, and woven in fresh layers. The result feels stronger and more faithful to the world I have always wanted to create.

The overall flow remains familiar, but new material now threads through every tale. As in *This Is Bob* and *Requiem for Lilith,* some roles are clarified, others are hinted at, and the stage is set for a saga that I hope will be as compelling as a whole as it is in each part. You may begin to sense where the story is heading and who the key players are, and I look forward to seeing what conclusions you draw on your own.

My aim has always been to let each story stand on its own—relatable, shareable, and open enough that you can jump in at any point and still know where you are. Certain connections and details, however, will only fully reveal themselves over time. I trust you'll enjoy the revisions and additions, and I invite you to accompany me on the long road to the finale.

Continue to exercise that free will.

Until next time,

RJM

P.S. You've been booped.

Look for the dark humor novel *This is Bob: A Guide to Not Dying (Mostly)*, available along with other titles.

Book One in the Willborne Saga.

Visit www.abnormalpublishing.com for free stories, information, and more.

Scan this QR Code for *This is Bob: A Guide to Not Dying (Mostly)*.

Read Book Two in the Willborne Saga *Requiem for Lilith*,
available along with other titles.

Visit www.abnormalpublishing.com for free stories,
information, and more.

Scan this QR code for
Requiem for Lilith

PROLOGUE

The Gambit

I WATCH HER. CARDS in hand. Every move ripples far beyond her knowing. The deck is quiet, but every hand is seen. Every bet, every bluff, every fold—etched into memory before it lands.

She sits sharp-eyed, clever, thinking herself the master of the game. Counting chips, reading tells, planning plays, believing the outcome rests in her hands. She is practiced. She is patient. She is proud. And yet, she forgets: the house always wins.

A chip spins, arcs through the air, and lands with a soft clatter. A card slides from the deck—sleek, secret, whispered only to the hand that deals it. Another card slides. Another chip clatters. Stacks rise. Stacks fall. Fingers hover. Hearts quiver.

Shuffle. Cut. Deal. Bluff. Raise. Fold.

The rhythm predates memory. The motion is preordained. The players believe they act. But the game moves them. The house moves them. The unseen hand moves them.

No one sees the croupier in the shadows. No one guesses the stakes are more than gold, more than pride, more than survival. This is a game of skill, of cunning, of guile—but not all hands are *theirs* to play.

And I—

I will record it all. Every chip, every fold, every shadowed movement of the pieces yet to fall. They do not see me. They do not know. They believe they play.

And the final hand will be played. The chips will be counted. The table will be cleared.

And the house—ah, yes—the house always wins.

1

♠

THE SQUEAL OF THE storefront door escaped into the late-night streets. In the cafe window, there patiently sat a dim red-and-blue neon-lit sign that read OPEN. Inside, the bubble-faced wall clock's tired hands rested on the eleven. Closing time was near. Justine and Wade's was a grand place for a classic cheesesteak sandwich. Especially when it came to the hunger pangs that violently struck a particular man at night, it was a relatively quaint place—small but held many surprises.

The yellow walls seemed to amplify the cheesy aromatherapy. Red and green tiles formed right triangles that drew a perfect arrow to the back of the joint. Various square tables were arranged in rows, with chairs placed in pairs, and menus and paper cards were perfectly littered across the tabletops. A long counter with several black barstools ran parallel to the back wall, keeping the kitchen secret. A small trove of treasure tucked itself into the counter's far-left nook. One of the gems was in its showcase: fresh-baked cookies—most had been picked over, save for a handful—and the old-fashioned cash register. Justine and Wade's was vacant except for the few night owls here and there.

An odd pair of men stalked to the back counter in hot pursuit of their next catch of the night. The clicks and clacks of their heels on the tile resembled a fanfare—one fit for a diplomat. Reaching his target, the taller, more fit of the duo straddled a barstool and exhaled a sigh of relief. His larger partner fumbled for balance a bit before settling in. Having finally conquered the structure, he sat atop it proudly, grinning slightly at his counterpart.

"I'm telling you, Dana, between the recent cuts to the police and fire department budgets and the school district's cuts—oh, and let's not forget the 'recent unexplained failure' of the dam—we're looking at a complete governmental shutdown in the next few months." The more prominent man emphasized the quote from the local paper's recent headline with air quotes. "I swear to God, if they were to dig six feet below town square, they would find that the whole damn town is balanced on a fucking toothpick."

Dana rolled his eyes and ran his fingers through his hair dismissively. "So, Walt, what's so urgent we had to stop in so late? You know she's not going to be too thrilled about this."

Walter chuckled heartily. "Ah. She knows me. Besides, she knows I love her for it." He gently patted his belly with a smirk. "After all, what's life without a little risk, huh?"

Dana shook his head in disbelief. "Running a few red lights and flying through downtown to stop for a sandwich isn't exactly clear-cut protocol. Remember that last stunt you pulled when Brad was in the car with us?"

A tall, slender woman in her late thirties approached the counter. She wore a food-stained white T-shirt and black jeans, and her long chestnut hair was tightly wound up in a bun with a black hairnet. Her amber eyes crinkled with her bright smile, reaching her high cheekbones. Every time, the pair stopped for a bite here (Walter would often jest that Wade had married Justine to have her model for him instead of keeping it as a career). "Hello, boys, will it be the usual?" Her voice—sweet and friendly, as always.

Dana and Walter nodded and smiled. Justine replied with a slight nod before returning to the kitchen.

Walter grunted. "Protocol? Bah. You need to lighten up, Dana. Are you seriously going to lecture me on protocol while the world around us is going to hell? Besides, it's not just any sandwich we stopped for. . ." Walter trailed off as two glasses—sweet iced tea and Coke—slid towards him. "You know what I mean?" Walter grinned at Dana, leaned over the counter, and yelled toward the kitchen. "Thanks, Justine, baby! I love you that much more!"

"Next time, I'll make sure Wade's closing! Then we'll see if you still confess your love for me!" Justine yelled back. The starving duo giggled and sipped their refreshments.

After several moments, Justine delivered two trays of piping-hot cheesesteak sandwiches. "Here you go, boys. Enjoy."

With glee, Walter gave his newfound, genuinely handcrafted prized possession the once-over before setting out to devour it wholly. Dana looked on in sheer amazement. "I swear to God, Walt, where do you put it all?"

Walter chuckled as he took another bite, gently patting his belly again. "In one great way, then out another."

Dana wrinkled his nose. "Eh, I hardly say that's great, especially for me. I mean, damn."

Walter burst into laughter; flecks of lettuce flew out of his mouth. "Dana, you're going to kill me one of these days!"

The sound of his cell phone drew Dana away from the sight. He sighed as he wrangled it out of its warm bed, deep within his coat pocket. "Deupree, here." He snapped his fingers at Walter, who, like a sad puppy, put down his sandwich in obedience. "Got it. Yeah, we'll be getting back out in a few minutes." Dana tucked the phone back to sleep. Walter grunted as he went back to finishing the remnants of his food. "Five minutes, that's about all we've got. Then we gotta head back for some paperwork." Dana glanced down at his wristwatch. "The night's almost over, and I'd like to get some sleep."

After he finished his sandwich, Dana opened his wallet and laid out a twenty-dollar bill. He leaned on the counter and shouted to the kitchen. "Thanks, Justine! We'll see ya next time." He grinned at Walter. "You know, earlier."

Justine bellowed back from beyond the grill. "Thanks, love! You know me, always here!"

Dana stood up and gave Walter a pat on the back, sending him into a brief coughing fit, then strolled outside to light a cigarette. The cold air writhed its way past his warm lips, down into the depths of his lungs. He saw a shadowy figure fading into the distance as he ignited his Zippo. He exhaled a strong puff and shrugged it off as a late-night commuter before going to Walter's beaten-up brown 1971 Oldsmobile Delta 88 sedan.

)

"What are you doing? I said, keep your hands where I can see them!" The New England spring night turned the mugger's words into barely visible tufts of vapor. Beads of sweat dotted his forehead. The gun in his hand trembled as his gaze fell to the girl's hands.

They moved precisely: her pale right hand slid into the jet-black purse slung low on her side while her left hovered between them, a universal "hold on a minute" gesture. The tips of each of her slender fingers matched the darkness of her outfit.

As the girl's hands moved in the moment's tension, the mugger's gaze drifted beneath the typical high-school goth attire. She was attractive. Her dark-brown eyes were magnified by thin-rimmed glasses that almost seemed exaggerated, declaring, 'Here's a nerd, and she's proud of it.'

"This is all I have. Please, don't hurt me," the girl said, her tone calm. He might have noticed the unnerving calmness in her voice, but he wasn't focused enough.

His gaze snapped from the smooth curve of her cheek to her right hand, now retracting from her purse. The gun mirrored her movement. Her hand paused momentarily, then continued its path, revealing something that caught him completely off guard: a deck of playing cards.

"All life is a gamble," she began. "We go to sleep every night, comfortably betting that we'll wake up the next morning. When we hop in our cars, we take a chance that some drunk driver might be around the corner, driving a hundred miles an hour, about to end our lives." Her words sliced through the silence of 3:00 a.m. Something in the way she spoke and moved sent a chill down his spine. He hoped she hadn't noticed. He had the gun, he told himself. He was in control of the situation.

Her left hand dropped, meeting her right hand in front of her chest. Together, they began a rhythmic dance of cutting and shuffling the deck. As the cards slid between her fingers, an unspoken presence lingered. It wasn't just her making these choices—something, somewhere, watched with interest. The air shifted, pressure building behind her eyes as if something unseen smiled at her from the periphery of her vision. The cards fell on each other, flipping and turning in her hands. "Every day, loved ones and strangers die. Deaths in the hundreds, in the thousands, in the hundreds of thousands!" she continued, her voice taking on a manic edge. "Some deaths are obscure; others are known worldwide—murder, suicide, disease, old age. But one thing ties us all together—our very mortality. It makes us equal. We are all just fodder for the cause that is life, fodder for progress!"

A whisper brushed against the edge of her consciousness as the cards twisted and turned in her hands almost hypnotically. It was not words but something more profound—like smoke curling around the edges of her awareness. The sensation was intoxicating and exhilarating, as though the universe was holding its breath, waiting for the outcome.

Some of her words seemed to cut deep, dropping his guard as tearful memories resurfaced. Then came the dance of cards and fingers before him, the smooth paper and skin performing together. Occasionally, he glimpsed flashes of red and black. As the cards twisted and turned in her hands, the tension in his body slowly melted away. His gun slumped to his side. His guard was gone.

"Now, I'm going to offer you a rare opportunity," she murmured. "I'll show you just how fragile your life is." Her tone dropped, becoming almost casual. "I will determine your fate with five cards." She stopped, drawing four cards from the top of the deck. "Let's see." She showed him the first card. "Ace of spades." She drew the second card. "Eight of spades. But that's not important." She revealed the third card. "Eight of clubs." A sinister grin spread across her lips as she drew the fourth card, her voice low and predatory with each word. "Ace of clubs. Mister, you are a dead man, and this is your hand."

Her left hand moved back to the deck but didn't touch it this time. The man's head buzzed as the top card began to float. Like an avalanche closing in, her final words reverberated in his mind, louder and louder. He brought the gun up again, pointing it straight at her heart. The card spun slowly atop the deck, and the little goth girl's expression shifted from slight malevolence to sadistic glee; her eyes glowed a dim, demonic green.

His hands trembled uncontrollably. No matter how hard he willed it, his finger wouldn't pull the trigger. The card was halfway spun, and his right eye turned bloodshot as vessels burst behind his retina. He gasped, the realization dawning too late. *Damn it all . . . He told me I was only supposed to scare her!*

He clenched his eyes shut and, with all his might, willed his finger to move—and it did.

The crash was deafening. Scalding sparks erupted in the usually quiet alleyway. Warm blood splattered across the brick walls, across the now-visible ten of spades, and the girl's grinning face and glasses.

The mugger's lifeless body hit the ground, blood pouring from the right side of his face and from what remained of his arm. The ten of spades nestled back into the deck as she returned the cards to her purse. She pulled out a paperback book with the word HOYLE in large white letters on the cover and a pen. Flipping through the pages, she stopped at the chapter "Two Pair" and scribbled in the margin: Ten of spades makes guns explode.

As she turned away from the scene, a quiet hum remained deep in her bones, a dull green flicker in the dark. Somewhere, something was still smiling.

)

Dana groaned. *Three hours. Only three whole damn hours since I got to go home.* He flicked his wrist, setting his Zippo ablaze. Slowly, he brought it up to light his cigarette. He inhaled deeply, then sighed just as heavily. The smoke poured from his lungs into the night, swirling high toward the heavens before dissipating. He glanced up at the sky. Fire-escape ladders and clotheslines obstructed the view from the alleyway. The stars gawked at the bizarre scene below. He tapped his cigarette behind him, and a slight gust of wind carried the ashes away. He rubbed his broad, stubble-ridden face and stared down at the massive pool of blood, catching the glow of his figure. His black hair absorbed the pale moonlight but reflected off the blue in his eyes. He noted the sacks that had formed under his eyes and rubbed an eye briefly. He sighed again, shifting his weight. *For once, I'd like a decent night's sleep.*

A moment passed. Dana grunted as he pressed himself off the cold brick wall behind him. He spotted his partner coming from the car, which was well-equipped. Both were detectives first grade who'd soared fast up the ranks in their fifteen years since the academy. During those years, they encountered some of the worst (and best) humanity had to offer. To them, death came with the job, mostly while riding in the backseat. Dana puffed on his cigarette again as he turned to Walter—the man was indeed a wrecking ball as he plowed through the crowd, carrying two drinks in his hands and a doughnut in his teeth. Nearing middle age, he had well-trimmed salt-and-pepper hair, and his round face was adorned with square-rimmed glasses, subtly masking his dark green eyes.

"Move! Move! Oh, hey, Janice. Hey, hey, alright, alright! I want everyone to clear the area right now! C'mon, guys, get this section roped off already!"

"Alright, Walter, let's see what we got for us tonight," Dana said, attempting to clear his throat.

"You doing alright there, Dana? You don't look so well." Walter spoke in his usual low and relaxed tone, but to Dana, it was like nails on a chalkboard at that moment.

Dana shivered and shook his head. "Yeah, just lack of sleep. You know how it is." Walter nodded as he looked down the alley past his partner.

Dana took Walter's coffee offering, and Walter grabbed the doughnut from his mouth with his now free hand. The two began an intimate stroll, surveying the bloodbath of a scene scattered over a good portion of the alleyway.

A bloody shell of a man lay sprawling against an apartment building. The bricks were coated in their original red and in the crimson that had sprayed wildly in all directions. The ground—cold, brown, dirty, and littered with teeth, skull fragments, and fingers, as well as other various organs and tissues—was covered in a rusty pool proliferating under the man's blood-soaked tawny jacket, bloodied blue jeans, and blood-caked black boots.

Dana read the preliminary report aloud. "The victim is a John Doe, Caucasian male, late thirties to mid-forties, five feet eleven inches, black hair, eye color unknown. No form of identification was found on his person."

The baffled duo scanned the body thoroughly. The man's skull had been blown nearly utterly into oblivion. His lower jaw was obliterated. Strands of hair still clung to what remained of the right side of his skull. Skin and muscle, in a red-and-white marble pattern, curled outward toward the back of what was left of that part of his head. The right ear was gone somewhere. The nose dangled loosely from a small flap of skin. The left eye was too far destroyed to determine its color (what remained hung and swayed in the inner part of the man's gouged skull). The throat was exposed like an open hatchback, stopping just at the top of the sternum. The man's right arm was in shreds, while the area from the forearm to the hand was utterly decimated. Pieces littered the alleyway. The scene was a decoupage of death: a kaleidoscope in honor of murder.

"So, what do you think? Possibly another suicide?" Walter was the first to begin his inspection. He examined the blood sprays on the ground and walls and then the grotesque wound on what was left of the man's face, all while chomping down on his glazed doughnut.

"Nah, I think it was a mugging gone bad. Here," Dana pointed at the blood sprays— "you see how these run? It's as if something . . . inside of him exploded."

Walter lightly chuckled. "So, you mean to say his face just exploded clean off his mug?"

Dana leered at his partner. "Do you think that whatever gun he had would be able to take his face clean off, Walter? Perhaps he brought along a stick of dynamite? A little wiring here and there, light, set, and match! Oh, or maybe, yes, this is it—a group of baddies chased him down. Demons possessed all of them. Hell, even the devil himself was there! They all gathered around him and formed a pentagram, mumbled a bunch of nonsense about some sacrifice for 'his dark infernal majesty,' and made his gun explode—which ended up taking his face clear off. Why yes, that is precisely what happened. I can see it now." Dana made extravagant gestures of explosions and of the victim's face sliding off.

Walter rolled his eyes as Dana continued his rant. "And there he goes, folks . . ."

Dana began pacing in the immediate area. "See, he decided that since there was no other way, he figured, fuck trying to find an honest method of earning, with how the economy and life sucks for the average person nowadays. The guy found or stole a gun. He worked up the courage to mug someone, but then got the surprise of his life, which killed him. The damn thing must have malfunctioned. I mean, look at this place, Walt. It's a discreet location, very suitable for mugging someone. Who knows, maybe he did point the gun to his head, or perhaps he played a game of Russian Roulette with the victim, but since there's no bullet entry or exit wound . . . Ah, and look at this," Dana knelt and pointed at the remnants of a bullet chamber. "There wasn't a single fucking shot fired."

Walter sighed as he took an oversized bite of his doughnut and then mumbled, "So, he shot himself . . . with an exploding gun."

"TNT and all, baby," Dana smirked. Walter continued eyeing Dana with a straight face. "I'm just playing you, Walt. No need to get all offensive."

Walter giggled. "Don't you mean defensive, numb-nuts?"

"Touché." Dana grinned and began searching the area opposite the corpse.

"Someone was standing, maybe a witness—a victim or the murderer. Hmm . . ." He took a pair of white latex gloves from his pocket and began prodding around the spectacle. He turned his head back to Walter, who still loomed above the corpse. "Hey, Walt? Try not to get crumbs on the evidence this time, OK? I don't want to have to explain that again."

Walter mumbled something incoherent, and Dana smirked and returned to farming the small acreage in the back alleyway before him.

Walter finished his doughnut and started to poke at the remnants of the gun. Something out of the ordinary had caught his eye. "Hey, come here for a second." Dana rose with a grunt and sauntered to Walter's side. "Look at this. Is that a spade?"

Dana picked up the gun and studied it. He noted the spade pattern and number ten. He compared it to what remained of the man's hand. "Huh, it sure looks like it. Let's see here . . . number . . . ten. Yeah, that's a bit strange—maybe an imprint from the gun?"

Walter grunted. "Yeah, it's possible. Hot metal can sear flesh, causing it to leave a mark, you know, like how cattle ranchers brand their cows?"

Dana nodded. "Hmm, yeah, could be." He straightened his back, snapping the latex gloves off. "Ugh, alright, let's get the guys in to bag it all up. We'll get an imprint of the footprints here. It's circumstantial at best, and there's nothing else that can really place another person here. It may have just been a freak suicide, after all."

Walter nodded and picked at the remnants. As Dana started to head out of the alleyway, he turned back to Walter. "After I get the guys, I'm going to get Jerry so he can finish his thing. We'll gather whatever information they got later."

Dana winced as he walked toward the blinding parade of red, white, and blue. He rubbed his eyes and then pressed the palms of his hands tightly against his head—a migraine had begun to surge full-on. Something genuinely unusual had finally come to their neck of the woods. *Well, well, I'll be damned.*

2

♠

SHE GLIDED INTO THE empty classroom, flipping on the lights and sighing in disappointment almost at once. Long jet-black hair flowed down her back. Frills of ebony lace adorned the edges of her skirt. Charcoal lipstick and eyeliner marked her face.

That she had even shown up surprised the two, and despite her evident presence in the room, they could hardly believe it. It had taken them all month to convince her she had a secret admirer and that "he" wanted to meet her after school. They had been amassing silly string and water balloons in the usually abandoned classroom for over a week. The only thing she'd be greeted with would be disappointment, as it befitted a silly goth kid. But this pure excitement was too much, and their giggling immediately gave away their position.

She closed her eyes and spun around, hissing, "I know you're there" at the empty teacher's office door. With no other means of escape and the element of surprise now lost, the two boys solemnly filed out into the classroom, their eyes downcast, hoping she didn't recognize them, preparing for a harsh tongue-lashing. Her deathly gaze shifted from one to the other as if burning the images of their faces into her memory.

After dragging the moment out, she cleared her throat. "You think it's funny to toy with people's lives?"

"Look, Lilah, it was just a joke," one of the boys croaked out.

"I'll show you what playing with people's lives is like!" The dirty-brown-haired boy felt the hairs on his neck stand up. Though unsure of what he'd heard and felt was real or his imagination, he sensed something was amiss—a slight touch of something seriously wrong hiding underneath the innocent girl persona, a vague hint of a malicious duality. Her right hand reached into the little purse slung low on her side. It shot out once it had found what it was looking for, causing the boys to jerk in fear and relief simultaneously when they realized it was a deck of cards.

"Ooh, are you going to tell us our future with your *fairy cards*?" the brown-haired boy's oblivious friend chided, his face lit up in a stupid grin.

"Yup. However, these are no fairy cards. These are the real deal." Her hands began to dance, shuffling the cards rhythmically in their intricately rehearsed ballet. Once satisfied, her hand rested on the top card, and she rapidly drew four cards. "Let's see, the first card, a king of diamonds."

"Playing cards? What, are you gonna *poker* us to death?" "Henry . . ." The brown-haired kid attempted to silence his loudmouthed friend before he could cause more trouble for both of them.

The girl they knew, Lilah, allowed a smirk at the stray comment. "Next, we have the two of clubs, but that's nothing special." She showed the third card. "A king of clubs, not too important." She then revealed the fourth card. "Three of clubs, but that doesn't matter. You see, it's always the last card that's key!"

"Look, Gary, she's lost it. The goth girl's finally gone loony. She's—" He cut his sentence short. What was happening now was beginning to make him question his own sanity.

The top card of the deck was moving, but not by her hand— all by itself, instead. It slid until it stood upright on the deck, then back to the two boys. Slowly, it began to turn towards them. As this spectacle occurred, neither noticed the sadistic grin forming on the girl's previously blank face nor her eyes starting to glow a dull green. As the card hit the halfway point, the boys found they could no longer move, and sense of touch had almost wholly left their bodies. The card was nearly completely facing them now, and sparks of electricity arced from its corners. This card was all wrong—a series of sigils and symbols spun, scribed by something not of this world. Red and black intermingled within the spade, and in each corner was the number thirteen.

"Black Thirteen, boys. This is where we part!"

)

Dana flipped through the newspaper and sighed. *More tragedy? The whole goddamn world is a tragedy. Give me something worth reading on this goddamn toilet paper.* The rain beat angrily on the car, as rhythmically as drums in a tribal ceremony. Flashes of lightning here and there painted the gray-streaked sky. Dana leaned forward and looked up towards the heavens through the windshield, noting the giant blobs that pooled together and were swept away by the windshield wipers. He sighed again and let himself collapse back into the passenger seat. He looked out the window to his left. *Goddamn it, Walter! What the hell are you doing, ordering the whole damn store?* Dana rubbed his forehead and glanced back up to see Walter scurrying from the coffee shop to the car. As he got in, he handed Dana a warm paper coffee cup, set down a white-and-brown paper bag on the edge of the driver's seat, and placed his jumbo coffee cup in the cupholder. Walter buckled his seat belt, giddy as a schoolgirl. Licking his lips, he reached for his goody bag.

"Don't eat it all in one sitting now, Walt."

Walter sighed and slowly let his gaze drift to Dana. "Are you seriously going to do this every damn time I get a few doughnuts? I mean, c'mon . . ."

Dana snickered. "Easy, Walter, easy, I'm just pulling your leg. Don't go having a coronary on me."

Walter mumbled something about a third leg as he reached into the paper bag and grabbed a giant frosted raspberry-jelly doughnut. He eyed it, having already turned "Ignore Dana mode" on, and then took a massive bite. "Mmm, this one, man, it's so great." He licked his lips, catching bits and pieces of jelly.

Dana shook his head at the sight. "Use a damn napkin, man. God, you're acting like a dog."

"Yeah, well, at least I'm housebroken," Walter mumbled. Dana grinned.

The dispatcher's voice broke through the radio into their calm moment, sharp and cold. "Hey, Walter, Dana, get over to Middleton High. We have one dead male student with another in critical condition. Both were burned."

Dana growled as he reached for the radio receiver, holding it up close. "Copy that, dispatch." *This just isn't my week.* He placed the receiver back into its cozy holster on the dashboard.

"Well, alright then, we're off to a barbeque." As he finished his doughnut, Walter wiped his face with his brown coat sleeve.

Dana sulked in his seat. "Obviously, you're bringing the beef."

"I dunno, I think I'd bring the buns if anything," Walter said before sipping his coffee.

"You must be a riot at funerals." Dana sighed. "C'mon, fire up the roof." Walter took another sip from his coffee cup, casually glancing at Dana with a grin. "Sometime . . . today . . . Walter . . ."

Walter laughed as he put the car in gear and made headway in the onslaught of rain.

)

Middleton High School was massive, boasting four levels, a greenhouse, and a performing arts center, and of course, it was near its football and track field. The red-bricked titan seemed to bleed, the rain pooling around its base. The evenly spaced windows featured aesthetics resembling the bags beneath Dana's eyes. A few yellow signs claimed "Flooding," and holes were spaced systematically along with their orange cone partners, poised a traffic sign nearby declaring, "Work in progress."

The soaked duo sprinted into the crowded hallway. Walter dried his glasses with his handkerchief while Dana slicked his hair back and surveyed the immediate area—faculty and fellow police officers lined the hall littered with police tape. The hallway was dark, as it was after school hours (and the dreadfully dreary day outside didn't help the atmosphere much).

A young, petite woman broke off from a discussion with a group and made her way to Walter and Dana. She had curves, shoulder-length golden-blonde hair, and pale skin that amplified her bright emerald eyes—the whole package.

Shit, if that's the principal. Dana's mind drifted off momentarily before realizing she was standing right before him.

A melodious tone escaped from her ruby-red lips. "Hello, my name is Anne Wilson, principal of Middleton High."

For a moment, Dana didn't notice she had extended her hand. "S-sorry, I haven't had much sleep lately," Dana said, shaking her hand. He cleared his throat and revealed his badge and ID, as Walter had already done. "My name is Detective Dana Deupree, and this is Detective Walter Conway."

Walter and Anne shook hands and regarded one another, then awkward silence. Perhaps it was the lack of sleep, or maybe it was just a fantasy. Whatever the case, Dana was lost in a subtle moment of infatuation with Anne.

When she cleared her throat, he snapped back to reality, his fantasy thwarted. "So, I'm sure you will want to see where it happened?

Dana shook his head. "I'm sorry, what? Oh, yes, the scene—yeah—right, uh, please, lead the way."

Anne smiled and nodded, then led the lost pups down the hall to the classroom. Glass cases of trophies and other awards were carefully spaced among rows of lockers—twenty-some-odd, some dented more than others—and doors to various rooms, which were also battered and worn, aged from years of education.

"I have to say, Ms. Wilson, you're awfully calm for the situation," Walter said.

"I used to be a medical examiner in New Boston and decided it was time for a change of scenery. I had thought to have left that behind anyway." Anne sighed.

Walter scratched the back of his head. "Is fighting an issue here by any chance?" Walter asked her.

"No, despite the appearance of the school. You know how it is these days, budget cuts and schools being closed left and right."

Dana drifted behind a bit, noting the way Anne walked. *Cute.* He grinned and then picked up the pace, his hands in his pockets. "Is there anything you can tell us about what was found?" Dana asked.

"Two Caucasian male students, one 17 years old, and the other 16. Their names are Henry Chud and Gary Only. Henry was found dead, while Gary was found in terrible condition. He has severe burns covering his entire body. We really were surprised to find one of them alive."

Walter occasionally glanced down at the cracked tiling that split in various directions as he walked, avoiding the more distressing ones.

"It's nice to see that your skills haven't dwindled much since your change in fields. Thank you, Anne." Dana wiped his face with the wadded-up handkerchief from his coat pocket.

"No problem. What can I say? It's a gift and a curse."

They reached the classroom, where an outline of a body was taped to the floor; a smoldering corpse lay draped nearby.

"I'm going to have to ask you to wait outside, please," Walter apologetically told Anne.

"Oh, no problem, thank you both." Anne gave a smile that nearly melted Dana as she exited.

Walter nudged Dana and whispered, "Somebody's hot for the teacher."

Dana rolled his eyes. "Oh, shut it." As he wandered into the dilapidated classroom, he noted no windows—a pitch-black room. He flipped the light switch, igniting the room in a bright fluorescent white. There were chairs on top of the desks and some stacked one on another in the corner. The door to the teacher's office was closed; the boy was in the classroom's bowels—a charred, contorted silhouette of the once lively.

"What the hell could have happened here?" Walter scratched his head.

"Well, that's our job—to find out." Dana knelt next to the deceased, the pungent odor of burned flesh and bodily fluids relentless on his senses. "Oh God, I think I got too strong of a whiff." Dana fanned the air before his face, only exacerbating the matter. Walter handed Dana a surgical mask. "I hope you weren't saving these for anything special, Walt."

Walter grinned. "Maybe I was, who knows?"

Dana shook his head, the mask clinging to him. "I worry about you sometimes."

Walter and Dana crouched closer to the charred husk of a young man, burned beyond recognition. With its few strands of black hair, the head was unnaturally twisted far to the right; the lower jaw shifted to the left. The eyes were gone, hollowed out into a charcoal abyss; an expression of absolute terror was set on the blackened, putrid face. The clothes—fragments of denim and what seemed to be a T-shirt—were cauterized to the smoked flesh. Arms and legs lay contorted absurdly against the white tile—also scorched.

Walter looked over at his partner. "What do you think?"

Dana curled his bottom lip. "I don't know. Maybe it was suicide. Oh, wait. One lived."

Walter grunted as he rolled his eyes. "Not this again."

Dana grinned. "Oh, come on. Just look at it." He stood up, hands on his hips. "They could have gotten tired of life." He paused. "One said, 'To hell with high school, fuck trying to get laid!' And his buddy? 'Yeah, man, me too. Let's do this!'" Walter cocked his head slightly, interested to hear the rest of the fable. "So, what happened next?"

Dana smirked. "They got liquored up. Rolled up some tinfoil or wiring, stuck it in an outlet—a final embrace."

"Ding, a fresh batch of dead-kid hot wings?" Walter jokingly added.

Dana cracked a grin, nudging Walter. "Now you're cooking! Not too bad, see?" Dana sighed as he looked back down at the poor lad's twisted and seared body.

Walter looked back to see Anne peeking in from the hallway. Grunting, he glanced at Dana before walking over to ask her a few more questions. "Ms. Wilson, do you know if either of the two students were suicidal or depressed? Did they have any enemies or problems with anyone—here or outside school?" Walter's gaze shifted from his notepad to Anne; he held his pen at the ready.

She smiled. "Oh, please. Call me Anne." She thought for a few moments. "No, nothing recorded, at least. I heard through the grapevine that they were waiting for someone. Supposedly, they'd been planning to play a joke on a fellow student, but no one knows who."

Walter scribbled chicken scratch. "You mean no one's divulging anything for fear of consequence?"

Anne shrugged. "It's probable. Kids these days have a unique code among themselves. This classroom hasn't been used much lately, except for storing some desks and chairs."

"Hmm, OK, well, thank you again." Walter nodded and smiled before returning to Dana.

Looking the body over once again, Dana noticed a rather peculiar design on the young man's scorched chest. "Hey, Walt, come here for a second. Look at this shit." Dana looked up at his partner and pointed to the design.

"So, Anne says they were here after school waiting for someone. They'd been planning a prank or something, but no one is saying anything else."

Dana continued pointing to the design. "Again, what does that remind you of?"

Walt leaned in. "Huh, yeah, that is pretty interesting. You don't think that . . .?" Walter rubbed his chin.

Dana shrugged. "Eh, it could be coincidental. Let's not jump to any conclusions just yet."

Walter shook his head as he rubbed his face, letting out a sigh. "Bah, young people. You know, it's times like these that I feel so old."

Dana turned his head to Walter. "You're not that old. Besides, I like having you around."

Walter chuckled. "Oh, jeez, don't go and get soft on me now."

"Never. I know how much you love jelly on the belly," Dana smirked. Walter laughed. "C'mon, let's pay a visit to the other kid and see if there's anything we can learn. I'll wrap up what I can here. Get any other information from Anne, and then grab the boys for clean-up."

"Are you sure? I think she likes you . . ." Walter's lips slowly sprawled into a toothy grin.

Dana shook his head, amused. "Ha. What I think is that *you* are imagining things. Let's get going. I'll buy you another cup of coffee."

Walter nodded and left Dana alone with the smoked corpse. *Was all of this the result of a joke gone wrong? That's one hell of a punch line, alright. Poor kid.* Dana sighed as he stood up, took the handkerchief from his coat pocket, and wiped the sweat from his forehead. *Man, I need a drag bad.*

3

♠

A FEW DAYS AWAY from school were precisely what she needed. She wouldn't have bothered to go if it hadn't been canceled. It was during quiet time alone that she sought to gather her thoughts. The rain had finally let up enough for some dampness to leave the sullen earth. Scattered about were only glimpses of a far cheerier overworld peeking through the dense, overcast skies. Nevertheless, this was exactly how she liked it. It was in this sort of world that she thrived.

Alone, sitting on a lone boulder that topped a desolate, treeless hill overlooking the "fair town of Middleton," she found peace. It was her secret castle, her fortress of solitude. Her slender legs, covered in black-and-white-striped stockings, dangled over the edge of the smooth stone. Her hands clasped the copy of *Hoyle's Guide to Poker and Other Parlor Games*, which she had come to hold dear. Her notes lined the margins of many of the pages.

She'd never bothered to research this Hoyle figure—at least, outside of reading the new author's quick blurb at the beginning proclaiming that his work was comparable, thus warranting the inclusion of the long-dead figure's name. Lilah was sure, however, that despite his merciful slandering of the author, Hoyle was the kind of guy with whom she could see herself. He offered a rare kinship. She enjoyed how, rather than merely explaining a game, Hoyle dug into it, broke it down to its bare minimum, analyzed the components, crafted abstract strategies, looked for subtleties, and thus turned it into an art form. This was precisely what she was in the process of doing. Not that it would matter, Lilah thought sardonically. Though she was still young and considered herself relatively new to the subject, she was very sure that no form of ecstasy afforded by man could compare to what she was feeling now.

Quietly, she read over her notes while slipping a pen from her purse, ready to make any corrections that her last experience had taught her. She ignored the pages and sections that seemed to be written in a foreign language, dismissing them as possible doodles and designs she had come up with at some point in her past when she was a bit more naive.

She ignored the mental images and sounds of two boys from her homeroom screaming and twisting in agony as life was torn from their bodies. She repudiated her actions as justified; the boys were insignificant—on the level of millimeter-high insects crushed underfoot.

Lilah had known how this game of chance worked since the beginning of the deal. She knew that the cards inked in her blood represented her very life. Lilah felt the tug on her very soul with every pull of a heart or diamond. With every pull of the cards inked in the iniquity of the demon's blood, she could feel its grim influence slip into her subconscious, begging for release.

This game of tug-of-war offered her a rush, one she was familiar with—the subtle, thin scars running down her arms and legs could attest to this. However, the story of the closest she had ever felt to the sheer volume of this new high could only be told by the thicker, deeper scars planted below the palms of her hands, sliding around her wrists. These were all feelings she was familiar with, feelings that excited her.

She closed her eyes and let a long sigh slip between her dark-painted lips. Her legs gently squeezed together, causing the heels of her almost-knee-high, very-much-strapped black biker boots to click in unison in remembrance of the moment. "Black thirteen," she whispered, her voice gently trailing off. The card had added a whole new dimension to the game. The flooding of life as the constant tug on her heart abruptly released; the sheer exhilaration with every card she drew; the pure, enticing ecstasy of her lost time that poured back; the thrill of the unknown—Black Thirteen was all these feelings and more. This was all she would need to be satisfied; that was her conclusion.

At the end of her introductory paragraph, she added *that it was a renewal, a fresh lease on life, and a new dimension to the game.*

She flipped the book closed, keeping her pen on the page she was currently making notes on, and slipped it back into her purse. She removed her glasses and quickly slid off the enormous rock, landing like a genuine athlete on a great day. A grin lit across her face as she pushed the spectacles back on. One thing was for sure. She knew she no longer wanted but *needed* to feel it again, regardless of the odds.

)

The dynamic duo approached Middleton Hospital. The monstrous beast lay slumbering, waiting for the next victim to wander into its web of death. Its reddish-brown walls loomed high, and suffocated sunlight was absorbed wholly by its black-tinted windows. Beady eyes fixated upon the morsels, making their way slowly towards it. Foreboding, lifeless gray clouds loomed over the grand spectacle of death's pet. But at least it had stopped raining—for the time being. *Hospitals . . . ugh. I hate hospitals.* Dana's gaze dropped back down to the streets and his surroundings. He watched Walter walk into the lobby. The doors parted like an arachnid's jaws, preparing to close on their prey.

Walter turned around in the doorway and glanced over his shoulder. He sipped on his paper cup of coffee. "Hey, Dana, are you coming in or what?"

Dana dragged himself forward. "Yeah, I'm just spacing as usual."

Walter cocked his head in concern. "Are you sure you're alright? You look like you're about to fall on your face."

Dana yawned and nodded, rubbing his eyes briefly. "Yes, dear." He let loose another yawn. "Ugh, c'mon, let's see this kid. Then, maybe after, I can get some fucking sleep."

Walter grunted as he took another sip of coffee.

"God, Walt, how do you not piss and shit your brains out from drinking that much?" Dana shook his head as he followed a giggling Walter into the belly of the beast, depressing, gloomy, and rumbling with the echoes of hundreds of voices and machines. Two massive round gray-white marbled pillars stretched high to the bright alabaster-speckled ceiling, tucking away the gift shop and coffee shop near the entrance. The clacks and clicks of shoes and the thrumming of caster wheels heedfully carrying patients to their life-or-death destinations—were amplified on the marbled tile. Urns of various shapes and sizes filled with fake greenery adorned secluded areas, while more gray-white marble took the form of statues, some thinking, some lusting, some dying.

Light wooden chairs were strewn about in an orderly fashion, in good company with the small round tables near the coffee shop. More large, gray chairs and leathered, moaning, and groaning with their shifting occupants lined the massive front window that gazed out to the world of the living. A small line of people formed at an alcove in the lobby, where two windowpanes entrapped several white-coated professionals working relentlessly. Polished golden hands above the bay held an elegant oak scroll with calligraphy: *Pharmacy*. Nestled in the back of the lobby was a sizeable gray-white marble desk, its top a maroon marble. A big gold-plated sign in bold, black calligraphy was embedded in the above wall: *Patient Check-In/Out. Information.*

The two were "greeted" at the desk by an old woman. Time had been tough on the crone, the wrinkles deep, rigid, and etched into an unfriendly scowl. Her gray hair nearly matched the walls. It resembled a small beehive of makeshift silk. A silver chain clung to her tiny spectacles, which teetered on the tip of her pointy little nose. Her eyes were grayed, lifeless, having long fallen victim to the beast's venom—the stormy blue of a wild youth gone. On her white uniform perched a faded name tag: Gladys.

Dana studied the desk. *More marble. I guess that economic stimulus has paid off. Well, it's better than that old orange-and-green nonsense.*

"Can I help you?" Gladys asked with a rude tone.

What a bitch. Granted, being here would make anyone a bitch, especially with that sourpuss.

"Hi, we are—" Walter began, but Dana interjected.

"Detectives Dana Deupree and Walter Conway of the MPD. We're here to see the kid from Middleton High, Gary Only."

Dana matched her rudeness and raised the stakes by strumming the desk with his fingers while staring a hole into her head.

Walter turned his back to Gladys and leaned towards Dana, whispering, "What's the matter?"

Dana remained fixated on hollowing out her skull. "Don't worry about it," he whispered. "Anything yet?" he asked loudly.

Gladys slowly drew her gaze from the computer screen to Dana's smug smirk. Her head still faced down, oval glasses teetering. "Just a moment, please. Exercise some patience, sir."

Dana slapped the countertop with his palm, startling the woman. "Really? Can't you sift through the information any faster? Should I get someone to help you? Perhaps I should just wander around this drag and find him myself?"

Walter snickered.

"I apologize, sir. However, our computer systems are a bit sluggish today." A beep sounded. "Fifth floor, room 318," Gladys sharply muttered.

Dana smiled with glee. "Thank you, Gladys. Have a nice day—I know I will."

Walter nudged Dana with his elbow as they walked towards the nearby elevators. "Boy, what a broad. I thought you were going to deck her."

"Nah, misery loves company."

An elevator arrived with a ding before caressing the two and herding them into its bosom. It vomited them on the fifth floor. Dana and Walter looked at the signs that split the hallway in two.

Walter spoke to himself aloud. "Let's see . . . the right is ICU rooms 100 to 150 . . . and left is ICU rooms 151 to 200 . . . and further left is rooms 201 to 300 . . ."

Dana began walking. "Let's just go right. The place wraps around."

"Huh? Oh, hang on." Walter scurried to keep up, sipping again from his coffee cup.

Dana occasionally glanced into rooms as they walked. Everything about the place eerily suggested that death was busy, even following their every step. A frail old man sat in a wheelchair facing his doorway—smiling. As they passed, they could hear the loud, steady tone. They pressed themselves against the walls as hospital personnel rushed frantically into his room. In another place was a woman covered in bloody bandages from head to toe. A frantic female nurse ran to the wall and pushed the code blue button, as the patient's will had forfeited. Yet another room was filled with toys and balloons, and people were weeping around the bed. A child's small pale hand dangled off the side of it.

Assorted personnel pushed gurneys of the deceased, which seemed to number more than the living. It appeared today that the dead outnumbered the living. *It's more of a graveyard than a hospital*, thought Dana. The personnel had swiftness and force behind them as if they were phantoms.

The detectives arrived at long last in room 318. Inside, a mother and father sat beside the bed of their severely burned son. Walter knocked on the door, "Excuse me, Mr. and Mrs. Only." They flashed their badges. "We're Detectives Walter Conway and Dana Deupree. We're investigating the occurrence at Middleton High."

The parents rose from their seats and approached Dana and Walter. "I'm Fred," said the man, shaking their hands. "And this is my wife, Mary."

"Pleased to meet you both," said Dana. "I wish it were under better circumstances."

"Agreed, it's never pleasant meeting people in a hospital." Fred stood up straight as he spoke, almost in a military stance.

"What can you tell us about your son Gary, Mr. and Mrs. Only?" Walter removed a pen and his notepad.

Mary took a deep breath. "Well, he is very bright and has never caused trouble. His best friend Henry did, though, God rest his soul. He's a good kid, detectives. I just don't know how this could have happened to my baby boy." She cried, and Fred held her close, running his fingers through her hair. She sobbed into his chest, clinging tightly to him. "There isn't much we can tell you, detectives—nothing more than you already know."

"I see," said Dana. "Do you mind if we have a moment with your son?" He looked over to Gary, who lay wrapped in bandages, hooked up to various IVs and machines, and noted one that breathed for him.

"You won't get much from him, Detect," said Fred. "The doctor said he's brain-dead. He'll be a vegetable for the rest of his days . . ." He drifted off, then came back. "There was one peculiar thing. On his chest, the doctors found an imprint of a spade with the number thirteen."

Dana raised an eyebrow as Walter turned his attention to him. "Really? Hmm, yes, that it is rather peculiar." He recalled the dead John Doe. *This could just be a coincidence, though it seems unlikely.*

"Do you think maybe . . .?" Walter whispered to Dana. He went to sip his coffee and then realized it was empty. He tossed it in the waste bin not far from Gary's bedside.

Suddenly, beeps and bleeps went abuzz, blurring together like a natural disaster siren, and the parents were sent into a frenzy. Dana and Walter took a few steps back from the fast-fading young man.

Dana leaned towards Walter. "Perhaps. We'll have to start piecing it together soon and make it quick."

Doctors and nurses rushed to the room. "Clear out, all of you!"

One nurse rushed in with a crash cart while another removed the boy's chest bandages with scissors. Dana ventured a glance at Gary as he exited the room and saw vividly the spade and number thirteen etched in his scorched chest, pulsating in red-orange.

Dana and Walter leaned against the hallway wall. The hysterical parents cried and pleaded for their son's life with an invisible maker. After several moments that seemed like an eternity, the doctors and nurses made no further attempts. Slowly, they drew a white sheet over Gary Only and turned off the machines; the raging storm finally dissipated. Dana sighed as he rubbed his eyes.

Once setting foot outside, he reached for a cigarette; he thought of everything that had happened up to now. *Well, this is great, just fucking great. This is exactly what I did not need.*

4

ANOTHER FRIDAY NIGHT, ANOTHER anonymous card game. Once again, he found himself losing, and he didn't care. He wasn't sure why he attended these things, let alone hosted them. He'd never been good at any form of poker. Perhaps it was because of the regulars he'd started to consider friends despite the agreements: no names or attempted contact outside the apartment. Maybe it was because of her. He didn't have a good understanding of what she looked like. Unlike the others, she attempted to mask who she was, though these were hardly ever drastic—tonight was just a beanie she tucked her hair under and purple-tinted glasses.

The only way he could identify that it was inevitably her behind the disguise was through the things consistently the same about her. For one, the way she talked "like a sailor," he imagined his grandma would have said on more than a few occasions. He also knew the shape of her body, the curves, the faint tint of her skin hinting at a Mediterranean background, perhaps Greek. The most unusual thing was how she dressed—so simple: loose-fitting white tank top and snug blue jeans, as though she'd raided her dad's or boyfriend's closet. The entire ensemble was always topped off with her slightly oversized red tote bag, which she always had slung over her left shoulder except when playing the card game.

They all wore name tags displaying handles so that they had a way to communicate with each other. Some were comical, and some were clever. Two guys sat side by side and looked like brothers; their names were Clapton and Eric. There was a newcomer, a kid who couldn't have been more than sixteen years old and was always grinning like an idiot; his tag said Pepsi, as did the bottle he constantly gripped in his left hand. Meat was the big biker guy with the goatee and shiny bald head. Her, well, she had a different name every week. Last week, it was Mary Sue and Helena a couple of weeks ago, and this time, the tag said Mable. As for his, it simply proclaimed Mark. He thought no one would find out if it were a fake or real name, as he figured he wouldn't run into anyone outside the group's play night.

The dealer's rights had just passed to Mable, and she delighted the newcomer with a show of her exaggerated shuffling techniques. Stupid parlor tricks, true, but at least they broke the tension before everyone blatantly robbed each other of their hard-earned weekly paychecks. With the finesse and dexterity of a professional, she dealt with each player around the table. As the cards glided across the glazed surface, momentarily hovering in the air, the sole light in the room, strung low overhead, cast shadows that hinted at a hidden, darker game being played just below the surface of reality. The last card was dealt out, and they all fell silent. The game was on once again.

At first, it played out like it usually did. After several checks and one raise, Mark folded. He didn't have much money left, but he'd decided he would try to delay the inevitable loss for as long as possible. It didn't matter much anyway, not this time. His eyes settled on Mable, and he knew now why he bothered to attend these games. He just liked being around her and decided to say something to her this time.

He dropped his cards on the table and sat back, watching the game. As the stakes were raised, sweat began trickling down the faces of grown men. Pepsi wasn't doing too bad. He was definitely not new to the game or having any form of bad luck. The real star of the match was Mable; the large lump of cash continued to mount up in front of her. The call came around again, and Mable raised. Clapton was next and folded. Eric matched her, and then all eyes fell on Meat. He looked down at his cards and then slowly turned his gaze forward. Mark followed it and realized Meat was glaring at Mable. Her face was lit up with a smile, and though he couldn't see them, he knew her eyes were staring right back. The biker mumbled something under his breath, and his face slowly turned red. After a moment of silence, Eric asked what he had said.

"I SAID—" Meat stood up abruptly, flipping the table on top of Clapton and Mark. Cards and currency flew into the air like a strange blend of confetti. "THIS IS BULLSHIT! THIS BITCH IS CHEATING! THERE IS NO WAY SHE CAN COME IN HERE SO CALM EVERY WEEK AND WALK OUT WITH AT LEAST A HUNDRED AND FIFTY DOLLARS OF MY MONEY!"

As Mark struggled under the overturned table to achieve a better vantage point, he heard the foreboding click he knew could only have come from the hammer being pulled back on a revolver. It didn't take a genius to know it was pointed squarely at Mable.

"Fine, you think I'm cheating. How about this? Let's play one more hand, just you and me." Mabel's voice was almost melodic amid the chaos that had erupted in the room. Mark had managed to pull himself out enough to see her now. The low-strung light cast its glow across the lower half of her shirt and down her legs, fit in those slightly worn blue jeans. Meat cleared his throat and started to say something but was abruptly cut off. "If you win, you shoot me and get the money. If I win, you get the money and leave. We never see you here again." Judging by the silence, Meat had agreed to her terms, and Mark could see the outline of her face nod. She reached into her tote bag and pulled out another deck of cards, which she hastily shuffled. No card tricks this time, and he knew why. Meat had seen them before, and odds were, he wouldn't stand to watch them again.

As the shuffling finished, Mable rapidly drew five cards from the deck and peered at them. For the first time since he started coming to these games, Mark saw a line of sweat work its way down her forehead and lose itself in her finely plucked eyebrow. Slowly, she revealed her hand towards where Mark guessed Meat was standing. Then, the impossible happened. The cards began to glow—not shine, but literally glow. Mable's free hand went to her stomach, and she winced.

"What the? Argh! Ah!" Meat's voice reached a hysterical pitch as a white and orange light bathed the room.

There was a clatter as the gun dropped to the ground unfired. Mark's eyes settled on Mable. She had fallen to her knees and winced in pain, a small shriek managing to escape from her throat. Then, after a moment, she took a deep breath of air, gathered up the cards, and jammed them into the depths of her bag. Mable stood up in the now flickering orange and yellow. She looked around at everyone, staring back in sheer horror. Lilah turned and walked over to Mark and knelt before him. Her hand settled on a lump of cash, which she promptly shoved into the same place she had put the cards. Having retrieved what was rightfully hers, Lilah leaned towards Mark, and he could see her face was very much flush with color. She slid her glasses down to reveal dark-brown eyes. A small lock of black hair slid out from underneath her beanie and settled on her forehead, giving him a wink. Then, standing up, she spun on her heels until she was facing the door and walked out.

A single line of blood trickled down Mark's head from where the table had connected with it. As unconsciousness encroached on his mind, all he could think was: *Hit me.*

)

It was often a place of solitude. Then again, it wasn't as if he invited troughs of people over at any given time. Dana sat alone in his study. The ornate small crystal chandelier clung to the alabaster ceiling, dimly bathing the dark room with a soft amber glow. Shelves of books lined the wall behind where he sat, many of which he had read. One window gazed out to the front of the house and the street while the other opposite peered into the backyard. Each was a unique looking glass that offered a different world: sprawling suburbia in one and an endangered piece of nature that—knowing what the zoning authorities and city hall bigwigs cared for—could become another local supermarket in the other. He favored the latter, placing a small round mahogany table and two hunter-green leather recliners near it.

The walls of mahogany stretched and wrapped themselves around the room. The ensemble comprised more books, plaques, citations, commendations, medals, and a framed shadowbox. It contained a walnut baton with bronze accents and a brilliant yellow braided cord. On the bottom of the box, an engraved bronze plaque read:

Detective Dana Deupree,

When the night eclipses dawn in the final hour, hold your own and let no one—nothing—take your will. For we are all doomed to the curse of flesh. Never go quietly to your grave.

With the utmost gratitude and respect,

New Boston Chief of Police Marco Rodriguez

Near it was a newspaper clipping with the headline "*Cop Takes Gamble, Saves Fellow Officers. Fast-Food Killer Slain.*"

Light gray carpet covered the entire floor—a plastic mat nestled under Dana's black leather executive chair and massive mahogany executive desk. The old green glass desk lamp magnified the various pictures of the last couple of bizarre deaths. The thick cream curtains in the windows closed their eyes, preventing the outside world from gazing in.

He had already kicked his feet up on his desk, his eyes having repeatedly searched the crime scene photos of John Doe, Henry Reed, and Gary Only. Dana sighed aloud, frustrated. He glanced to his left at a small, empty glass. *Ugh, what a way to waste a Friday night.* He put his feet down and reached for a bottle of whiskey sitting not far from the glass. He unscrewed the top and poured a moderate amount. *Well, Walt, at least your gift set is of use.* Dana smirked as he brought the glass to his lips and guzzled its contents. He then set his gaze upon the crime scene photos again, focusing on the markings on all three victims. *How can it be? Each has some suit and a number, but where does thirteen factor in? Thirteen . . . there is no thirteen in a regular deck of playing cards. Maybe someone's gone off the deep end and is gambling peoples' lives away for some cheap thrill.*

Dana contemplated several theories and possibilities on a loose sheet of paper, ruling the three deaths were homicides rather than freak suicides. He reached for the whiskey bottle again and poured another glass. "Well, Dana," —he screwed the top back on the bottle and held up his glass in a toast— "here's to another splendid Friday night." As he consumed the contents of his drink, the telephone rang. He eyed it, grunting in discontent. "Deupree here."

"Hey, Dana, it's Walter. I know you're probably enjoying your Friday night home alone as usual, but we got some work for us."

What the hell do you mean, as usual? Dana rolled his eyes. "Dammit, Walt, is it that important that you have to disturb me?"

"Take a trip with me, and you'll find out."

Dana growled. "Fine, I'll be there in ten minutes."

"*Or* . . . you can just get your jolly ass outside, and we'll go." Walter let a slight chuckle escape before letting loose into a hacking frenzy.

"What the—you're outside?" Dana scrambled to his feet and rushed to the window that faced the street to see Walter waving by his beat-up sedan.

"Hey-y-y baby, you want some action?" Walter laughed as he waved at a peering Dana.

Dana smirked, closing the curtains and returning to his chair. "Ha, don't you call me baby, darlin'. I'll be out in a few."

He sighed as he hung up. He stood up and wrangled his suspenders over his shoulders, then grabbed his long brown overcoat off the back of the chair, causing it to spin a little. He picked up his gun and holstered it before pocketing his keys and cell phone. He ran his fingers through his hair—his frazzled appearance tonight was the opposite of what he wanted to appear as during the day (he often thought of himself resembling a gun for hire or a personable old gangster from a twenties flick). He rubbed his eyes and forehead before shaking his head clear of such childish fantasies. Dana turned off the lights off and exited the room.

Dana stepped out into the darkness, catching the silhouette of Walter sipping on a cup of coffee and possibly nibbling on a doughnut. He noticed the round shade munching faster. He opened the passenger door opened and plopped down next to Walter.

Dana looked over at his partner; the dashboard's green lights reflected off his glasses. "You missed a spot there, Walt. Raspberry again, I take it?" Dana grinned at Walter and clicked his seat belt into place.

Walter rolled his eyes and shook his head as he put the car in gear, red Cyclops eye on the roof flashing and spinning, and pulled away from the curb, speeding into town. "We got a call about a disturbance at some apartment. I guess a poker game was going on, and, well, things got hot, but not in a good way. If you want to peek at the dispatch report, it is on the dash." Walter sounded annoyed and yet a bit interested in where they were going.

Taking the bait, Dana reached for the file. The caller stated, "A series of shouts in the neighboring unit, followed by a loud crash and a lot of screaming."

Dana looked over at Walter. "Is this all? I mean, we hear about this stuff all the time, and half of it is just a kid stuck in a well."

Walter shrugged as he turned sharply. "Yeah, well, I don't know, 'Lassie.' That's all we have to go by at this point.

Although"—Walter paused as he cleared his throat— "EMTs did respond to a burn victim . . . if that's any consolation prize for ya."

Dana looked to his right out the car window at the shops and buildings buzzing by. "A burn victim . . . again? C'mon, Walt, give me something else."

Walter shrugged again as he slowed down and stopped at the Village Hill Apartments complex. "Well, we're here. Time to get us some information on this heap." Walter heaved as he exited the car, taking his cup of coffee.

Dana stared out the window at the apartment complex. It looked like any other in the city—typical dull reddish-brown brick stacked up to five floors. Windows were sparse in the front, six per floor, some embedded at ground level, some morphing into doors leading out to tiny decks. Lights were on in several apartments, probably due to the ruckus caused. Some people gathered on their decks on the top floor to watch the entertainment below. Dana finally got out of the car and closed the door. His eyes scanned the area, noting limited parking space. All over the parking lot were law enforcement and support vehicles: fire trucks, ambulances, police cruisers. He glanced down at the cracks that split the parking lot. To him, the building seemed like an oversized shell for a lot of cockroaches, if that could be considered. *It looks more like a poorhouse. City living, bah. It isn't what it used to be, that's for sure.*

As Dana walked along the new concrete sidewalk, he saw the sign displayed on the side of the building: "The Village Hill Apartments is under new management! Coming soon, improved look to the interior and exterior!" It also notified residents of dates for when the parking lot would resurface. *I may stand corrected.* Dana smirked as he accompanied Walter into the building and up the stairs.

"Are you sure you're doing alright, Walt? You're not going to quit on me now, are you?" Dana said jokingly as Walter caught his breath at the top of the fourth floor.

"Fuck you, Dana." The two had a chuckle at Walter's expense.

Dana motioned. "Here it is, unit 4C."

He glanced at the door's broken and burned-out buzzer, where a new one was underneath it. A few other police officers were venturing in and out of the apartment, leaving the door open. Several people sat in chairs, all of them with blank expressions on their faces. Dana and Walter surveyed the interior from the doorway.

"What the hell happened here?" Walter asked.

"Well, that's kind of our job—to find out." Dana nudged his partner in the gut.

Dana entered to find a table overturned, miscellaneous playing cards, and some cash strewn about the floor like a piñata had been smashed open. Scorch marks painted the off-white carpet and white ceiling; the room smelled of burned flesh and hair. *Not again. Please, no more of this.* Dana sighed. He eyed the floor once more, noticing something peculiar. Dana withdrew a pair of white latex gloves from his pocket and stretched them over his hands. Dana started rummaging about the mess on the floor, shuffling food, beer bottles, and a bottle of Chartreuse aside until he found a familiar gun. He carefully examined it before rotating the revolver's cylinder and ejecting the rounds. Dana searched for Walter and saw his partner questioning a witness wearing a name tag with "Pepsi" scrawled on it. "Hey, Walt, come take a look at this."

Walter turned around and cautiously stepped through the mess. He took a sip from his coffee cup. "What did you find? Anything good?"

Dana gave his clever smirk. "A .45 revolver—still loaded, unfired, and in pristine condition."

Walter shrugged. "So?"

Dana fixed his gaze upon Walter. "So? This is the same gun the John Doe used." He turned it over and held it out to Walter. "Look at this—no spade."

Walter studied the gun carefully. "You're right, no spade. Do you think that it might have been a custom job?"

Dana thought about his partner's remark. "Possibly, I wouldn't exactly shell out a bunch of cash just for an etching of a spade, though. Different strokes for different folks, I guess."

Walter nodded, scanning his notepad. "Anyway, the scrawny kid over there, his name is Pepsi—real name Sheldon Johnson. He says they were playing a few rounds of poker, and this giant flipped a lid on some girl. All he remembers is the girl and the big guy playing a solo match, and then the guy just went up in flames. Sorry bastard became a giant barbecue chicken, and she split the scene."

Dana examined the room. "Who was running the game?"

Walter pointed. "That kid over there. His name is Mark or something, whatever's on his tag. If you want to deal with him, I still need to talk to other people."

Dana nodded. "Sure, have at 'em, big guy. Maybe after, we can stop and get some grub if you're up for it."

Walter nodded. "Yeah, make it a date." He laughed.

Dana shook his head and removed his smirk as he went through the obstacle course to talk with Mark.

Mark was jittery. He shifted side to side in the chair, holding an ice pack to his forehead, where blood had dried. Dana took note: white, dark hair, tall, thin—a bit scraggly. He approached him and extended his hand, glancing at the name tag. "Mark, I'm Detective Dana Deupree. Do you mind telling me what happened here this evening?"

"Y-yeah, M-Mark, Mark Colley," he said in a low voice, shaking Dana's hand. He winced in pain as he readjusted the ice pack. "I host poker night every Friday and have some people come in—ah." Mark winced again. "People come in, and we all play until we're out of cash . . . just our usual."

Dana nodded as he wrote down Mark's answer. "And this girl and the big guy, do they have names?"

Mark smirked a bit. "Oh, you mean Meat? He's a really, really big biker guy: bald, goatee, pretty ripped. I dunno how old he is. He was a regular, though, along with Clapton and Eric." Mark paused. "Now Meat's a tad crispy. The only real newbie is Pepsi over there."

Dana held back a smirk. "Do you guys always use such . . . abstract names?"

Mark shook his head. "No, not always. It varies depending on who shows up."

Dana nodded again as he continued writing. "And the girl, what about her?"

Mark paused for a moment, reluctant to divulge anything about Mable. "She comes every week. Her name is different every time: Helena, Mary Sue . . ." Mark drifted off.

Dana gazed at him sternly. "And tonight, what was it?"

"Mable . . ." he muttered.

"And what does she look like?".

Mark's eyes darted around the room. "Uh, she has kind of dark-tinted skin but not too dark, like olive or tanned." His gaze locked onto Dana's notepad. "She's young, I guess. Look, I don't really ask people for their details; they just show up," Mark said defensively.

"Description, please."

Mark grunted. "She wore a beanie, um, loose clothing—a white tank top, blue jeans, purple shades."

Dana sighed. *That's great. That's only about half a million other girls in the world.* He finished writing. "So, what happened? From the top. Go."

This time, Mark sighed. "We were just playing cards. Mable was beating all of us. Meat suspected she was cheating, flipped the table, and then pulled a gun out and threatened her. I was trapped under the table and dazed." Mark sifted through the video that replayed on his mind's reel. "She said, 'If you win, you shoot me and get the money. If I win, you get the money and leave. We never see you here again.' Right after that, I saw her reach into her purse, pull out a deck of cards, and deal, and then Meat just . . .'" Mark drifted off, trying to recall if what transpired did. "He . . . ignited into a ball of fire. Then she took her money and left."

Dana gazed upon Mark. "Anything else?"

"She . . ." Mark paused. "She looked like she was in pain when it happened."

Dana raised an eyebrow. *In pain?* He rubbed his eyes. "Can I get any clarification on that?"

"I don't know," Mark snapped back. "I said she just looked like she was in pain."

Dana nodded. "Alright, Mark, thanks for your time. An officer will ask you for an official statement, so stick around." Dana walked away from Mark, who groaned in acknowledgment and strolled to the apartment's entryway. He looked down at the doorknob. "Hey, can one of you guys check this for some prints?"

One of the officers on the scene hollered aloud, "On it, Chief!"

Stepping outside, Dana noticed a flimsy laminated adhesive name tag in the door's gap that read "Mable." He knelt, withdrew a pair of tweezers from his coat pocket, and picked at the name tag that lay partially hidden. *C'mon, damn you . . . there!* Dana held the label up and read it aloud. "Mable . . . hmm." As he crouched in the doorway, he caught Mark eyeing him and turned away.

You know more than you're willing to part with, Mark. Dana looked down at the name tag and let a small grin escape. He stood up and called out for his partner. "Walter! We're done here! Let's go already."

Walter hobbled through the people and obstacle festival in the apartment, making his way to Dana. "Jesus, it's like a pack of marshmallows in there." Walter wiped his brow of the sweat that had built up.

Dana chuckled. "You would think of mallows, Walt. C'mon, let's go get some grub—I'll drive, you buy." Dana patted his partner on the shoulder as Walter growled. Dana laughed harder, securing the name tag into a small baggy and then into the depths of his coat, obscuring it from Walter's view. *Mable, Helena, Mary Sue—it seems she likes to keep it classic.*

Dana reached into his coat for a cigarette and flicked his Zippo. He inhaled deeply as he began descending the stairs back to the car, sighing as he trailed down. *It's going to be a long, long night.*

)

Dana pulled up along the curbside of a small dark-bricked building, soothing the brown beast to sleep.

"Now you're speaking my language, Dana." Walter grinned out the window towards the diner.

A large ruby-red neon sign brightly proclaimed Grave's Diner. In the window hung a fuchsia-and-azure neon light that flashed OPEN brilliantly in various sequences as though sending out a coded message to the famished people of the night. Before them stood a shining beacon of hope to those struck by the tyrannical hunger beast late at night. The sign let them know that a friend was there. The parking lot was deceptive. From the front of the diner, it looked small.

On the contrary, it stretched further, harboring more for the merrier. Dana looked over at Walter, flashing his sly grin. "Don't worry, Walt. I won't spend too much." Walter grunted as he opened the passenger door, sighing at his partner's shenanigans. "Ah, come on, you know it's all in good fun."

Walter shook his head as both made their way to the door of Grave's Diner. "You're a son of a bitch, you know that, Dana? A real, classy son of a bitch."

Dana smothered his cigarette butt in an ashtray before entering the establishment, lightly chuckling to himself. Inside, it was vacant; there were only a few people here and there. A small sign read, "Please seat yourself." Naturally, Dana and Walter waltzed over to a smoking booth, where they removed their coats and placed them on the coat rack. Dana adjusted his suspenders before sliding into the booth. The place was an old-fashioned diner: classic 1950s styling complete with a working jukebox in the corner, low bar stools at the front counter, and red, blue, and mellow-green neon signs. And it was all topped off with a neon Coca-Cola clock, which hung above where Walter and Dana sat.

"I'll be right back, Dana. I gotta take a leak." Walter motioned behind him.

"Ha, you only now have to piss? Christ, you just guzzled like a hundred gallons of coffee. I'm surprised all you have to do is take a piss." Dana rubbed his eyes, fatigue slowly setting in, his eyes tired of looking at his partner. Walter giggled, his little chubby pouch bouncing up and down like a water balloon. Soon, he vanished from sight, and Dana sighed peacefully, leaning his head back on the booth.

At last . . . peace and quiet. Then, his stomach growled. *I guess I am pretty famished.* He opened his eyes slowly and forced himself to sit upright.

Within a few minutes, the server came over. The woman was young, in her late twenties, maybe. Short and skinny but not so thin that she was a toothpick. She had some meat on her bones. Her hair was long and golden, bundled up in a sloppy ponytail. Eyes brown; very attractive. Her uniform outlined her illustrious curves from top to bottom. The top of the navy-blue blouse, with matching buttons like pointy little teeth—open, showing the crease of her bosom and exposing her bare neckline. A sweet voice revived him. "Hello, my name is Julie, and I'll be your server for this evening. Dana smiled at her as she bent over, placed the utensils before him, and caught a hint of fruity perfume. He closed his eyes briefly, wondering where he had smelled such a scent. "What'll you have, sir?" The angel's melodic voice jerked Dana back again.

"Oh, a Coke with a lemon wedge, please. I'm waiting for my partner to return."

Julie scribbled down a few words before nodding. "OK. I'll be right back, sir." She sprinted off to the kitchen.

Cute girl, Dana thought, letting a sly grin show as he fiddled with the napkin containing his knife, fork, and spoon. Walter soon exited the restroom, adjusting his belt and suspenders, and briefly stopped at the jukebox. He deposited a few coins, pressed a button, then turned around and returned to the booth. A song came over the airwaves, resounding throughout the still silence in the dining area. Dana glanced up. "Meat Loaf? Nice choice, Walt."

Walter scooted into the booth, and soon, the server came by with Dana's drink. "And here you are, sir. Are you ready to order, gentlemen?"

"Uh, I'll have a cup of coffee, regular, please." Walter eyed the server up and down subtly and glanced at his menu. "Uh—uh—er . . . I'll have a triple bacon cheeseburger, steak fries, and a side Caesar salad."

Dana shook his head in disbelief. "Jesus . . . a whole cow and just a salad?"

Walter leered at Dana. "And what are you getting, Mr. Health Fanatic?"

Dana looked up at the waitress. "I'll have a jalapeno pepper-jack patty melt. Ask Mike, he knows how I like it. Oh, and a side of curly fries, please."

Julie smiled as she finished taking down the orders. "I'll get these right in for you, boys." She left them as the song preached on: "Hot Patootie."

Dana ran his fingers through his hair; Walter looked like he had something on his mind. "Dana, do you think this is all linked: the John Doe, kids, and the poker game?"

Dana sighed as he reached into his coat pocket, pulling out his cigarettes and Zippo. "Maybe. We still got to talk to this Meat fella if he hasn't gone and died on us." He placed a cigarette between his lips, gave a flick of his wrist, and the Zippo erupted into a torch. "The truth is, I want to get something in my stomach before I think any more about this bullshit." Dana brought the lighter up to the cigarette's hairs, puffing strong. With the same fluid motion of his wrist, he flicked the Zippo case closed, snuffing the single flame.

Julie returned with Walter's coffee, a small bowl of creamers, and a new sugar container. "Here you are, sir."

"Thanks, little lady." He winked. Dana rolled his eyes, and Julie giggled.

"Your order will be up soon. If you need anything else, don't hesitate to let me know, OK?" Julie smiled as she swayed back to the kitchen, the doors trembling like flowers in the breeze.

Dana couldn't help but smile.

Several minutes passed, and before long, Julie returned. She held Walter's and Dana's dishes within her possession and served them accordingly.

"Need a refill?"

"Coffee for the fat dolt and more Coke for the half-wit, if you would please, miss. And that will be all, thank you."

Julie nodded and returned to the kitchen. Walter licked his lips and took a large bite of his burger as Dana took his knife and carefully cut down the middle of the sandwich, not letting the handle slip from his tired hands. Watching Walt was almost enough to make him lose his appetite.

A handful of Coke and coffee refills later, Walter patted his full belly while Dana rubbed his eyes. The night had trickled into the early morning of Saturday. *Man, I thought the caffeine would have helped by now.* Dana sighed as he lit another cigarette and dug his wallet out of his back pocket.

Julie came by again to drop off the bill. "You boys have a good night, OK." She smiled brightly.

"Thank you, Julie. It has been the utmost pleasure." Dana smiled back at her, absorbing some energy to loosen the tiring grip that had tightened on him.

As she walked away, Walter eyed Dana. "That's probably why you're being such a Debbie Downer! You need a lady, yeah—that's it!"

Dana rolled his eyes. "Got an answer for everything, don't you?"

Walter shrugged. "What can I say? It's a gift and a curse."

Dana chuckled, removing a twenty-dollar bill and one of his detective cards from his wallet. He placed both on the table with Walter's ten-dollar tip. *Maybe she'll call, no matter if not. It's not like I'll be alone on a Saturday night.* Dana yawned. "Ready? Let's check on Meat. I got a text message from Chad a little while ago that he was in stable condition."

Walter nodded. "Alright, the better we start on it, the earlier we can maybe get some sleep."

"Exactly. God knows I am one for sleep." Dana yawned heavily again. Walter led the way to the exit.

Dana turned around, faced the kitchen, and hollered, "Thanks for the grub, Mikey! Say hey to Amy for me, will you?" A muffled "will do" echoed through the server station.

Dana offered to drive, and Walter volunteered shotgun. The air was cool and crisp. Traffic was nonexistent. Dana stared at the early-morning sky as Walter unlocked the car doors and passed the keys to him. He spotted stars twinkling and a close full moon—a cosmic night light that blinded his eyes. The two strapped themselves in and began their next adventure to a familiar place—Middleton Hospital.

I wonder if Gladys is working tonight, Dana thought with a smirk as he parked. "Let's get this over quickly. I'm bushed."

Walter nodded. "Right, we'll make it a quickie."

Dana grinned. "Now that's what I'm talking about."

)

The extravagant duo made their way into the lobby, where the lights were dimmed, creating a haunting setting. They shuffled lazily to the receptionist's desk, where a familiar old crone sat—waiting. "Ah, well, well, if it isn't my favorite. Gladys, how's the night shift?"

Dana strummed his fingers across the desk, expecting another exciting bout as Gladys eyed him and Walt.

"Can I help you, detectives?"

"We're here to see a patient who came in under the assumed name Meat." Dana tilted his head as he scratched his scalp. Gladys hacked a series of coughs. Dana growled as he retracted his hand, feeling some spots of saliva land on it. *I don't need what you have infecting you, lady. I'll be damned if I'm going to get sick and feel MORE like shit than I already do.*

A beep came from the computer system. Gladys eyed Dana again sternly and gave him a noticeable fake smile. "ICU, room 149. Good day, detectives."

Only a few nurses occupied the nurse's station in the ICU. They sat computing, measuring medicine, and watching heart, blood, and brainwave functions.

In 149, Meat lay bandaged from head to toe. A foul stench wafted through the air—a smell that Dana and

Walter knew from not too long ago. *That smell always gets to me. Disgusting. Ugh.* Dana fanned in front of his nose, then removed his handkerchief, placing it over his mouth and nose.

Walter examined Meat. "Well, another burner."

"Ya think? Christ, you can't smell all that and not make that conclusion."

Walter giggled. "Alright, well, I'm going to go find a nurse and see if anyone is checking on him regularly, then check the ME's preliminary report."

Dana nodded as Walter exited the room and continued to examine the burned Meat. *Well, you sure did have a number played on you, buddy.* Dana checked his limbs and then peeked at his face. His eyes were shut. Sleeping, no doubt—or overly pumped up on morphine or both.

But suddenly, the slumbering giant awoke. His eyes widened with panic; he sat up and grabbed Dana's arm tightly. His bloody, bandaged, scorched face crackled as his jaw moved to the words. "It was . . . it . . . bright . . . one . . . a one . . . a heart . . . fire! That . . . bitch!" Dana struggled to writhe his arm free from the ragged sentinel's vice grip, but soon, the colossus collapsed back onto his bed, fast asleep.

What does a heart, a one, it, and fire have to do with this? Dana recollected the puzzle pieces as Walter entered the room again.

"Guy's name is Ward Estrada, part of some local biker gang. He has severe to damn-near-fatal burns all over his body, and you're not going to believe this, but the nurse said that on his chest is an imprint of a heart, and it isn't an 'I Love Mom' tattoo, Dana."

Hearts and spades. Great, now we need clubs and diamonds, and we have a real Texas hold 'em match. "Thanks,

Walt." Dana sighed. "I don't think we'll get any more out of him. He's back fast asleep."

Walter cocked his head. "Back asleep? Did he wake up?"

Dana nodded. "Eh, yeah . . . something about an it, a one, a heart, and that bitch."

Walter shifted his weight to his left. "One of hearts? Ya think he means an ace of hearts? Think maybe this goes with the others—the spades?"

"Probably. We're now up to our balls in crusty jokers, and they're not queens."

Walter grunted. "Well, if we can somehow find out about that Mable chick, we can maybe get somewhere."

Dana turned and faced Walter. "We will. Prints are running. Let's hope she touched that doorknob."

Walter nodded. "Yeah. What do you say we get out of here? I'll drop you off."

Dana smirked. "Oh, such a chivalrous prick. Don't expect to come inside, though." Walter giggled as he turned and exited the room. Dana reached into his coat pocket and withdrew the baggie with the name tag. *Who are you really, Mable?*

5

♠

THERE ARE NUMEROUS WAYS *to murder someone—a few are similar, but still, they work just as well.* Lilah stared at this latest entry, an addition to her introduction. She'd written it last night after she got home from her little adventure. Lilah had never felt her heart race like it had that night, and when she finally found herself in the safety of her room, she flipped open the book and wrote the first thing that came to mind. Looking back at it after a good night's sleep, she could only feel disgusted. In this book, such words seemed like blasphemy.

The book had been a gift—the last one he had ever given her. It was as good as holy.

She had spent all morning putting herself back together. Thick coats of white on her smooth skin touched up with black around the eyes, fingers, toenails, and finally on the lips. To her, this felt like coming clean. This was the real her.

Friday nights were a form of venting. Such things were a necessity. She always considered it a hiccup in her personality, the need to become someone she wasn't. It was like releasing a bunch of un-Lilah-like feelings consistently bottling themselves up in her head. A *girl's gotta have her secrets*, she supposed. She tapped her pen against her lips as if waiting for the silly thoughts to pass before continuing her inquest into any other late-night leavings she might have left herself in the margins of *Hoyle*.

As she flipped through the book's first pages, something immediately caught her eye—an unusual usage of red ink amid a swarm of black, a quickly scribbled drawing of a heart, and the following passage: *Ace of hearts replaced with one of hearts. I guess it's the opposite of the thirteen of spades. It feels like a Mack Truck to the gut.*

Upon reading that last line, she instinctively winced in pain. If there was one thing she remembered clearly, it was that feeling. In fact, she still felt it; she felt a lot weaker overall now. She'd even noticed that morning while looking at herself in the mirror that her skin was much paler. Her eyes were also red, though she supposed that could have been from the smoke from the late-night burned Meat.

She realized she would have to toughen up if she continued playing like this. Although she wasn't sure how to accomplish such a feat as making one's soul stronger, she figured trying something like meditation was worth a shot. It's not like concentrating on not thinking could hurt anyway. *Perhaps on Sunday, I'll head up to Hazel's store and pick up some incense and a book on Zen, well-being, and peace of mind.* Her eyes drifted to the clock hanging on the wall above her desk. It was only seven. Hell, maybe she'd make the trip tonight.

Still thinking about that first line she'd written, she slipped on her biker boots, tightening one strap at a time, then stood and patted her ebony skirt, straightening the laces on the end. She slung her black hoodie over her dark blouse. She took care to tuck her long hair into the hood, which she pulled over her head. *You can't be too careful, especially with the weather's shenanigans this time of the year*. After placing a wad of cash into her black purse, she looked down at the desk and reached to grab the lone book.

As she looked at the handwritten words scrawled across the two revealed pages, an image popped into her head: the face of an older man with wrinkles cut deeply down his cheeks and beside his eyes and white tufts of hair poking out from the sides of his mostly bald head. She remembered her time with him when her parents were out caring for their duties. She remembered how he entertained her with those old-fashioned card tricks, remnants of his antiquated practice as an amateur magician. She remembered opening the present two weeks before he passed away: within a shoebox wrapped in newspapers, the copy of *Hoyle's Guide to Poker and Other Parlor Games*, and a little package that contained a deck of playing cards and poker chips. There was something she had forgotten to say to him, and now her grandpa was gone. As she snatched the book and tucked it into her purse, warm tears ran down her eyes in black streaks of salty eyeliner. She didn't bother to wipe them away or touch up the makeup. She would go out like this. "Besides, I'm not the only person out there crying tonight."

)

"Are you sure you're alright?" the man behind the cash register inquired again.

"Yes, I'm fine. I just forgot to finish up my face before I left." His concern genuinely touched her.

The organization of the shelves was simple but still seemed unusual to Lilah. Next to copies of the Bible and sets of prayer beads were books on the occult and atheism. It was down this aisle of books and meditation devices that she found the first item she was looking for. Upon selecting the text on Buddhist meditation practices, she went to the decoration section, where smells of potpourri and scented candles overwhelmed her senses. Making her way to the far end, she picked up a package containing a set of burning incense and a clever little stand to place it on. Satisfied, she made her way to the counter.

The hesitant cashier accepted her money and bid her a good night. At this, she offered the man, slightly graying, a hint of a smile and exited the shop. The sun had finally sunk below the horizon, dragging its slowly dimming orange glow behind it like a heavy burden stuck indefinitely to its back. The cool air of the cloudless night was a sweet refreshment to her nose and lungs. She inhaled deeply and set off for home. Gentle breezes caressed her face, and she allowed her eyes to gaze upwards at the open sky; she pulled her hood off her head.

Overhead stretched a vast expanse of darkness flecked with dimly glowing white lights shining down from an unfathomable distance. Darkened faces of vacant shopfronts drifted by as Lilah walked along the sidewalk. The town was bathed in silence, only interrupted by the conversations of random pedestrians and the hum of the occasional automobile as it weaved between the silent, hulking structures like ants marching around blades of grass. Streetlights began to flicker on with *pops* and *whirs*, illuminating circles of pavement and curb regularly, creating an illusion of an alternating world of light and dark.

Lilah's trek ended abruptly at the corner of Constance Avenue and Main Street, a prominent intersection on her journey to her sanctuary. As she waited for the orange

No Crossing sign to change its face to the white Walk, the rugged hum of a thoroughly used engine crept up behind her. Curiosity struck her, and she glanced over her shoulder and saw a beat-up brown sedan. A relic straight out of the seventies had stopped at the light, another wanderer merely waiting for an orange light to change to something a bit brighter. Through the glow cast by the traffic light, she could see the passenger's face—pale and haggard, with dark circles hanging low under the eyes, almost darker than the ones she had painted around hers earlier. His face was thoroughly spotted with stubble. Perhaps it could be called the beginnings of a beard. His gaze slowly drifted up and met hers, hidden behind her ever-present wide glasses. For a second, their eyes met, and Lilah felt a shiver run deep down her spine and thought she heard a growl. Immediately, she turned her attention forward, and in that exact second, both lights announced that it was safe to proceed.

Beside her, the car rumbled and rolled off, making its way down Constance Avenue, then hung a right until it was entirely out of view. Lilah sighed in relief, gracefully stepping off the curb and crossing the street with a slight sense of urgency. Again, she found herself in that desolate world alternating between light and dark, rimmed with the grim and silent sentinels. One more block now, and she would be home. Lilah figured she'd try the incense tonight, maybe read the first few pages of the book, and then tomorrow, funeral-willing, she would get to practice this newfound hobby; her purse and shopping bag swung with new intent. She made her way home with renewed vigor.

)

"No, no, no, son of a bitch!" Dana picked up the pot off the stove as it boiled over. "Another reason why I get take-out, fucking hell!" He tossed the pot angrily in the sink, and globs of old cream of corn sloshed up on his T-shirt. "Oh, for fuck's sake!" Dana threw his arms up in disbelief. He removed his shirt and tossed it aside on the floor, then reached for a sponge to clean up the water that had pooled around the element on the stove. He sighed as he went back and forth between the sink and stove. *I swear, I need a dishwasher. I don't have time for this. I can't take a piss without having . . .* Dana's mind rant was interrupted by the ringing phone.

"Deupree! Make it quick!"

"Cheese and rice, Dana, what crawled up your ass and lodged itself sideways?" Walter growled back. "Ya, prick."

"Oh, sorry, Walt. I . . . I'm just cleaning."

Walter chuckled. "I have to say, that's a first. You cleaning on a Saturday night—well, hell, cleaning anything in general."

"Yes, Walt, I thought that I would, just for the hell of it, clean my house . . . on a Saturday night." Dana cradled the phone between his shoulder and ear as he cleaned up the last bit of water. "What do you want?"

"Alright, Dana . . ." Walter began, then sighed. "Well, I wanted to see if you wanted to catch a flick, but if you're busy cleaning, I can call up old Beatty."

Dana paused. *Hmm . . . I could get something to eat. It'd be a chance to get out.* Dana scanned his kitchen, noting the dishes piled high on the counter near the sink and layering the bottom. *To hell with this mess.* "N-no, Walt. Sure, I'll come with you. Uh, come and pick me up if you don't mind. I have to get something for dinner, though—" Dana was interrupted again, this time by the doorbell, followed by a series of knocks.

"Hang on. Someone's at my door—it's you, isn't it?" Dana spoke to dead silence. He hung up and sighed, shaking his head with a grin. Dana cursed again as he picked up his T-shirt and trudged through the kitchen towards the front door. He rounded the corner and answered the door to find Walter holding a Chinese take-out bag.

Walter raised an eyebrow at a shirtless Dana. "You're, uh, you're doing some pretty hardcore cleaning, I take it?" He poked his head inside.

Dana rolled his eyes. "No, Walt. I went to take a piss. Which ended up turning into a number two." He turned around, motioning Walter to follow. "The damn pot boiled over, and I tossed it in the sink. Shit got all over my shirt."

Walter nodded. "Ah. Yeah. Well then, I got dinner, no problem." He placed the bag down on Dana's small octagonal oak dining table. "I got your favorite as well."

Dana grinned. "Ah, jeez, thanks. It makes me feel all warm and creeped out at the same time." He sighed contentedly. "No matter. Here, I'll be right back with some whiskey."

Walter removed his coat and placed it on the back of his chair, sitting at the table.

Dana flipped a switch that sparked a low, dim light above the table, slowly brightening to a reasonable level. He then walked to his room, at the back of his house, to fetch a shirt and make himself more presentable. Dana wandered into the bathroom as Walter babbled, ranting about something related to the case, but it went in one ear and out the other. He stared hard at himself in the mirror, at the dark circles under his eyes, the face stubble from having not shaved in the last couple of days. Dana turned the cold-water handle, ran his hands under the frigid flow, splashing his face in the icy water, and stared back at himself. He rubbed his eyes, grabbed a towel, and patted his face dry. Dana put on his black T-shirt, which was a bit unusual—given he usually wore dress shirts. *Ah, what the hell, it's relaxing for a change*, he thought as he lightly brushed back his hair and made his way out to the dining area, but not before swinging around the corner into the kitchen to grab the whiskey he'd promised.

"Grab me a bottle of soda if you can, Dana," Walter shouted. "Liquor hasn't been agreeing with me lately."

Dana paused, rolled his eyes, and grabbed a bottle of Coke for Walter. He retraced his steps to the dining area, sat down, and handed Walter his refreshment.

Walter smiled as he unscrewed the cap and took a few sips. "Thanks."

Dana nodded as he retrieved the Styrofoam box containing General Tso's chicken. *Finally! Man, it's been a while.* Dana sat back and enjoyed his meal, which was far more successful than he had planned.

"Thanks for the grub, Walt," he said as he finished. "Movie tickets are on me." He wiped his mouth with his napkin.

"No problem," Walter said with a nod. "I know you're as helpless as a kid stuck at college, always feasting on Ramen noodles when all you want is a good meal." Walter laughed heartily and then checked his watch. "The movie starts in forty-five minutes. Want to get a head start?"

Dana nodded. "Sure, let me clean this up, and we'll head out. If you want, I'll meet you outside."

Walter coughed into his hand. "Alright, I'll see you out front then." He stood up and stuffed himself inside his coat, seemingly tighter. He grunted. "The only thing I hate about eating Chinese . . . ugh. It's so great, but it makes me so damn bloated." He headed out to his beaten-up car. Dana often joked about how it would randomly blow up one day.

Dana rushed to the kitchen for his white trash can and cleared the mess in the dining room with a single sweep into the pail. He rebounded to the kitchen for the finale—placing the trash can back underneath the sink. As he snatched his keys from the oak coffee table, he retrieved the lone gun that sat adjacent (and in need of good company) and placed it in his holster.

The evening air waltzed gracefully across the lawn as Dana stepped outside. The sky was clear, and the stars were beginning to peek out from under the day's blanket—one by one—across the bed that sprawled for miles unending, with dabs of a low-hanging cloud here and there. The sun had set into a red-orange placement, disappearing beneath the horizon from sight. "Alright, Walt, let's hit it." Dana situated himself comfortably in the passenger seat. Walter nodded, and they headed into the heart of Middleton. Maple Street led the pair through the nightlife of Old Middleton. Though some shops were vacated for the night, others were bustling: the bars, a dance club, and a few mom-and-pop shops. At night, the town was beautiful—to Dana, at least.

The wrought-iron lamp posts were spaced evenly down Main Street, their silhouettes illuminated under the soft amber glow. The layered brick crosswalks weathered under the stress of time and commuters. At the town's epicenter stood the lone courthouse in solitude, the clock at its peak speaking at the top of every hour. The clock's slow, ever-gazing eyes watched—attentive—the area below and the timberline that stretched towards the outskirts of town. Trees were trimmed and landscaped to perfection. It was the ideal town, a town of dreams.

The beat-up car clattered down the slightly occupied streets, past silhouettes of passersby, those leaving shops or going off to the bar. A light turned red, and Walter slowed to a halt. Dana stared blankly ahead.

In his peripheral vision, he saw a figure. He slowly turned his head to his right, catching a glimpse of her silhouette before she came into focus—slightly above average height, slender legs, pale under the evening's light. She stood just outside a dark emblem of light. She met his eyes through thin black spectacles. Mascara streaks ran down her cheeks as if she had been crying. She was enshrouded in darkness: black skirt, hoodie, jet-black hair. A sense of familiarity overcame him, making him wonder if he knew the girl from somewhere. As he stared for that moment, he felt a strange pain in his right eye that began to overwhelm him. He winced, and then the light turned green.

Walter continued to cruise the streets, making a few turns here and there until they finally completed the journey to Romero's Theater. As he and Walter exited the car, Dana still thought of the girl he saw at the crosswalk, remembering where he had seen her before, if he even knew her, and why his eye raged with pain. He shrugged it off as he neared the entrance. Now was not a time to worry about such coincidences.

Glitz, glamor, and excessive pizzazz greeted them—the enormous red-and-orange neon Romero's Theater sign that displayed its namesake and depicted the daily features stated in black-and-red print. They entered the lobby to hear thundering speakers and bright screens playing trailers and smell the scent of fresh popcorn and butter. Two high school students sat talking in a small box behind the cashier's station while four others did their jobs and attended to customers. *Typical*, Dana thought with a sigh.

He shuffled to an open cashier station. He could feel Walter practically salivating.

"Good evening. How may I help you?" asked the young man behind the counter.

Walter whipped out his wallet as he eyed the electronic movie board above the station. "Uh, get us two—"

"Walt, you know I'm buying, right?"

Walter looked at Dana with confusion. "Oh, yeah, sorry, heh." He put his wallet away, chuckling at his forgetfulness.

Dana traded places with Walter and also eyed the board. "Two tickets for *Machete*, please." He handed a wad of cash to the teen as the machine spit out two tickets. "Keep the change, kid."

"Thank you, sir!" The deep voice rose, almost cracking out of its range.

The detectives made their way to the concession stand, where the employees bumbled around like a group of busy bees—the honey was fresh and appetizing. The two assumed an attack formation, with Walter as the point man and Dana as the wingman.

A petite young girl who looked to be just out of high school approached the counter to wait on them. Her long jet-black hair was secured in pigtails with elastics, each containing an alabaster skull, stark amid the ebony strands. She wore a spiked black leather dog collar, upside-down crosses hung from her ears, and thin-rimmed oval glasses sat on her nose, adorned with a skull stud. Her plump lips were as dark as death. Her face was soft and elegantly round. *Hell,* Dana thought. *In her dark way, she is a model.* Her pale complexion contradicted the vibrancy of her red-and-black checkered leggings. Her tall boots clunked against the overworked floor behind the counter. She seductively leaned over and gazed upon the two detectives. Her name tag was decorated with skulls and crossbones in a purple glittered ink that also scrawled out *Lynaly.*

Before them stood a modern-day succubus rather than the stereotypical modern classification of a goth. She spoke smoothly and seductively, her voice dark, sweet, and alluring with a slight raspy undertone. "What can I get you, boys?"

Maybe it's her I've seen before. Enthralling, entrancing, enticing. Dana was mesmerized and dumbstruck by a stray memory. *That sounds so familiar, but where exactly was it?* He thought again about the girl at the crosswalk.

Walter checked himself before opening his mouth and straightened. "A jumbo tub of popcorn—saturate it with butter—and an extra-large Coca-Cola, if you would be so kind, Lynaly." He finished his order with a big smile.

Dana rolled his eyes, silently laughing to himself. *Christ, Walt, she's thirty years younger than you. You cradle-robbing son of a bitch.*

Lynaly then turned her gaze to Dana, her tone more alluring. "And what can I get you?" She smirked.

"Hmm, a small popcorn, light on the butter, lightly salted"— Dana gazed past Lynaly—"and a medium Coca-Cola with a lemon wedge, if you would, please, miss."

Lynaly smiled at Dana as she slowly pushed off the counter, showing a bit of her cleavage. She turned to fulfill the requested order, and Dana and Walter noticed the wiggle she gave when she took a step. Her miniskirt did the curves of her hips justice, while her tight blouse amplified her bosom.

"Boy, I wish I were ten years younger. I looked good then, you know," Walter whispered to Dana.

Dana rolled his eyes. "I think you'd need to be at least thirty years younger for it to be legal with her. Jesus, man."

The two shared a laugh before Lynaly came back bearing their demands. "Is this separate or together?" She eyed Dana—slowly.

"Hmm? Oh, split, please, heh." Dana smiled.

Her lips cracked into a slight grin. She seemed to mutter, "Mmm," and Dana could have sworn she was mentally undressing him.

As they paid, he noticed her glance at their MPD badges, and she scribbled something down on a piece of paper, giving Dana a wink. "Enjoy the show . . . detectives."

"Thank you, Lynaly. Have a good night." Dana smiled and nodded, turning his back to her. As they walked away, Dana noticed the slip of paper in his change. It read:

You can use the handcuffs on me anytime, sugar.
—Lynaly

Dana giggled as his eyes ran over the note and phone number. She was cute and mysterious, too. He tucked the piece of paper in his wallet with his paper currency.

Halfway through the show, Dana's mind drifted, much like his eyes, and he fell asleep. Grotesque images were projected on the backs of his eyelids. From the city morgue emerged a very dead yet newly reanimated John Doe, who was missing half of his face—or rather, head. His right hand was replaced with a high-caliber gun, as though he were some cyber-zombie. A pair of rabid, brain-eating, electricity-shooting zombie kids mindlessly (and slowly) wandered the streets. And all the while, Dana was pursued by a giant flaming brute bellowing for bloody vengeance. Ultimately, an unknown but familiar girl who wielded a poker deck of life and death saved him. She drew a royal flush, banishing the monsters. Their screams of agony and determination haunted his ears until they became nothing more than a puff of wind.

A soft voice echoed from the girl's dark silhouette. "This is only the beginning, Dana."

He startled himself awake.

Walter looked over at him. "It's about time you woke up, sleeping beauty."

Dana scowled at his friend, who sat with a grin on his buttered lips. He rubbed his eyes, focusing on the screen before him. "I'll be back. I'm going to the bathroom."

"Bah, c'mon, it's gonna be over by the time you're done—can't ya hold it?" Walter munched on another handful of popcorn. The tub was nearly full again, having been refilled not long ago.

Dana shook his head and descended the stairs. As he exited the theater, he saw Lynaly talking to another girl. She saw Dana and stared. He felt as if her eyes were groping him, investigating places unseen.

He went to the bathroom and could still feel eyes upon him as he relieved his bladder. Turning his head back, he saw nothing but black-and-white-checkered tiling. Feeling uncomfortable, he finished up quickly and washed his hands. Dana stared at himself in the mirror. The circles under his eyes were slightly lighter, but he hated the idea of having paid to sleep in a chair. *Tomorrow, I think I'll shave for a change.*

He reached into his coat pocket and pulled out the plastic baggie that contained Mable's name tag. The ink had nearly vanished—undoubtedly, she hadn't wanted to leave a trace. He tossed it in the trash. *I'll wait for you to slip up, Mable, or whoever you are. It's only a matter of time.* He exited the bathroom and went back towards the theater. Using his peripheral vision, he couldn't see if Lynaly was still at the concession stand, but when he glanced behind him, he saw her come out of the women's bathroom, adjusting her clothing. Her gaze connected to his. He casually turned his attention forward and almost ran into Walter.

"Holy shit, I would have leveled you if you were some other prick!" Walter said jokingly.

Is the movie over already?" Dana looked back towards the bathrooms. There was no sign of Lynaly.

"Yeah, it was great too. There were even spoof trailers of a few sequels." Walter sighed, seemingly let down yet pleased. "Here's your coat. I guess"—Walter yawned— "I'll take you home."

"Thanks, Walt, that's really sweet of ya, but don't think you're staying over at my place. I don't think your ex wants to know you're next door." Dana laughed. "She might believe you still care or something."

Walter joined in on the laugh. "That broad? Bah, she's a skank. I'm just glad I didn't have any kids with her. If anything, she'd probably get jealous. Besides, I'm sure Quinn gives it to her more than enough." Walter shook his head. "Good old Double D. Debbie."

The two exited into the chilly night. Up high in the heavens, the night's umbrella was fully open now and sparkled brilliantly, much like the moon, which bled into the darkness of the night. A cloud continually shrouded it from view, but a silvered lining emanated. Serenity was this night.

"She wasn't that bad—not that I know, but she seemed alright."

"Ha, that's because she wanted to nail you," Walter added as he chuckled.

"No way, I was not her type. You're just making that up."

Walter shook his head. "Didn't matter to her, as long as you had a dick made of wood. She'd do anything that could drill her. I thank God I'm rid of that parasite," he said as they approached the car. "She sucked me dry." He laughed. "And I don't mean like a blow job either. Granted, she was just like a Hoover."

Dana laughed as Walter unlocked the doors. "You're an animal, Walt, a real animal."

As Dana searched the parking lot, he noticed a silhouette near the corner of the theater just before it disappeared into the shadows. He shrugged it off and got into the car.

)

As the duo drove off, she emerged. The once poor high school massacre victim, Beth, had been there, watching from the darkness. She'd tracked her quarry for weeks, watching, learning, waiting. She knew she was close when she watched the girl known as Lynaly enter Romero's Theater. The sick, burning hatred that coiled around her heart whenever she thought of the massacre never let her forget. However, a new hold had her in a grip that seemed to will its way through her body.

Tonight, she was done waiting.

The treetops and rooftops of Middleton offered the hunter a clear vantage point. The cold of the night bit into her bones, but she ignored it. She followed behind Lynaly as she left the theater, moving silently above her, a predator stalking her prey.

As Lynaly crossed into the empty lot behind the theater, Beth made her move. A single gunshot shattered the night.

Lynaly stopped mid-step, her head turning slowly toward the direction of the shot, a wicked smile playing at her lips.

"Well, well," she murmured, eyes gleaming. "It seems a little mouse has come out to play."

Beth, surprised, readied a shooting stance again. "I'm going to kill you," Beth said, her voice cold and hollow.

"Are you, now?" Lynaly asked, amused. "Try not to miss again, little mouse."

Before Beth fired another shot, Lynaly moved faster than Beth could track, a blur of shadows and magenta flame.

Beth barely had time to drop the handgun and draw her silver dagger before Lynaly was on her.

The two clashed violently, Beth slashing wildly while Lynaly toyed with her, blocking with graceful ease. A smirk never left her face.

"You've got spirit," Lynaly cooed, deflecting a desperate strike. "But you're out of your depth, little girl."

Beth lunged, screaming, her blade aimed for Lynaly's heart.

Lynaly caught her wrist with inhuman strength and twisted. The sound of bone cracking filled the night. Beth cried out, falling to her knees.

"So fragile," Lynaly whispered, crouching beside her, eyes burning with cruel delight. "And you thought you could kill me? You—a pawn who doesn't even know her place."

Beth gasped, her vision swimming from pain, but her hatred burned brighter. She spat blood onto Lynaly's boots.

"You killed them," Beth shouted, tears burning as they streamed down her cheeks. "You killed them all. I'll send you back to Hell."

Lynaly chuckled darkly, tracing a single finger down Beth's cheek.

"Poor, little broken thing," she murmured, rising to her feet, towering over her. "You don't even realize . . . the hell you already live in."

She raised a hand, magenta flames licking her fingertips, ready to end it.

"That's enough." The voice was calm but commanding.

Two fiery embers flickered and danced as they stepped out of the mist, charging the air around the young man with an unseen energy.

"You? I had told you to run and run far away. I'd advise you to stay out of this," Lynaly warned, not turning to face him. "This doesn't concern you."

"Shane?" Beth said through the pain.

"It concerns me when you kill someone who doesn't deserve it."

"She tried to kill me, and if you're going to get in my way, then I'll extinguish both of your miserable lives."

"Because you murdered her friends," Shane said simply, stepping between Lynaly and Beth, whose body trembled on the pavement. "And mine."

Lynaly's eyes narrowed dangerously. "You're making a mistake."

"I've made many of those," Shane whispered, but his stance was firm.

A tense silence passed, the night holding its breath.

Then, with a soft, infuriating laugh, Lynaly lowered her hand, the flames extinguishing. "Another time, then," she whispered, stepping back, her gaze lingering on Beth with something akin to pity. "You won't be so lucky next time, little puppet." She vanished into the mist.

Shane turned to Beth, kneeling beside her. She flinched at his touch, but her body was broken—she couldn't fight him off.

"Let me help," he said gently, touching her shattered wrist. A faint warmth pulsed from him, and Beth, though wary, felt the bones begin to knit together.

"Why . . . why are you helping me?" Beth whispered, staring at him with burning hatred and confusion.

Shane met her gaze, his own filled with regret and something darker.

"Because there are things you're unaware of."

Behind Beth's eyes, Amii stirred, observing Shane. *You'd do well to keep him at bay, child. He's a dangerous one.* Her presence was cold and predatory, but there was a glimmer of satisfaction beneath the warning as though Shane's hesitation had pleased her. Beth disregarded the comment. And Shane, despite his healing touch, felt that wrongness in Beth—something that didn't belong, something twisted. He had a hunch, thanks to the Man with the Red Right Hand, but nothing was definite.

He said nothing about it. Not yet. His voice was gentle, "The important thing is that I've found you . . . and now that I have a second chance, I'm not going to let it go. We lost everything, Beth, so let's start over from scratch. Together."

A flicker of doubt passed through Beth's eyes for a moment—so brief it was nearly imperceptible. But it was there—a slight dip in her fiery resolve.

"I'm sorry, but I can't," she said, much to Amii's delight.

)

Atreyu stood alone in a small neighborhood, homes silently dozed, resting from the day's events to prepare for the next while he waited to meet destiny. The air seemed to hum with an unnatural pressure as if the world knew what would happen and dared not interfere.

He wouldn't have to wait long.

A slow, measured footfall echoed on the pavement from behind him. Atreyu didn't turn immediately. He knew who it was. The air had already shifted—cold, metallic, and tinged with decay.

"Tell me, boy. Do you think you can disrupt the order of the universe without facing consequences?" Albedo's voice was like crushed glass, sharp and unpleasant. The tall, gaunt figure stepped into a broken overhead lamp's faint, sputtering glow. His presence assaulted the senses—a dense, suffocating pressure that made the shadows recoil.

Atreyu sensed a danger that went beyond the usual. There was something about Albedo tonight that felt. . . off. His movements were precise, yet too fluid, like a marionette whose strings were pulled with practiced ease. The way his eyes caught the dim light, they were too glassy. But Atreyu, ever focused on the game at hand, dismissed the unease as anticipation.

"It's funny you bring that up, dear Albedo," Atreyu said with a smile and a thin, dangerous curve on his lips. "In any case, try not to get too poetic. I know you've been snooping around my affairs for too long. Therefore, I thought it was time we had a talk."

Albedo sneered, the pale skin of his face stretching taut. "You've grown too arrogant, boy. The Order tolerates your ambition because you produce results. But you seem to have forgotten your place."

"Oh, I never do," Atreyu murmured, finally facing him. His icy blue eyes gleamed faintly, reflecting the dim light like a predator's. "After all, you've been there in service to the Master for as long as I have. I think, though, perhaps you have. Otherwise, you wouldn't have come alone."

A flicker of something passed over Albedo's expression—fear, maybe. But it was quickly masked with disdain. "Pah," he spat. "I don't need an entourage to deal with a man-child who thinks they're playing soldier."

Atreyu laughed softly, a sound like dry leaves scraping across stone. "Good. Good. Then you won't see this coming."

Before Albedo could react, Atreyu was on him, moving with inhuman speed. The first blow cracked ribs; the second sent Albedo sprawling across the cold, damp pavement. He skidded, coughing black ichor, eyes wide in disbelief.

"What . . . what are you doing?" Albedo snarled, clutching his side.

"What I should have done long ago," Atreyu whispered, advancing slowly. "You've been a festering sore on the Order, my plans . . " A shimmer of something sinister further flickered in his eyes, his mask emphasizing the night's glow. "And my uncle for far too long. But don't worry, you'll still serve a purpose."

Albedo tried to rise, but Atreyu was already there, a hand around his throat, lifting him effortlessly. Power crackled in the air, ancient and dark.

"No," Albedo gasped, realization dawning too late. "You . . . you can't . . ."

"Oh, but I can." Atreyu leaned in close, his voice a cold caress. "The Order won't mourn you. And as for your soul . . . well, let's just say I have . . . other plans."

"His Excellency will hear of this!" Albedo cried out before . . .

A violent surge of energy erupted between them. Albedo's scream was brief, a ragged, wet sound that cut off abruptly as his body convulsed and collapsed inward, the flesh dissolving into black ash, leaving behind only a tiny, trembling mass of raw essence. A soul stripped down bare.

Even as he had forced Albedo into that corner, driving the fatal blow, there was a fleeting moment—an instinct—that whispered this wasn't right. Albedo's reaction lacked the depth of fear or rage Atreyu expected. It was almost . . . resigned. Yet before Atreyu could process the thought, the universe delivered its cruel convenience, and as such, he took it, believing the problem was solved.

Nearby, a chocolate lab barked incessantly with concern for the neighborhood. Atreyu knelt, cradling the soul gently, almost reverently. "Yes, I think a more . . . obedient form will suit you."

With a whispered incantation, the soul shuddered, twisted, and flew into the yapping dog. It yelped and rolled on the ground before slowly collecting itself. A low growl echoed from the chocolate lab, its eyes burning faintly red.

"Perfect," Atreyu murmured, stroking the dog's head with deceptive gentleness.

As he did, the faintest hesitation rippled through him—a flicker of doubt, like a cold finger tracing his spine. What if this was too easy? What if this was a step into someone else's design? But he pushed the thought away, savoring the moment, believing himself the master of the board.

"What have you done?" the beast whimpered.

"For all your knowledge, supposed foresight, you fell so easily into my trap." Atreyu grinned. "Now then, if you value your life, use that demon sense of yours and go. Find that green-stained cur and . . . convince her. Be useful for once."

"Fine. But know this: the Master will learn of this betrayal, boy," Albedo said, bound and broken, as the beast's form whimpered a few times before obediently slinking into the shadows.

Atreyu watched him go, the cold smile never leaving his face. Still, though everything was falling into place, he couldn't shake the ominous feeling of eyes on him. The thought that the Master would come to learn of Albedo's fate had crossed his mind, but he had words and evidence to support his reasoning for why he did the task.

Unbeknownst to him, through the eye of a nearby crow perched high above, the *real* Albedo observed silently, a small, knowing smile playing on his lips. The imposter had served its purpose well. He'd need to alter his appearance now; it wasn't difficult, but it was amusing nonetheless. The Order was always willing to accept . . . patrons . . . and indeed, a new one of his caliber would be welcomed with open arms. After all, the game was far from over.

6

♠

SHE DIDN'T MIND THE incense. If anything, it was a nice change of pace. Lilah's father was surprised and pleased, as always, when she started doing something he didn't view as occult-related. The book she had found was a bust, though. After glancing through it, she realized it was just a ridiculous collection of words she could have read in one sitting. The whole text, about two hundred pages, was easily summed up in one piece of advice: Close your eyes, open your mind, and let your worries and fears drift away until there is only peace.

Her dad was snoring steadily down the hall of their three-bedroom apartment. Her younger brother had long since gone to a sleepover at a friend's house. This night was as peaceful as it got at the Dean's residence. Nights like these made her wonder if things would have been different had her mother been around. But she never asked, and her father never offered. It was easier that way. Some memories, she thought, were better left unsaid.

She moved across her room without urgency, closing the curtains and her bathroom door. Searching several drawers, she pieced together a set of pajamas and slipped into the sleepwear.

Then she reached into the red tote bag, shoved into the corner of her closet, and pulled out a lighter. After a few attempts, she managed to spark a flame and promptly used it to light the end of an incense stick, which she placed on the little stand she had set up on her desk. The smoke drifted upward in a thin, scraggly line before contacting the ceiling and drifting into several tendrils.

The smell immediately filled the room, filling every corner with the sweet scent of white sage. Lilah pulled two red candles out of a drawer in her desk, set them up on either side of the incense stand, and lit them. When she turned the lights off, soft white-yellow became a dim, flickering orange as the tiny flames danced with miniature air currents.

Lilah climbed onto her bed and coaxed her legs into a crossed position. She glanced at the clock: 11:15. She then placed her hands on her lap and closed her eyes. White sage filled her nostrils, and memories of the previous days, weeks, and months flooded her mind—horrific images formed of faces exploding, blue light arcing from her hands, and burned hair. Voices and sounds followed, but silence and darkness slowly began to work between the memories as she searched for them. Black gaps wedged their way into her thoughts and forced the harmful thoughts out. Images dimmed, and voices became whispers.

A wave of warmth rushed through her body, filling her head to toe. Darkness poured in like a blanket and surrounded her, bathing her in its absoluteness. She drifted into it and felt her muscles relax. The grip loosened until she could hardly tell it was there, making her happy. She allowed a simple smile to take her and relaxed even more as the warmth washed over her.

"*So, you have finally come looking for me?*" A voice boomed all around her, rattling her from her calm.

She retracted from it but remained in her shadow world. "Who . . . who are you?"

The voice lightly cackled. "*You know very well who Mullin is, you foolish little girl!*" A hard shiver jolted Lilah's spine, and cold began to creep over her body, replacing the newly found warmth. "So, *what brings you to me, child?*" With each word, the grip on her being tightened exponentially until it choked a small scream from inside her mind. Only then did it loosen a touch.

"But why are you here?"

"*I am a part of you now, girl. You should know by now.*" She winced, and a shriek released itself within her consciousness as the grip once again tightened. "*I ask you again. Why have you come searching for me?*" The voice echoed through her head, tearing into the silence like knives through silk.

"I was just seeking inner peace—"

The voice erupted in maniacal laughter, which rang through her head like the horn of a truck about to collide with an unwitting pedestrian. "*There is no room for such a thing in your life anymore. Now, there is only you and me, child.*"

"But why? Why like this? I-I don't understand."

The disembodied voice seemed to have a hint of a grin in reply. "*Because, little one, that was the deal we made. Although, I suppose I have always enjoyed being in the company of people like you. Ah, yes, people looking for pleasure, risk, and power. Never to worry about the consequences or even knowing them, but under no circumstances ever minding them—never bothering to feel remorse for their actions.*"

"Those people—it was always in self-defense, never for mere amusement. I am not a murderer!"

"Ha, *then why do you bother to gild your actions?*"

Lilah scrambled for a response but found none. In a world that held only truths, lies had no power.

"*Very well, I will demonstrate it to you then. I will show you just how much you and I have become ONE!*"

With that final word, Lilah's body rattled violently. She found herself lying on the carpet as she tried to force her eyes open. She flung her arm out, searching for something to grab ahold of, and her hand found the comfort of her bed. With some effort, she pulled herself to her feet and made her way to the light switch, stumbling on clothes and a book that lay in her dark path.

With the flip of a switch, her room was illuminated in soft white-yellow. The incense had long burned out, and the candles had become twin puddles of melted red and gray wax. She turned her gaze to the digital clock: 8:00. She had blacked out for almost eight hours. She made her way to her bathroom, and before opening the door, she bent down to pick up a shirt on the floor.

As she did, she noticed something peculiar—her pajama shirt wasn't hanging loosely. Instead, it stuck to her stomach. She stepped into the bathroom and immediately switched the light on. She froze in terror as she stared at herself in the mirror. Blood was strewn across her shirt and matted in her hair, and streaks of brownish-red ran up her right arm, across her face, and down the corners of her mouth.

)

The sun peeked through the chocolate-brown drapes that clung to Dana's bedroom window. He winced, silently cursing his tormentor. *Morning always comes all too soon.* Dana sighed as he rolled over from his left to his right, hoping to catch a few more minutes of slumber before the usual torrential downpour of events each day. Still, he found himself unable to resume his precious activity. *Every time.* Dana sighed again, throwing the covers off and sitting up. *Now I bet Walter's "Dana-is-up radar" is going off.*

Dana yawned loudly. It had been a while since he had gotten some rest. Then Dana remembered he needed to shave today . . . and the very sexually explicit dream he'd had about Lynaly—at least, he thought it was her. He smirked at the thought of bringing home such a girl. He had no room for a committed relationship. He was married to his job, but it did have its advantages now and then.

He grunted as he stretched. Gathering himself, he shuffled into the main bathroom. The light made him flinch and clench his eyes shut as he flicked it on. After rubbing his eyes, he stared at himself in the mirror. He noticed faint red markings on his chest—ten parallel lines that dragged downward. *Well, that is rather strange. . .* He ran his fingertips over the slightly raised skin; no pain flowed in return. He shrugged it off, thinking he might have scratched himself during the night. He retrieved his shaving cream and razor from the mirrored cabinet. After lathering up a wad of cream, he turned on the cold water from the faucet, but as he reached for the razor, he noticed something peculiar stuck to his shoulder: a single strand of long black hair. *Weird. Maybe it was from when I put my coat on the seat at the theater or from work. Terra has the same-colored hair . . . and she likes to give hugs.* Dana smiled as he thought of Terra.

She was energetic and petite, had shoulder-length black hair and bright green eyes, and possessed a Mona Lisa smile that could soothe the most savage predators. She also had voluptuous curves that many said were just wrong for her age and for someone who was a traffic cop. He couldn't remember a time when she didn't have a smile on her face.

As Dana shaved and his mind wandered, blood trickled down his cheek and into the sink. He looked down at the slightly bloodied water and the mirror. A vertical cut, like a number one, marked his face. *What the hell?* Dana placed his hands under the faucet and ran water over the wound on his cheek. He finished shaving and patted his face dry. The cut, relentless, continued to bleed. He threw the blood-spotted towel on the counter beside him. Opening up the mirrored cabinet again, he removed a package of Band-Aids. As he closed the cabinet door, he caught a glimpse of a dark silhouette behind him, grinning a Cheshire cat smile. He quickly turned but found only the shower vacant. *I must be losing it. This case is probably just getting to me.* Dana ran his fingers over his face and hair and skipped showering.

He wandered back into his lonely room, but while he took his time changing, he felt as though someone's eyes were upon him, the same feeling he'd had at the theater. He looked around the room but knew it to be empty. Dressed in a black-and-white pin-striped dress shirt, a crimson tie, and pleated black pants, he turned off the lights and exited for the kitchen, where he found the dishes washed and put away neatly. His kitchen was spotless. *Well, this is just getting stranger by the minute...* He walked over to grab the telephone, but it rang. Startled, he flinched and dropped it on the ground. He fumbled it back up to his face, sighing. "Deupree here."

He sighed with relief as he heard Walter at the end of the line. "Hey, Dana, been up for long?"

Dana ran his fingers through his hair. "No, not really—Hey, Walt, did anyone come in after us? Like, I mean, did anything happen after the movie?"

There was a long pause. "Uh . . . no, but you did go on a cleaning frenzy in the kitchen." He laughed. "It was like you were on a mission from God or something."

Whew. Thank God. Dana rolled his shoulders back, then leaned against the wall. "Interesting. Well, I was going to call you, but I doubt this is about wanting breakfast. What's up?"

"Animal Control was called out this morning." Dana could hear Walter take a sip of coffee. "What they found was probably the last thing they'd ever expect, at least around here."

Dana rubbed the back of his neck. "You mean like some kind of sacrifice or something?"

"Eh, kind of. I'll swing by and pick you up." Walter coughed a bit before continuing. "After we check it out, we can head to Cheryl Ann's Place for breakfast."

Dana nodded. "Alright, Walt, I'll be out front. I gotta grab my coat."

"Alright, I'll see you in a bit."

Why can't I remember anything? I remember that dream of that girl . . . and that's it. Dana rubbed his head as he hung up.

Strapping on his holster, he looked himself over in the mirror in the hallway to make sure he looked presentable, at least below the neck (his hair would still be classified as "bed hair"). Dana shrugged and left, locking the door behind him. Walter was already waiting outside.

The day was bright, with the sun nearing its peak. Clouds had been annihilated from the sky, and vibrant blue populated the view. The air was crisp with a few drafts of wind. Dana stared at his partner, whose green sunglasses and posture made him look almost as if he were waiting to whack him.

"You really have to stop this, Walt. It freaks me out sometimes," Dana said as he approached a cackling Walter.

They hopped into the car and sped off toward the neighborhood in question. "So, what was it that Animal Control couldn't handle?" Dana reached into his coat pocket and pulled out a pair of wire-rimmed black sunglasses as he turned his head towards his partner.

"They said it would be better if we were to see it—that it looks more criminal than anything natural or accidental." Walter sipped lightly on his coffee, his cup smaller than usual.

"What's with the small cup?"

"The doctor called and said I got to watch my intake. They said something about my blood pressure or whatever being high, the bastards." Walter shook his head. "It's like when they say eggs are good for you, then bad, and, oh no, wait! Now they're good for you! They can't make up their fucking minds. I swear."

Dana laughed. "Yeah, it's a whole lot of shenanigans, but that's good you're doing something about it."

"Meh, I could give a rat's ass. Plus, this was all they had this morning when I stopped by at eight." Walter smirked.

"That's my, Walter, alright." Dana giggled.

Arriving at the scene, the duo was greeted by an Animal Control specialist, who took his ball cap off and wiped his brow on his sleeve. He spoke as if being rushed. "Pleased to meet your acquaintance, detectives. The name's Ed." A small smile hid under his mustache.

"Ed." Dana nodded. "Detectives Dana Deupree and Walter Conway." Each extended a hand to Ed.

"So, what can you tell us about what you found here, Ed?" Walter whipped his notepad and a pair of latex gloves from his coat.

Ed turned around and motioned for Dana and Walter to follow. "I know this isn't the sort of thing you boys would usually deal with, but it definitely seemed out of the ordinary, and, well . . ."

They ventured behind Ed's truck. "My God, what is that?" Dana held his handkerchief to his nose.

"Well, it was a dog. The name was Rily. He was this here neighborhood's little gem. Great with the kids and ain't ever caused any fuss. A group of kids found him this morning. Apparently, this little fella was barking up a storm last night, and then there was a series of whelps and cries. Well, that's what the neighbors here said anyway." Ed knelt beside the carcass. "He was bitten too . . . Not sure by what, though. The bite mark almost looks human, doesn't it?"

Walter and Dana knelt beside Rily, his fur matted and crushed down under dried blood, his skin clawed and torn, his insides torn and draped out, marked with what seemed to be bite and further foreign impressions. The throat was slit deep and wide, nearly decapitating the poor chocolate Labrador.

"Who or what in the world could have done this?" Walter looked down at the Lab's head. Its blue eyes were open wide as if its life had been ripped from his body, and its tongue hung lazily out of its mouth.

"Dana, this is just wrong. Why would anyone go to such lengths to butcher a dog?" He was trying hard to keep his composure.

Dana shook his head. "I . . . I don't know." He looked up at Ed, who wiped his eyes. "We'll take it from here, Ed. We'll let you know when we're done so you can get on with your job."

Ed nodded and retreated in haste back to his truck. Jazz music played loudly, and Dana could hear crying in short breaks. Dana pulled out his latex gloves, and the glum pair examined the canine further. *Ah, damn it, always a sucker when it comes to animals.* Dana sighed as he turned the dog's head slightly. On it was a pattern similar to another he had seen before. This was, however, not a spade but a club.

"Well, Walt, we almost have a full playing deck." Dana set the dog's head gently onto the ground.

Walter looked at Dana, puzzled. "What do you mean? Is it connected?"

Dana nodded. "He has a club engraved on his head, and I don't think it was done with a knife, nor was his throat. It's like something or someone just ripped him open using its nails. Ugh." Dana stood up straight and turned away. "Take some pictures if you don't mind. I'm going to talk with Ed real quick."

He knocked on the truck door and stared in another direction, allowing Ed to wipe his eyes. Ed stepped out of the truck and looked at Dana, his eyes red.

"I'm sorry, Ed. I know you're not used to something as brutal as this." He gave him a pat on the back.

Ed shook his head. "No, sir, first time finding something like this." He sniffled, trying to maintain self-control.

Dana looked Ed in the eye. "Hopefully, it will be your last, too. Trust me, we'll get whoever is responsible." He glanced over his shoulder to see Walter come up behind him, the camera hanging loosely around his neck. "We're done here, so we'll leave you to your job."

Ed nodded and shook their hands, and Walter pat Ed on the back.

Noting the time, Dana sighed as Walter started the car. "Well, we may want to make that lunch instead."

Walter nodded as he drove the car and tossed the camera in the back. "Yeah, it's alright"—he grinned— "since you're buying."

Dana glared at his partner. "Bullshit, you have money. Get it yourself."

Walter frowned. "But I got your dinner last night."

"Fair enough, lunch it is," he said, nodding abruptly.

Walter smiled, and Dana stared out the passenger side window. *Did you do this "Mable"?* Dana shook his head. *What . . . who made you do this? Why?*

)

He was moving fast. Not because the hospital had told him he had to leave when his insurance didn't go through. And not because of the warnings that the pain medication would wear off in five to ten hours, although that could have been part of it. He stormed through the wards, desperately searching for a way out, a way to go down. Finally, through the red haze—he wasn't sure if it was the rage or some side effect of the medicine or something; he hadn't bothered to pay attention to those eggheads—he spotted an elevator.

He took a few moments to formulate a plan of vengeance. Under his finger, the down button lit up in a dull green. Now, he had to play the waiting game. In front of him, the numbers above the doors danced to a tune that could only be the creation of a madman. There shouldn't be this much activity this time of day—at least, that's how he figured it.

Behind him, a woman at a desk stopped typing. He knew this type, what she would say, knew he was at his weakest, knew she would know where to find the wounds, and would dig her claws into them solely to make them far worse and only for her satisfaction. She was going to say something, and he was sure that in the red haze of the world, his rage would be unleashed, and this was not something he wanted, not quite yet.

"Sir."

His muscles clenched up. He could feel his hands digging into his palms beneath the bandages, the medication barely keeping the feeling at bay. Underneath his burned-on-the-edges leather jacket, underneath the bandages that wrapped his whole upper body, his arms, his face, his skin shrieked in agony, but the cries fell on drug-deafened ears. He wasn't sure if his nails were drawing blood—hell, he wasn't even sure if he still had nails.

"Sir."

The doctor had said parts were missing; they were burned off—whatever that meant. He was a roasted marshmallow, and no amount of health care would reverse that.

"Sir."

What good would the absence of any part mean when your body looked like Silly Putty anyway? No, that didn't matter. What did matter . . .

"Sir? Mr. Estrada?"

His rage was hitting a fever pitch now. He could see himself digging his fingers into the old bat's eye sockets; her screams would be a cold refreshment or a tasty appetizer before the main course. Underneath white cloth, bandages, a horrific parody of a smile lit across his face, and he knew that—DING! A silver door slid open before him, and a storm of white coats and metal crashing snapped Ward Estrada from his fantasy. He waited for the stragglers to exit, then entered the tiny vacant room. The nurse stood up and waved her arms at him. Silver quietly slid into place, stifling her attempts to gain his attention. He took in a raspy breath before hitting the 1 button. The elevator hummed to its destination, and Ward's mind began formulating plans again.

The door opened, and he stormed out, moving like a man with unfinished business. He brushed past two men in matching long brown coats, knocking the wider of the two enough to spill hot coffee out of his tiny cup and onto his hand and shirt.

"Hey asshole, watch where you're— "

Estrada was out the front door before the man could finish his sentence. He had less than a week until Friday and had to set up a date with a particular person, though "coerce into" would be more accurate. Estrada waved down a taxi, which lazily pulled up to the curb. He opened the door, and the car shifted as his bulk strained the suspension.

"Holy sh—"

"The Nomads Motorcycle Club." Ward's raspy yet deep voice interrupted the driver. He reached into his pocket and fished out a fifty-dollar bill, which he handed to the man.

The driver nodded. "Nomads Motorcycle Club it is." What did matter was that Ward was moving fast, not because of bad news or drugs, but because he couldn't wait to hear that bitch Mable scream.

7

LUNCH HAD COME TO pass. Dana and Walter were satisfied, and their bellies were content. As they sat at their usual booth at Grave's Diner, Walter's cell phone sounded with the ringtone he had programmed for emergency calls. He answered it with haste.

"Walter here. What happened?"

"Conway, Officer Terra was found severely injured in her home. I need you two . . . to go and check on her. They just left for the hospital a few minutes ago." A shroud of silence fell over the phone.

"Captain, are you OK," Walter asked.

"Yes, Walter, just please . . . go . . . and check on my daughter. I will stick around here and find out exactly what the hell happened." Their captain hung up, severing the connection.

"We need to leave—now!" Walter said.

The two rushed for the exit, and Dana turned back and hollered into the restaurant. "Mike put it on our tab! We got a call!" Dana glanced over at his partner as they ran for the car. "Maybe I should drive."

"What, are you saying I can't drive to an emergency?" Walter replied sharply as he hopped in the driver's seat.

"No, Walt, I'm just saying I'm a bit out of practice." Dana sarcastically said as he opened the passenger door and jumped in. Walter simultaneously put the keys in the ignition and slammed the red Cyclops eye on the roof.

They tore out of the parking lot, the Cyclops' eye blinking every which way while the siren wailed for everyone to get the hell out of their way. "Walt, will you put your damn seat belt on? I don't feel like seeing you go through the fucking window for being reckless." Dana gripped the handlebar above his head as Walter sped through the streets, weaving through cars and red lights.

Walter glared at Dana for the remark. "What? Oh, oh, thanks, Dana."

Dana shook his head, smirking. "We'll get there. She'll be alright, OK? She's a tough gal."

Walter wiped a tear from his right eye.

The two arrived at Middleton Hospital in a few minutes, with Dana's hair practically standing straight up. They rushed inside the lobby, passing Gladys, who was waiting for them. "Detectives, hold on!" The adrenaline-frenzied pair froze in place and glared at her as they hastily retreated to her desk. Gladys spoke softly. "I'm sorry, but she's undergoing surgery. The doctors will notify me of any changes. Perhaps in the meantime, you should situate yourselves here."

Walter spun around; his head hung low, and the frenzy turned to grief.

"Gladys," Dana asked, "is there any information you can divulge?"

She sighed. "I only know there were many injuries—that was all I was told."

Dana nodded. "Thanks." He flashed a brief smile, then searched for Walter, who had dragged himself to the small corner coffee shop in the lobby and ordered a cup of coffee.

He poured his cream and sugar, hands trembling. Dana came up behind him as he finished stirring.

"Walt, we will see her alive. Now, drink your coffee and get a grip, alright?" Dana placed both hands on Walter's shoulders, staring through his glasses, noting Walter's pitiful look. "This. Is. Our. Job."

An hour or so passed, along with a few cups of coffee. Neither was sure of the time, but both agreed that it seemed like an eternity. Finally, the reception desk's telephone rang. Gladys answered it immediately. "OK, yes . . . yes . . . right away, thank you." She hung up and waved the detectives over. "She's out, and all examinations are completed," Gladys said, compassion in her voice. "You can see her on the second floor, Room 120."

Both men thanked her before sprinting for the elevators. After another eternity, the doors parted to reveal a giant. He was heavily bandaged and wore a burned leather jacket. The hulk of a man barged his way past them hard enough that Walter's arm got caught, and what was left of his coffee spilled on his shirt.

Walter turned and cursed at the man already out the front door. "Hey, asshole, watch where you're going!" Walter flicked his hand at the mess and then frantically wiped at it. "Son of a bitch!"

The two finally clambered into the elevator, rode to the next floor, and rushed to the nurse's station.

"I need Officer Terra Branigan's status!" Walter pounded his fists onto the counter, causing all the nurses to jump up. A nurse with her nose buried in a folder pointed to a room. The two rushed inside to find doctors and nurses cluttering the view.

Walter started forward, but Dana grabbed his arm. "Walt, we can't just go up to Terra. Give them some space and time." Dana patted his gloomy partner on the shoulder as Walter's head sank again.

A short and pudgy nurse approached the two detectives. Her hair was nestled under a scrub cap, and she wore a white surgical mask that hid any honest expression and nearly blended in with her pale skin. The only notable contrast was the blue latex gloves stretched over her small hands. She spoke with knowledge and assurance. "Detectives, it's never good to meet under these conditions. I'm Agatha White. I see you're here about Terra Branigan?"

They nodded. Walter looked restless, ready to pounce like a tiger and reclaim his lost cub. "Yes, how is she doing?"

The nurse hid a smile under her mask. "She's going to be fine, detectives. Although she's suffered several severe injuries, none are life-threatening."

Sighs of relief escaped from both. Dana smiled and nodded. "That's great to hear, Agatha. Thank you, and everyone who helped, for all your hard work."

Walter turned to Dana. "I'm going to call the captain." Dana nodded as Walter exited into the hall.

Agatha began to turn back into the circle of white, but Dana stopped her. "Nurse . . . can you describe her wounds?"

She trembled slightly. "It . . . it didn't seem like any attack I've ever seen in my career, Detective. It was like something straight from a Hollywood horror film. She has several lacerations, though the strikes and marks missed her vital organs. Her face is badly bruised. Thankfully, she had no broken bones, but she was beaten relentlessly, especially in the face. Her breasts are also . . ." Agatha paused and cleared her throat. "Her breasts are clawed in a crisscross manner, and her back is scratched, right down to the muscle in some regions."

Dana cocked his head slightly. "Were there any strange markings, by chance? Perhaps a heart, spade, diamond, or club, like playing cards?"

Agatha shook her head. "Hmm, no, only what I described to you, Detective."

Dana nodded. "May I see her? For just for a moment?"

"You may . . . I warn you, though—she's not looking like her usual self."

Dana silently approached Terra's bedside and looked at her face: ravaged, swollen black, blue, and everything in between. She appeared lifeless. "She's sedated and medicated for the pain. She's fine." Dana glanced at Agatha and nodded.

Terra's Mona Lisa smile flashed before his eyes—she'd always been so happy and outgoing, so lively. Now, she lay helpless, limp, battered, and broken in a hospital bed with tubes, wires, and all the essentials that could run an engine. Machines beeped and bleeped at a steady pace. *Who did this to you, Terra?*

Dana felt a warm sensation run down his left cheek. He ran his fingertips over it and looked down to see red smeared on them. *What the hell?* Dana turned to Agatha. "I need something to stop this, please."

Agatha looked Dana over. "Are you alright?"

He nodded. "It's a razor cut I got from shaving. It bled for a while when I got it." Agatha retrieved a bit of gauze and surgical tape and placed the ensemble on Dana's face. "Thank you again, Agatha." He turned and left the room to find Walter out in the hall on his phone.

"OK, Captain Branigan." He nodded continuously. "Yes, sir. Yes, will do, Brad . . . Don't worry, I promise you." He hung up and approached Dana, still patting his coffee stain with a handkerchief. "The hell's with your face?" Walter eyed the monstrosity as if it were a contagious facial plague.

Dana pointed at Walter's shirt. "What the hell's with your shirt, piss on yourself? You have terrible aim, Walt." He grinned as Walter rolled his eyes. "My razor cut started bleeding again. Strange, it happened when I got near Terra."

Walter looked at Terra, "Hey, would you mind if I had a minute with her?"

Dana nodded and waited outside the room for a moment.

The two made for the elevator, and Walter pushed the down button. "I don't know, Walt. I've been seeing, hearing, and experiencing strange shit. I thought it was just the case getting to me—" Dana was interrupted by the elevator's bell ringing, and they entered. Walter pressed the 1 as Dana continued. "For example, I dreamed about that girl from the movie theater. Then I found a long black hair in my bathroom, and I sure as hell don't remember cleaning my kitchen."

Walter listened attentively. "It could all be a coincidence?"

Dana shrugged. "I don't know, Walt. I think I might stop at Hazel's shop."

Walter nodded. "You might want to. Debbie used to have books, charms, and all that sort for warding off evil spirits, demons, and whatnot. You do have sleep problems too . . ." Walter paused as they exited the elevator. "What it could be is old folklore. Ever hear of a succubus?" Dana nodded. "They like to feed on men's spirits when they sleep. They drain you of your life, sexually, of course, and there are all sorts of crazy hoodoo around them. That might be your problem. Who knows?"

Dana chuckled. "Maybe, Walt. I feel like lately, someone, or something, is always watching me."

Walter also chuckled. "Ha, I get that every day. Then I realize I'm the one who watches everyone else."

Dana grinned. "Yeah, you sure have a way of catching people off guard. Especially when you pop by my place."

"What can I say? What are friends for?" Walter patted Dana on the back.

Outside, the sun shined brightly and beat down on the detectives' faces. It was soothing and comforting after the latest rush they'd endured. Dana reached for his sunglasses and studied the block. Traffic had built up. Motors hummed, revved, and clanked; concertos blasted from within the cars. Dana couldn't help but smile inside at the beauty the day offered, and it was still relatively early—at least for him.

"Hey, Walter, do you mind stopping by Hazel's shop now?" Dana asked as they approached the car.

Walter glanced up at Dana, hesitant, as though he'd been lost in thought. "Sure, no problem."

"What's up, Walt? Is something bothering you?"

Walter squinted as he unlocked the doors. "Yeah . . . that asshole who spilled my coffee reminded me of someone who should still be in bed." He climbed into the car and fastened his seat belt.

Dana followed suit. "You mean Ward Estrada, aka Meat?" He thought back on the rush and bump. "Hmm, yeah, now that you mention it, did resemble him."

"Yeah, next time I see him, I'm going to bill him for a new shirt and give him an ass-kicking, courtesy of Walter Conway."

Dana giggled. "Yeah, Walt. Well, let's make this quick."

The duo ventured through the network of downtown streets to find themselves at Hazel's Holistic Shop. Dana looked over at his partner. "I'll be back in a few."

The shop's front was old-fashioned and rustic. Sporadic flecks of orange painted the outside walls, faintly covering the light oak finish. Various signs promoting protection, prosperity, and health covered the walls. Up above the store was another level where the owners lived.

Dana entered and was greeted warmly by Hazel, who stood behind the cash register. Hazel was in his late fifties. The white of wisdom had begun to speckle through the silver of his hair. His face was broad and noble, and his eyes were brown, like an oak tree's bark. Like the tree, he was tall and fit, and his skin was slightly wrinkled. His voice always seemed humorous and enthusiastic; he still had a story to share—especially if you mentioned his old dog, Sparks.

"How's work been treating you?" Hazel asked.

Dana smiled in reply. "Good, Hazel. I've just been having some trouble lately."

"Mmhmm, yeah, well, I got all sorts of things. Tell me, if you don't mind, what's been happening." Hazel sat down on his stool behind the counter and folded his arms.

"Well . . ." Dana took a deep breath as he approached, glancing at all the knickknacks that populated the counter and register. Shiny jeweled towers spun in unison, sparkling in the light like small, tamed clusters of stars. "I have a case that may be getting to me. I haven't slept much, and strange things are happening."

Hazel cocked his head slightly. "Oh, like what? Doppelgangers?"

Dana cracked a smile. Hazel was always talking about stories of doppelgangers. "No, like, I had a dream. That I had this gorgeous woman in my bed—"

"Ha, any dream with beautiful women is troubling. But no, go on."

Dana chuckled heartily and continued. "I dreamed that she was in my bed. We had sex, and when morning came, I went to shave. I ended up cutting myself, and it didn't stop bleeding for a while. Then, today, it was bleeding profusely when I was visiting a fellow officer in the hospital."

Hazel jutted out his lower lip. "Hmm, well, was this officer female?"

Dana nodded. "Yeah, it was when I was at her bedside that it started again . . ." Dana paused. "Come to think of it, I'd been thinking of her when I was shaving."

Hazel nodded. "Is there anything else?"

"Yeah, I found a long black hair in my bathroom. I figured it was a loose strand from Terra, the officer I saw today, but I don't know. Then, there's this uneasy feeling that someone is watching me, and I see shadows and silhouettes of figures. Shit moving in the corner of my eye, but nothing is there." Dana rubbed his eyes.

"Sounds like maybe a succubus, Dana. I know it's folklore and all, but maybe some aromatherapy and some items for protection will help." Hazel stood up and walked from behind the counter onto the sales floor. "Come with me." He motioned for Dana to follow and stopped in front of a rack that contained protection charms. Hazel's eyes carefully examined them, one by one. "Here." He reached for a necklace that contained two amulets, the hands clasped: one a circular medallion with various signs on it, the other a hand with an eye in its center. "This is a Solomon Seal," he said, holding the necklace up. He pointed to the hand. "This is the Hamsa hand, and this"—he pointed at the medallion— "this is a protection seal." He handed the necklace to Dana. "Wear it at all times. Also, line your windows and doors with these." He crouched and retrieved several pins lined with feathers, leaves, and markings. "These are protection pins." He explained how to place them around the house. "Lastly, I want you to sprinkle salt around your bed; if you want, this is optional, maybe your windows and doors as well."

Dana nodded. "Thank you, Hazel. How much will all this run?"

"It will cost you nothing this time, my friend." Hazel smiled. "I'd rather see you through this than have you pay and die on me." He chuckled. "A dead customer is of no use."

Dana smiled and joined in on the laughter. "Thank you again, Hazel. Tell the missus that Walter and I say hello."

Hazel nodded. "Mmhmm, sure will. Say hi to Walt for us, too."

Dana gathered his protective relics and placed them in a small cloth bag, courtesy of Hazel. As he was about to exit, he heard a woman's voice bellow above the store. "Hank? Hank! Is that Dana?"

Dana smiled and waved goodbye as Hazel hollered back. "Yes, dear, he and Walter say hello!"

Dana trotted back onto the street feeling renewed, a spring in his step. He always found conversations with Hazel to be enjoyable. He saw Walter sitting in the car, sipping coffee and wiping his mouth.

"Hey, all set?"

"Sure am. Hazel and Adriana say hi," Dana said, hopping in the car and fastening his seat belt.

"Ah, those two are such a cute couple. Hazel's great." Walter smiled as he put the car in gear and sputtered away from the curbside.

"You can drop me off at my place, Walt." Dana yawned. "I'm going to try and get some sleep."

Walter nodded. "Okie dokie. As you wish."

Not long after Dana walked into his apartment, he felt eyes piercing his being again. He searched around and behind him for anyone but saw no one. *I really hope this works out, Hazel.* He tossed his coat on the rack, anxious to remedy the situation that kept him from slumber and plaguing his life. Walking around his house, he placed the protection pins as directed and equipped himself with the necklace. He entered the kitchen and rummaged through his spice cabinet to retrieve his salt container. In his bedroom, he sprinkled a circle around his bed. *I think that should be fine.*

A sense of freedom overcame Dana. For the first time in a long time, he felt good. He didn't feel the pressure, anxiety, or feeling of hostility that he'd previously had. He climbed into bed and fell fast asleep.

Dana slumbered for hours. His mind ran rampant, and his body became aware of something foreign. He saw images of people and places. He saw a massacre at a high school auditorium. Then he saw John Doe, Estrada, and the boys again. All were pounding on his front door in the darkness. He answered it to see a silhouette of a girl standing in the doorway facing the monsters, keeping them from entering. She started slowly turning to face Dana but vanished as he was startled awake.

He lay in bed. Night had come—or had it? All around his bed was darkness, nothing but raw darkness. He rubbed his eyes to check if his eyes were open and sat up in the sea of nothingness—light obsolete, absorbed. As he scanned the room, a gray shade appeared before his bed.

It laughed hysterically. "So, you think a few cheap relics will offer you protection from me, mortal? Oh, I love it when such pathetic wretches cling to any shred of hope using seals and banishment spells. You are so cute, my pet."

Dana peered back at the shade in disbelief. "Who . . . what are you?"

"It is none of your concern, my dear, other than that you belong to me. You are my property, Dana Deupree. You are my precious consort. Mmm, Dana." The voice spoke seductively, and the shape of the shade was curved most sultry. "You are mine and mine alone, my sweet Dana. You and I are together. We are so close, Dana. Soon, we will be as one in time." The shade drew closer to his bedside, stopping at the circle of protection.

"Mmm, come to me, Dana. Mmm, oh yes, Dana, come to me. I can help you. I can make you feel oh so much better." The voice allured Dana, enthralled him, warped his mind to its harmonizing tune, and clutched him almost certainly. His guard dropped.

But a distant yet familiar voice echoed in Dana's mind. No! It allowed him to grasp his senses, "No!" He shook his head. "Whatever you are, whoever, leave me alone!"

Startled, the shade hissed. "You sniveling, pathetic little worm. Today, you saw merely a glimpse of what power I possess—a small glimmer of what I am capable of. Remember this, you frivolous sack of flesh. Every thought you come to possess is mine, just as much as you claim it to be yours, fool! Go ahead. Dream, slumber, and think that you are safe all you want. You will find no haven anywhere, Dana Deupree. You are mine!" The shade shrieked and hissed violently as it and the darkness vanished.

Dana snapped up, sweating profusely, his bedsheets soaked. He turned and looked at his alarm clock: 3:18 a.m. He dropped his head back onto the pillow with a sigh. His eyes scanned the ceiling. *Maybe it was just a nightmare?*

)

Once again, Mark found himself at the computer, staring at all the evidence he'd collected. It didn't amount to much, but he figured there had to be enough information to find out who she was. The web page he'd set up to organize the weekly card tournaments allowed him access to small tidbits of information: IP addresses, emails, and private user contact information. She had been smart, though, choosing to direct communication through an instant messenger service, which she hadn't used since the incident. These clues merely afforded slight hints.

Her digital names, he supposed, contained some clues. The email address she had registered with was lanturnholder@gmail.com, and her messenger name was lying_shame03. Both came complete with a tiny cartoon icon depicting a female vampire. Not very unusual, he figured, since it seemed like nowadays, people everywhere were latching on to the vampire fad: books, shirts, posters. You name it, they had it. *Still, there's something there.*

Memories flashed in Mark's mind. Deep-brown eyes peered out from behind dark shades, a single lock of jet-black hair slipping onto her smooth forehead. *Vampires* . . . He had a feeling this girl had a theme in her life.

He sat back in the chair, letting his fingers run through his /curly, dark-brown hair. Frustration ate away at the edges of his sanity as his mind ran over the evidence again. He felt that he needed to figure out who this girl was; he felt it at the bottom of his soul. "Mable, Mary Sue—is it a code? What can all this mean?" he murmured.

After flipping the monitor off, he went to the kitchen to retrieve a beer bottle from the refrigerator. He popped off the top, and as he took a swig of the cold brew, he went to his couch. The apartment management had worked wonders, replacing his carpet and putting a fresh coat of white on the ceiling. However, despite the collection of air fresheners plugged into several sockets in the room, he could still detect the faint hint of burned hair and flesh. It had been bad at first, but now it was bearable, and for this, he was eternally grateful.

He took up his plastic wand and, with the wave of a finger, made the black box in front of him light up and illuminate the dark room in a blue glow. Sounds burst forth as the screen depicted a slightly pudgy boy in an orange wet suit swimming in a large glass tank with dolphins. As he made his way towards the camera, he opened his stupidly grinning mouth, but all that could be heard was the sound of dolphins chirping. A narrator's voice interrupted the scene to announce how New Boston Tuna was revamping its efforts to protect these "angels of the sea" before declaring consumers should buy the company's product. Mark motioned with his finger again, and the screen flashed to a young woman with wavy blonde hair sitting at a desk; stock market numbers scrolled across the bottom of the screen. A box appeared next to her head, declaring tragedy on America's East Coast.

"It appears yet another tragedy has befallen the quiet town of Middleton this week as we get reports that a police officer, Officer Terra Branigan, was brutally beaten in her residence," the woman announced in a blunt, emotionless voice. "She is now in intensive care at Middleton Metropolitan Hospital as the police force works around the clock to solve this disturbing case. This is following the recent string of mysterious deaths and the near-fatal burning of a local motorcycle enthusiast, as well as the vicious slaying of a beloved local dog over the past week. The cause of the tragedies remains a mystery as the police chief proclaimed there have been very few leads in the cases . . ."

Mark's concentration broke again. He sipped his beer as his mind wandered back to that night. He kept seeing her eyes, one quickly closing and opening as if beckoning him to try to uncover everything, the smirk on her face upping the wager. He could see her standing defiantly over him as everyone cowered in fear, withdrawing her cards and dealing them out as she dealt with the lunatic who'd threatened them with a gun—*like a guardian angel, smiting evil before returning to someplace on high. Ever-present but unseen until another situation calls for her.*

Somewhere outside, the low rumble of multiple motorcycles grew and then abruptly fell quiet. After a pause, Mark shrugged, and with a slight motion, he made the glowing box fall dark and silent once more. He stood up and surveyed his surroundings. The computer in the corner seemed to beckon to him, and Mark needed to answer its call.

After another swig, he seated himself at the desk. Outside, the shuffling of feet grew loud and quieted just as quickly. He reached out for the switch to turn the monitor on but was interrupted by a loud knock on his door. He shot up immediately. The interruption to his silent world sent a shiver through his body. *Who could that possibly be? It's nowhere near Friday.*

Then, an explosion of knocking. Cautiously, Mark made his way to the source and lined his eye up with the small peephole. As his vision focused, a loud crash signaled that the door was coming open by force. Bright lights flashed across his vision as his head connected with the swinging door. Mark was sent flying in the air, landing on his right shoulder on the coffee table and spinning onto his stomach on the floor. Warmth poured from his nose onto the brand-new carpet, painting it a fresh shade of red. As the loud ringing of the new concussion rattled through his mind, he attempted to push himself up. A sharp pain ran out from his right shoulder, and his effort was thwarted as a big boot planted itself on his back.

"Where is she?" The low, raspy voice sounded vaguely familiar. "Where's the bitch with the cards?"

"I don't know . . ." The muffled words began making their way out of his mouth but were interrupted as the boot lifted off his back and slammed into his rib cage, stealing the air from his lungs. He rolled and slammed into the coffee table again before settling on his back. His attacker stood over him, a hulking cross between a mummy and a biker. Under matching black leather and chains were strands of white gauze with the occasional splotch of blood where wounds hadn't quite healed. A shudder ran through the biker-mummy, and he brought up a baseball bat and pointed its end at Mark's badly bruised and beaten face.

"Where is that bitch 'Mable'? The bitch who did this to me. I want her NOW!" The low, raspy voice had turned to thunder.

Mark tried to push himself up and away from his assaulter, but his body felt like a ton of bricks, and he was now sure that his right arm was useless.

"I'm telling you, I don't—" The garbled words hadn't entirely escaped his swollen lips before excruciating pain shot through his left knee. As wood connected with bone, Mark felt something give, somewhere between the pain and the crunching sound.

"Well, then, I guess we're just going to have to keep breaking things until we find out, huh?" the biker-mummy gleefully replied.

From behind the biker, men in similar leather jackets entered the apartment through the broken doorway and split up. The apartment erupted in loud crashes as furniture was flipped; glasses and bottles crashed against the walls and tile.

"You see, I know you know who she is—and more importantly—*where* she is." The thunder had become a low, raspy sound again.

Mark looked up through his swollen eyes and saw the baseball bat held over the biker's head. Mark clenched his eyes shut in anticipation, and fresh pain exploded from his right shin. The pain was beginning to blend, and Mark realized he couldn't muster the strength to open his eyelids. His throat choked out a weak scream as blood ran into his mouth.

The world began to spin, and as it went faint across the dark expanse, he heard a voice. "I think I got something, Gigan!"

)

The morning had finally come. The sun poured into Dana's room relentlessly. Light sloshed against the chocolate walls and covered most of the cream carpet. Dana sat on the edge of his bed, dressed for the day. His eyes were heavy. He occasionally startled himself, leaning forward or backward too much. He rubbed his eyes and let loose a heavy yawn. His tired gaze lazily scanned the room.

Every window was open—free from the usual curtains that barred them shut. They were the eyes that peered out into the world, which in turn peered right back in. From the window in the back of his room, Dana could see the seven-foot gray-brown privacy fence that lined his backyard and that of his neighbor, Debbie Butler—Walter's ex-wife. The crisp azure sky stretched to the blanket of the horizon. The moon could still be seen, high and slowly being devoured piece by piece by the day.

He sighed. His mind flashed cryptic images from the previous night's events. Again, he had seen the ghastly visuals of the ill-fated people coming to attack him, and twice now, he had seen the same silhouette of a girl outside his door. *Who are you?*

He rubbed the back of his neck as tension mounted, weighing him down. He felt the necklace Hazel had given him still clasped around his neck. He picked up the amulet and gazed down at it, staring at the eye in the hand, and seemed to feel some of the tension ease off. *What was that all about?* He recalled some of the events in his dream: a massacre at a high school and a fatal car accident. They shared the color red.

He climbed to his feet, staring at the faint amount of salt lining his bed. Shaking his head for believing such superstitions, he casually stepped over the line and walked towards the picture window, looking out to his backyard. He examined the window, noting his placement of the protection pins, then reached atop the windowsill for one of them, feeling about for it. "Ah, damn it!" He retracted his hand when he felt the pinprick and examined his index finger. Blood was starting to bead from the small poke. He sighed again. "What a way to start the day off." He grabbed the pin and held it before him. When it first came into his possession, the pin was an amber-bronze; now, it was as black as death.

He stared out into the backyard. The glass reflected a flash of a face that sadistically smiled at him. He took a step back, startled by its sudden appearance. But when he approached the window again, only the day and the sun were present. He let out a sigh of relief. *I swear. My mind has got to be on overdrive or something.* He turned around and ran his fingers through his hair, pacing.

The doorbell rang. *Who the hell could that be?* He meandered through the narrow hallway and into the living room to the front door. The bell chimed again. "Hang on a second!" he yelled. "Damn it, do people not have patience anymore?" he mumbled as he unlocked the door. The door's opening revealed someone he had not expected to find on his doorstep.

At first, all he saw was black—the sunlight seemed to be swallowed whole by this . . . person. Familiarity set in. A look of total surprise had set in on her face, followed by that soft, angelic voice that sang to Dana's ears once again.

"Oh, what are the odds of that?" Lynaly smiled.

Dana melted, then regained himself, rubbing his eyes. "Sorry . . . can I help you?"

"We met before. Back at the theater? I seem to have lost my cat. I live in the neighborhood." Lynaly turned and pointed up the street towards the outskirts of Middleton. "I've been going door to door to see if anyone has seen her."

Dana gave her a quick once-over as Lynaly batted her long, dark eyelashes. Her smoky eyes radiated in the day. She had her hands in front of her, and they held a small black-and-red spiderweb purse; she swayed gently like a beautiful flower in a breeze. She appeared slightly different from when he'd last seen her. She wore a low-cut ebony button-down blouse with white lace frills embroidered around the neckline and short sleeves. Underneath were black fishnet sleeves that covered her arms and hands until they met at points that rested on her middle fingers. On her waist sat a black-and-red plaid miniskirt. Her slender legs were dressed in sheer black leggings and lace-up leather boots that reached the middle of her thighs. Her complexion appeared almost doll-like—white porcelain—in the day's light. Her voluptuous lips were bathed in a ruby red that could nearly be mistaken for blood, coated even and perfect. Her hair was wrapped up tightly into a bun held together with two crimson lacquered chopsticks. On her ears dangled silver upside-down crosses wrapped around her neck was a choker with a matching cross and a garnet teardrop at its tip.

"Oh yeah, Romero's Theater, yeah, now I remember. Lynaly, right?" Dana ran his fingers through his hair. A feeling of uneasiness overtook him. "I'm sorry, I haven't seen or heard a cat around here recently."

Lynaly's eyes seemed to glaze over like a sad puppy. "Oh. I'm so worried about her. She's been missing for days." She frowned and dropped her head to look down at the ground.

Dana glanced at his watch. "Well, I guess I could help you look for her. I don't have anything going on, and I don't have to go to work for a few hours."

Lynaly beamed. "Really? That would be great. Thank you so much."

Dana nodded. "No problem, let me grab my coat, and we'll go."

Lynaly nodded and turned around. Reaching into her purse, she brought a pair of tiny purple-tinted octagonal sunglasses and put them on, smiling under the sun's bright gaze.

Dana closed the door briefly and grabbed his essentials: gun, keys, and wallet. As he threw his long black overcoat on, he patted it down to ensure his cell phone was in one of his pockets. *Just in case Walt calls*, he thought.

Trotting down the steps, he met with Lynaly at the end of his walkway. He glanced to his left to see Debbie outside by her mailbox, stretching.

Debbie was a real fantasy. Standing side by side, Dana would tower over her. She had the body of a young woman with the moves of a sexually mature woman. Her long blonde hair was tied into a taut ponytail that bobbed up and down with every step. She was in her jogging outfit: skin-tight white sports bra and equally tight gray shorts. Through his sunglasses, the outline of her ass seemed to shine like the perfect melon. She turned around and waved. He flashed a smile and waved back while Lynaly only stared on. *Damn, Debbie. Walter, you sure were one hell of a dog.* He felt a sharp pain near his razor cut and winced slightly before disregarding it.

They continued down the sidewalk, and Dana searched the neighboring yards for any signs of a cat. "Your cat, what does she look like?" He turned his head to Lynaly as they walked.

"Hmm? Oh, she's black." Lynaly glanced over at Dana, flashing a smile.

Dana smiled back. *A black cat, how could I not have guessed?* Lynaly seemed dismal—shuffling her feet along, head-heavy. Dana put his hand on her shoulder. "Hey, now, I'm sure we'll find her. Everything will be alright."

She looked up at Dana with sad-puppy eyes, half smiling. "Thanks."

So far, there was nothing, not a hint of her cat. They stopped at a red light, where some passersby glanced at the seemingly odd couple. Dana pulled his cell phone out of his coat pocket and glanced at the time on its display, noting it was near lunch. He turned to Lynaly. Her arms crossed her chest, and she lightly clung to her shoulders. "Hey, do you want to get some lunch?" She nodded with a smile.

Dana often frequented Marie's Delicatessen, a gourmet sandwich and deli shop on the corner of Main Street and Ash. It was where he and Walter went when they wanted a taste of the Ritz. It housed its restaurant and was neighbored by Lisa's Book & Coffee Shop and Candy's Malt & Ice Cream Parlor.

He and Lynaly approached Marie's. Wrought-iron tables and chairs lined its patio, where people spoke to each other over the slight dings and jingles of shop bells.

Dana held the door for Lynaly, and the scent of freshly baked bread immediately hounded his nostrils. They simultaneously removed their sunglasses as they surveyed the shop. The place was compact yet roomy for what it offered.

Dana smiled as his gaze swept the racks of bread and cases of meats, cheeses, and prepared foods. *Walt would kill me right now if I didn't tell him where I was.* He reached for his phone again.

But Walter's line rang and rang, not going to voice mail. Dana raised an eyebrow. *Strange.* Walt always answered. He held his phone before him. The display flashed a small phone icon, and he pressed a button and returned the phone to his ear. "Hey, Walt, I was just trying to call you. Are you hungry?"

"Hey, are you busy?" Walter replied, oblivious to Dana's question.

"Uh, kind of. Why? What's up?" Dana shifted his balance to his right.

"Well, we got a report from the Criminal Response Division. It seems that someone got pretty angry at our poker host." Dana could hear Walter close his car door and begin walking.

"Sorry, Walt, I'm not home," Dana replied quickly. A short silence was followed by mumbling, and then: "Oh . . . well, where the hell are you at then?"

Dana grinned. "At Marie's place."

"Oh, what the fuck, Dana," Walter growled. "You know I absolutely fucking love that place!"

Dana laughed. Lynaly looked over and smiled at him, and he flashed a smile back. "Hey, I told you I was calling you and asked if you were hungry. Don't go getting your knickers in a twist."

Walter grumbled. "Alright. I'll be over there in a few."

"See you in a bit," Dana smirked as he hung up.

Dana glanced about, searching for Lynaly, and noticed she had already ordered her sandwich and was browsing the selections of wine in the wine vault. *Well, I guess*

I can put Walt's and my orders in. Dana walked up to the far end of the deli case, thoroughly scanning the sizable pieces of paper that listed different sandwich combinations. He glanced at his usual—roast beef, bacon, white cheddar, lettuce, and onion on wheat bread with horseradish mayo—before noting Walter's favorite: double meat pastrami/corned beef and double Swiss cheese with sauerkraut and Russian dressing on toasted rye bread.

The middle-aged woman behind the deli case approached and greeted Dana with a smile. Her bleached apron was stained with flour and streaks of oil. "Hello, Detective Deupree. How are you doing today?"

"I'm doing pretty well, thank you, Marie." Dana smiled back.

"Ah, and how is Detective Conway? Usually, you're in with him." She put on disposable plastic gloves.

"Oh, he'll be in. You know how he loves you, Marie." Dana and Marie both chuckled.

Tilting her head to her left, she asked, "So, will you be having your usual today?"

"Yep, #21, and also Walt's #19 if you would, please," Dana said, glancing at the menu again as he spoke.

"Alrighty, I'll have them up in a few moments." Marie smiled as she began preparing the sandwiches.

"Thanks, Marie." Dana nodded. "Oh, and could you also place her order on mine?" Dana motioned with his head towards Lynaly. Marie nodded.

Lynaly was still looking through the wine selection in the back corner and clutched a bottle of root beer. He grabbed two bottles of cream soda and came up behind her. "Hey, find anything good?"

"There's so much to look at. It's impressive."

"Yeah, it is. Marie has a great selection." Dana scanned the cellar with Lynaly. "Hey, I covered your lunch. It should probably be ready. We can take you back to your house once Walter gets here."

Lynaly smiled. "Thanks."

They headed to the register and were greeted by a young man who looked no older than seventeen. He was small and relatively thin, and his dark-brown hair was short and spiked. He had Marie's dark green eyes and good manners.

"Hey, Aaron, how have you been doing?"

"What's up, Dana? You on a date?" Aaron smirked, noting Lynaly's presence.

"Maybe, Aaron, just maybe." Dana chuckled. "How's your dad doing?" He handed Aaron payment for the meal.

"Alright. Mom says he'll be back from New Boston soon, some business trip or whatever." Aaron rolled his eyes.

"Ha, well, tell Michael I said hey. Walt will be by soon. See you later." Dana circled back to where Marie had completed Dana's lunch requests. "Thanks, Marie, take care."

"You too, Dana. Have a nice day." She smiled and waved goodbye.

Dana and Lynaly walked outside. The door slowly closed behind them. They simultaneously equipped themselves with sunglasses and giggled. Walter arrived, pulled up in the parking spot, and reached for something next to him in the car.

Dana approached while Lynaly surveyed the car from the sidewalk. "Hey, Walt." Dana tried to hand Walter his soda through the car window, but Walter shook his head. "What's wrong?"

"Well, I found this little gal wandering around your place while talking to you. It looks like you had a pussy prowling around. It might be why you've been hearing and seeing things." Walter cradled a medium-haired black tabby cat. He patted her head while she continued to purr in his pudgy comfort, her eyes closed.

Lynaly hopped down off the curb excitedly and came up to Walter. "Oh, it's her!" While the girl patted the cat in his arms, Walter gave her a once-over and then looked at Dana, his lips and facial features saying, "Score!"

"Really! That's strange, though. I didn't see her. Maybe she was hiding somewhere." Dana cocked his head and pondered aloud.

Lynaly set her lunch and soda down on the hood of Walter's car. Walter raised an eyebrow at Dana, who only shrugged in return. "Come here, Sheila. There's my baby." The cat instinctively climbed from Walter's arms into Lynaly's, revealing her bright golden eyes.

"Now, there's a happy kitty if I ever saw one." Walter brushed himself off, and cat hair drifted in the subtle breeze.

"What's the matter, Walt? Don't like pussy . . . cat hair?" Dana smirked.

"Don't look so smug. I just happen to like my pussies shaven, is all," Walter replied with a toothy grin as he finished brushing himself off.

Dana laughed, noting that Lynaly was oblivious to the innuendos.

"Thank you, Walter," Lynaly said, smiling at Sheila and running her fingers down her back. Sheila turned her head towards Dana, and he couldn't help but feel uneasy about how she stared at him. The cat purred as Lynaly stroked her, her gaze still upon Dana. "Thank you both. Especially you, Dana. I hope to see you again—soon." Lynaly smiled and placed the cat down on the ground. Sheila obediently stuck close to her master as if waiting for a command. Lynaly reached for her lunch and soda before smiling at both men and giving Dana a seductive look-over and a wink. "I am afraid that this is goodbye for now, boys. Places to go, people to see."

And there goes a girl and her cat. Dana grinned as he watched them cross the street, then looked at Walter. "What are you grinning about, old man?"

Walter laughed. "Now you know why they call me the Silver Fox."

Dana rolled his eyes. "Oh please, don't flatter yourself. For God's sake, she's more than half your age."

Walter giggled as Dana handed him his sandwich container and cream soda. They retreated to the inside of Walter's car. "Bah, forgot to nab a paper," Dana said, putting his lunch on the dashboard.

Walter reached behind him and pulled from the seat pouch a current newspaper. "Do you mean this?"

Dana nodded. "Yeah, do you mind?"

"Go for it." Walter tossed it on the dash. "So, how long were you two together today?" Walter took a big mouthful of his sandwich.

"She came by earlier and asked me about her cat. So, we went looking, and well . . . we ended up in town." Dana took a bite of his sandwich, lightly brushing the antipasto salad aside with the other half of his sandwich.

Walter nodded as he continued to chew. "Mmm, man . . . Marie . . . makes some awesome sandwiches. Michael's a lucky prick." Dana smiled as he took another bite. "What did she get? Do you know?" Walter asked through his incessant chewing.

Dana fished a wad of paper from his coat pocket as he balanced his plastic lunch container on his lap. He looked at the receipt. "Hmm, looks like the same thing I got."

Walter cocked his head. "Really? Well, it seems you two have something in common. Shame, really, she doesn't know what she's missing out on." Walter went back to devouring his sandwich.

Dana rolled his eyes. "Oh jeez, Walt, like anyone would want your shriveled, crippled pastrami stick." Walter laughed. "Alright, so what's the deal with Mark? Did something go down?" Dana unwrapped his white plastic spork and napkin, ready to dive into his antipasto.

Walter nodded as he scooped some of his salad with his sandwich and shoved it in his mouth. "Mmm, yeah, got his ass beat to kingdom come and back, and then again."

Dana scooped up a sensible amount of salad. "Any witnesses?"

Walter shook his head. "Not who want to come forth . . ." Walter paused. "And you'll never guess who's on the case."

Dana dropped his spork and glared at his partner. "Don't tell me . . ." Walter curled his lip and squinted. "Really? Ugh, well, isn't that great." Dana rubbed his eyes and face with a groan.

Walter took a big bite of his salad. "Yep, Captain Branigan said they'd be good for the case."

Dana rolled his eyes again with a sigh. "For making us want to blow their fucking brains out? Ours? Or just everyone's?"

Walter stared at his salad. "I'm sorry, Dana . . ."

"It's alright, Walt. The election of the pricks of the department isn't your fault."

Taking another big bite of his salad, Walter spoke as he chewed. "No, I'm sorry, Dana . . ."

Dana sniffed the air a couple of times. His brow formed into a scowl, and he slowly turned his head to a smiling Walter. "Fucking eh, Walt. Come on! Really?" Walter laughed as Dana rolled down his window, gagging.

"I'll stop doing it when you stop laughing."

Dana chuckled. "I'm not laughing, I'm dying. Jeez. What the hell did you eat? Or what did that thing eat before it died up in your ass?"

Walter's laugh surged in a frenzy. "Oh, wait, I think there's one there. Oh—and it's starting to crown! Ah, can't drop it here!"

Dana shook his head. "Serves you right. Karma is a real reckoning bomber, or in this case, a real shit."

Walter laughed harder. "Stop it, Dana! You're going to make me shit myself!"

"That's why it's called schadenfreude, Walt!"

"I'll be back in a bit, you rat bastard." Walter's laughter settled as he exited the car and entered Marie's Delicatessen.

"Ah, come on, Walt!" Dana hollered out the window. "Don't do that, especially to them! What did they ever do to you?"

Walter just waved.

Dana's thoughts turned to Lynaly and their short time together. *Lynaly . . . hmm . . .* A small smile crept across his face but then slowly retracted as he recalled the nightmare he'd had earlier. He shrugged it off again and reached for the necklace that Hazel had given him. He then thought of when he'd seen Debbie earlier that morning with Lynaly and the sharp pain that had originated near his wound. He swung the sun visor down and stared in the mirror. His eyes looked saggy, though not as bad as the day before. He tilted his head to the right slightly, noticing the second mark on his cheek, next to his old cut. There was no trace of blood, though—just slightly raised skin, reddened and irritated. *What the hell?* Catching a glimpse of Walter rushing out of Marie's, he pushed the visor up. Walt's face was paler than ever. Dana turned his head towards his partner as he returned to the car. "What's the matter, Walt? Take a shit so bad all the color left?"

Walter stared blankly out the windshield. "I just found out . . . Debbie . . . she's dead."

Dana turned his body towards Walter. "What the hell are you talking about? I just saw her this morning. She was fine. Damn fine, at that."

Walter nodded. "Quinn just found her. It hasn't been too long because she was still warm."

"Any notion as to what happened?" Dana asked.

Walter shook his head, "He didn't say much. He just wanted to let me know she had died."

Dana turned and faced the front. *What the hell is going on?* He recalled what the shade had said. "*Today, you saw merely a glimpse of what power I possess—a small glimmer of what I am capable of. Remember this, you frivolous sack of flesh. Every thought you come to possess is mine, just as much as you claim it to be yours, fool!*" The wraith's voice echoed limitlessly in Dana's mind. "I'm sorry, Walt."

Walter shook his head. "Don't worry about it, Dana. I mean, yeah, she was my ex-wife, but . . ." Walter rubbed his eye. "She was still a person in my life." He sighed.

Dana looked at Walter. "Are you going to be alright?"

Walter nodded. "We got a job to do. There's plenty of time to grieve later." Walter flashed his classic jokester grin, "Although, I wonder if Quinn would give me at least five minutes with her . . ."

Dana tossed the plastic containers in the backseat, shaking his head. "You really know how to turn on the charm."

Walter smirked. The two strapped themselves into their seats and began the familiar journey to the hospital.

)

At first, she thought that she'd finally gone insane. By some miracle, the police hadn't caught on to her little escapades, to her indulging in the bloodthirst that had begun to itch at the back of her instinct. Now Lilah was doing things that she couldn't remember. And there was the new little persona that had surfaced in her head.

Lilah was pretty sure that there were no doctors or psychiatrists who would know how to diagnose a patient who explained she could shoot fire from a deck of cards and had been going around dispensing capital punishment at the behest of a demonic entity currently inhabiting her brain. Part of her wished that maybe she was just crazy, that her recent actions were perhaps just a grand delusion. However, as Lilah opened the book of Hoyle and examined the contents, she couldn't help but put such fanciful thoughts to rest.

She thumbed through the guide to card games and parlor tricks, in awe of how much had been written and how little of it was decipherable by a human mind. Entire pages were marked over in what appeared to be a reddish-brown ink that she was now sure was her blood. Page after page was lined with pagan symbols and unknown figures that spanned back to times long before mortal life came to populate Earth.

On occasion, she would pause and look at her fingernails. They were ordinary, pink, and white, like any other healthy set of fingers. But Lilah couldn't shake the image of the blood and fur caked underneath them, the blood in her hair, on her face, the taste . . . Her body rattled violently at the thought, but she recuperated and set her mind back to the matter at hand.

The only pattern she could pick up on throughout the text was the repetition of certain significant characters next to and covering illustrations and images of specific cards and card hands that dominated the book's pages. She tried to consult Mullin, who had come to inhabit her mind, but there was only silence. Lilah could only assume that it was during a fit of unconsciousness, or perhaps several, that the thing had taken advantage and used her and her blood to fill the gift from her grandpa with the arcane and cryptic text that now haunted nearly every page, even covering most of the pages where she had placed her careful annotations. The moment of quiet contemplation and introspection threatened to encompass her when something caught her attention. It brought her back to reality, nearly causing her to drop the demonic text.

Ever since the incident at her last poker match, she kept the radio on whenever she was home, alone in her room, and tuned to a local AM news station. It was the tail end of an announcement on the radio that had caught her attention.

She stepped into her private bathroom and stared at her reflection, imagining the girl stained much redder who had gazed back at her earlier in the week. After that image was put to rest, she set to work on her makeup and clothing

—preparation for the journey to the hospital to visit an old friend.

8

♠

WALTER PULLED UP IN front of the hospital, where their usual parking place was occupied by another vehicle, a black 1977 Dodge Charger. Both glanced at the car and grumbled, knowing well whom it belonged. Dana entered the hospital first this time; Walter slowly drifted in behind. Dana turned around and waited for his partner. "Hey, Walt, want to get Terra something from the gift shop?"

Walter picked his heavy head up. "Hmm? Yeah, you know, that's not a bad idea."

Dana waited in the lobby as Walter hurried off to the tiny gift shop tucked back in the corner near the adjacent coffee shop. He paced, surveying the lobby and examining faces, then wandered to a small alcove, growing impatient. Dana brought his head up only to catch a glimpse of a girl disappearing into an elevator. Thinking nothing of it, he continued pacing back and forth around a pillar. Walter finally returned with a small package wrapped in brown paper.

"Are you all set now?" Dana said, his tone annoyed yet anxious. He was surprised that his partner hadn't retrieved a cup of coffee.

"Yep, let's go see how she's doing."

Gladys, who was busy taking calls, "waved" at the dynamic duo with a flash of her eyes. Dana turned to Walter as they waited for the elevator to answer their call. "So, what did you get, Terra?"

Walter smiled. "It's a secret."

Dana raised his eyebrows. "Oh, really now, Walt? Did you slip in an engagement ring or something?"

Walter laughed. "Nah, I think I'm doomed to spend the rest of my life being single"—he fiddled with something in his coat pocket— "or at least part of a food club."

"I don't know, Walt. I think she's good for you." Dana glanced up at the falling numbers.

"Do you think so?" Walter cocked his head to the left, shyly scratching his scalp.

The doors opened as the bell dinged perfectly in tune. They entered, and Walter pushed the button with a 2 on it with a little smile. As they exited on the second floor, Dana sighed. "I really hope we just missed *them* . . ."

Walter puckered his lips. "Who?"

Dana stopped and looked at Walter. "You know damn well *who*."

Walter stopped and thought, and then an angry look manifested. "Oh yeah. *Them*. Pricks."

The two picked up their pace as they entered the giant hallway that housed Terra's room. Dana knocked on the door, and Terra and two men in long coats turned their attention to them. "Well, well, I didn't know it was going to be a reunion, or I would have brought cupcakes and sprinkles," said one of the men.

"Hey, Terra, how are you doing?" Dana asked. "Oh, and what a pleasant surprise to see you too . . . Elias . . . Ellis." Dana gave a fake smile and laugh while Walter glared at Elias, who had his hand on Terra's.

Elias White and Ellis Waters were detectives from the Criminal Response Division, investigating what Dana considered "an inconceivably boring series of events."

Ellis stood lopsided with an "I make this look good" attitude. He was tall and scraggly but clean-shaven with feathered sandy-brown hair, bright blue eyes, and skin tanned to a golden brown—a real pretty boy. He wore a banana-cream-colored long coat, a poor attempt at mimicking Dick Tracy in Dana's eyes. His attire was mismatched: a vanilla-cream dress shirt, brown dress slacks, and dark blue dress shoes. Dana and Walter often made fun of him, saying he could have tried out as a model instead of a detective without his poor fashion judgment. As a prank, when they were all on a case together one time, Dana and Walter stuck zit stickers on his face while he slept in the backseat. When Ellis woke, Dana suggested a mirror. The ensuing fight compromised the stakeout and the case. As a result, Walter and Dana were assigned to the Homicide Division, and they came to love the reassignment.

Then there was Elias—Walter's arch-nemesis. With every woman Walter came to develop feelings for, Elias was always there to try to hone in and steal her away. He was shorter than Ellis, thin, and looked like he spent too much time at the tanning salon. Elias wore his strawberry-blond hair slicked back and had a matching thinned "Zappa" beard. He was a cocky, smart-mouthed wiseass. Elias did dress better than Ellis, though, sporting a solid jet-black dress shirt, black dress slacks, and dark-brown dress shoes. He completed his ensemble with a crimson tie and a long black leather coat.

"Well, if it isn't Tweedledee and Dumbnuts," Elias said with a smirk.

Walter rolled his eyes. "My, my, if it isn't the Cabbage Patch twats." Walter took a few more steps into the room while Dana pressed his back against the doorway, watching. Ellis walked away from Elias and towards the lone chair.

"Boys, please play nice," Terra said, glaring at Ellis and Elias. "Hello, Walter"—her gaze shifted— "Dana." She forced a smile through her badly bruised face.

Walter walked a few more steps closer to Terra's right; Elias still stood on her left, holding her hand. Elias noted the package Walter was cradling. "What's that?" he said with a laugh.

Walter glanced down at the gift, then at Terra. "I—I got this for you. I hope that you get better. I know you will." He extended his arm to give the gift to Terra.

Elias began laughing hysterically. "You're pathetic, Walter, you know that? You go and bring her *that*? You may as well have taken a shit, thrown in some nuts—that you don't have—gift-wrapped it, and then given it to her." Walter dropped his arm and head.

Dana pushed off the doorway. "Hey, Elias? What did you bring again, exactly?" Elias readied himself to say something, but Dana cut him off. "Right, nothing except yourself. Boy, it sure is ironic talking about pieces of shit, isn't it?" Dana grinned.

Walter joined in the grinning while Terra snickered quietly to herself. Even Ellis let a slight chuckle escape before Elias glared at him, causing him to stop. "It doesn't matter what I did or did not bring—I came for a friend and fellow officer," Elias snapped back.

"No, the only thing you typically come for is yourself,"— Dana strolled towards Elias — "and we are here for an investigation. So, I do believe your visit has come to an end, Detective. Perhaps you should be checking on your victim instead of flapping your gums at us." Ellis raised his eyebrows and mouthed, "Damn." Terra's monitor seemed to beep with a giggle as she restrained herself from a healthy laugh.

"I will talk to Bradley about this . . . this preposterous outburst of yours. Mark my words, Deupree!" Elias stormed past Dana, who stood there with a big smile.

Dana turned around as Ellis walked to the door with Elias. "Outburst? Detective White, you're the one who's yelling and throwing a tantrum, but hey, if you want to talk to the captain about this, by all means. There are witnesses, unlike in *your* case. Besides, remember who outranks whom, half-pint."

Elias's nose wrinkled, and his lips curled as he grunted in disgust at Dana and left the room.

Walter stood in awe as Dana turned about to face him and Terra. "Goddamn, I love having you in my corner!" Dana and Walter shared a laugh; their goal was always to make their unsavory co-workers' lives as miserable as possible.

"Walt, I'm going to wait outside here. Find me when you're done, alright?" Walter nodded. "It was nice seeing you, Terra, and I hope you get better." He gave her a small wave. "Take care."

After Dana had left, Terra rolled her head to the right to look at Walter. "Is he OK, Wally? He seems troubled."

Walter shrugged. "I think he just doesn't like seeing you like this." His gaze softened under Terra's fixation. "I have been worried about you. Your dad has been, too." Terra nodded. "Did you see him yet?" Walter shifted himself slightly, eyeing the battered Terra with heartfelt eyes.

Terra sighed. "No. I think he's obsessed with finding out what or who did this to me." Terra moved her hands slightly towards Walter; they were seemingly heavy from all the medication. Walter knelt beside her bedside and picked her hand up, rubbing it against his cheek. A tear flowed and met with the warmth of her hand. She smiled at Walter. "It's going to be alright, Wally. I'll be out of here before you know it, and then we'll go. Just have patience."

Walter nodded as he absorbed the sensation of her hand caressing his face. "I know. Tomorrow will be here, and then it'll be today that we'll pack and go." He smiled tearfully back at Terra and handed her the package. She accepted it, forcibly smiling through the pain. She slowly placed her hands on the package, and Walter put his on hers and helped her tear it open. Inside the little box was a tiny ruby-red velvet ring box tightly packed in tissue paper. Terra glanced back up at Walter, who got down on a knee. "Terra, I know it's been only two years, but you mean the world, no, life—everything to me. I live for you, and I want to spend the rest of it with you." Walter struggled with his words, attempting to keep his composure. "I want to share every moment with you. I—I—damn it, Terra. I love you so much." Walter slowly opened the box to reveal a white-gold, two-karat, marquise-cut, solitaire diamond engagement ring.

Terra's heart monitor picked up in rhythm as she shed a tear. "Oh, Wally, you're so cute when you try to be romantic. You know I'd marry you any day."

Outside the room, Dana smiled to himself. *That a boy, Walt, you sly dog, you.* Then, he noticed irregular movement in his peripheral vision. He turned his head to face down the hall only to see Ellis and Elias leaving a bathroom near where he was. He could see Elias was pissed off, and he slapped the back of Ellis's head and cursed as they fast-tracked down the hall back to the elevators. Dana turned his head slightly back towards Terra's room. *Bah, I'll leave the lovebirds alone.* He decided to check on Mark.

He slowly approached the closed door when he heard a conversation taking place. "I am telling you, young man, you are absolutely very, very lucky to be alive," said a man with an Indian accent. "Yes indeed, and to have such company of a lovely lady, excuse me, if you don't mind my saying, Miss—?"

Dana heard the soft reply as he stood in front of the door. "Lilah, Doctor Jaymes. Lilah Dean."

>)

Here, Lilah sat in a small room in Middleton Metropolitan Hospital. Her pen tapped on what had been a blank page at the back of the book of Hoyle. She had just jotted down: *It is inside my mind. Its name is Mullin.* When read aloud, it sounded like pure insanity, but then again, there was nothing sane about the situation.

Lilah glanced up from the book. Across the small room from where she was seated lay the person she knew as Mark, real name Mark Colley. She didn't think she would have been able to recognize him. A nurse had given her his name and room number after Lilah told her they were good friends. The information on his beating and the location in which he'd been found were both given to her courtesy of the very same radio that had delivered what she considered decent news a few days back.

His face was swollen, so he looked like nothing she could remember. His right shoulder was wrapped tightly in bandages, and both legs were in a cast up to the hip.

According to the nurse, he had been unconscious since he'd been picked up and brought in. Lilah smiled as she thought of how unrecognizable she had to be to him. Her hair hung loosely down her back, with two locks hanging just forward from her ears and down her cheeks. Her face was painted its usual white with charcoal lipstick and eyeliner. Her clothes were also a total reversal from what he had known. The ivory tank top had been replaced with a murky blouse and corset laced down the front, and blue jeans had been replaced by a black skirt puffed out by pale padding. Her legs were covered in sable-and-violet striped stockings that ended in her heavily strapped dark boots. Her dusky brown eyes were presently exposed behind her "nerd" glasses. Quite the change from the poker-playing, trash-talking Mable he knew.

Outside the room's curtains and glass, the sun shined brightly, casting yellow and brown across the room, beating back the constant glare of the fluorescent white lights overhead. Coupled with Mark's gently beeping heart monitor, the sun's warm glow seemed to signify that everything was right in this small room.

Lilah glanced across the sea of calm, and on the other side, Mark's eyes fluttered and then attempted to open fully through the swelling. Disoriented, they scanned the room, seemingly looking for something familiar but failing in this task. She noticed his gaze finally come to focus on her. At that, she laid her pen in her book between the pages, closed it, and stored the small package in its home.

Mark made several weak attempts to clear his throat. Lilah smiled and went into the bathroom, where next to the sink was a stainless-steel spring-loaded device that dispensed conical white paper cups. She popped one out and ran the faucet until cold water poured out, which she then captured in the paper cup. Satisfied, she made her way to Mark's bedside and offered it to the hand, which was not attached to the arm that was bandaged. He accepted it graciously and put it to his lips. Immediately, two thin lines formed down his cheeks as he tried to down the whole thing through his swollen lips.

"Easy." Lilah's voice spoke soothingly. "You're going to get more on you than in you."

Once the cup was emptied, Mark's arm dropped back into his lap, and the paper cup rolled from his grasp and wedged itself between his sheets and the plastic guard rail that ran along the sides of the bed. He gasped for air, and each breath sounded terribly painful. Enough so that Lilah almost winced.

"Mah . . . May?" He closed his eyes and grimaced. "Ah . . . are . . . you . . . May . . . Mable?" Lilah let a smile escape, and Mark's face put on a show as it attempted to reflect relief, happiness, and affirmation. Now, it was her turn to attempt conversation. She opened her painted black lips but was harshly interrupted by quick knocks on the door.

The door opened partway, and a somewhat round, brown face with a bushy black mustache poked in. The doctor opened the door fully and closed it as quietly as possible. His gray hair told tales of years of experience. "Ah, yes, I see you are awake, Mister Colley. This is very good. I am Dr. Vir Jaymes. My staff and I hope to help you to make a full and speedy recovery."

Lilah took a few steps back as the doctor took her place at Mark's bedside. She watched as he poked and prodded, occasionally taking notes and flashing a light in Mark's eyes before taking more. After finishing his writing, he slipped his pen into his shirt pocket and walked to the foot of the bed to face Lilah and Mark. He glanced down at his clipboard and rustled through a few pages. "I am telling you, young man, you are very fortunate to be alive. Yes indeed, and to have such company of a lovely lady, excuse me, if you don't mind my saying, Miss—?"

"Lilah, Doctor Jaymes. Lilah Dean," Lilah responded calmly and coolly.

"Oh, yes, very lovely," the doctor responded cheerfully. "I'm afraid, however, that visiting hours for Mister Colley will be over soon at the request of law enforcement. However, I will leave you two alone for now." Dr. Jaymes made his way out, closing the door gently behind him.

"Well, I guess I should leave, but don't worry—I'll come back to visit tomorrow after school. I hope you're doing a lot better by then." Lilah gave Mark another smile and checked her person before moving towards the exit.

"Li . . . lah . . ." Lilah stopped and turned enough to look over her shoulder. "Lilah," Mark repeated, "Meat, he's looking . . . coming after you." He struggled to clear his throat. "Please . . . be careful."

Lilah nodded, waved, and resumed her journey towards the exit. After shutting the door behind her as carefully as possible, she turned down the hall towards the elevators, only to be startled by a man. He leaned against the wall, eyes wandering to everything but her. His disheveled, dingy hair and stubble hinted at a person having trouble sleeping. Lilah closed her eyes and marched past him, her chin held up as if to show that she wasn't scared if the police were on to her. As she walked by, she could feel his eyes settle on her and follow. When Lilah got to the elevator, she pressed the down button and turned to look at Mark's door. The man was gone, so she shrugged, returning her attention to the glowing numbers. Far in the back of her consciousness, Mullin growled something incoherent.

)

A man's voice came from near the room's entrance, followed by a few grunts. "Walter Conway, how are you doing?" Walter and Terra turned their attention to the man who stood before them, offering a smile. He was in his late fifties, tall and clean-shaven with a high receding hairline, short, swarthy hair, and bushy, dark brows to match. The man wore a royal blue police uniform, proudly displaying his Middleton Police Department badge. He removed his black officer's cap.

"Beatty." Walter smiled, wide-eyed with joy, and laughed. "How are you, old friend?" Walter walked over and shook Beatty's hand firmly.

Terra forced a smile onto her swollen face as the officer sauntered into the room with a big teddy bear. "Oh, Beatty, you shouldn't have."

He chuckled. "Nyah, I know how much you like your teddy bears, Terra," Beatty grunted as he looked at the massive fluff ball.

"Well, thank you. Did you see Dana on the way in?" Terra asked, accepting the plush gift.

"Hmm, nope. Is he here?" Beatty searched the room.

"Well, he was outside the room. He might have gone to check on that kid who got his ass rocked." Walter moved back to Terra's bedside.

"Hmm, I heard about that case. It seems you guys got Ellis and Elias slinking around." Beatty motioned with his head outside the room.

"Yeah, they were here, but they found themselves . . . to have more pressing matters." Walter chuckled.

"Let me guess—Dana used that good ol' silver tongue of his?" Beatty gleefully grinned.

Walter laughed as he nodded. "You know how he is, Beatty."

Beatty laughed as well. "Nyah, the man is a good friend, Walter. He should know better, though, than to bother with such a trifling. Especially when it comes to those two." Beatty grunted again in rapid succession.

"Well, Beatty, it was nice seeing you again." Walter smiled and shook his hand once more.

"It sure was. I see you finally asked her?" Beatty glanced at the engagement ring on Terra's hand, then raised an eyebrow at Walter.

"You bet your ass." Walter stood proudly, beaming with a bright smile.

"Well, I wish the best to both of you. I have to be on my way, though." Beatty smiled as he placed his cap back on his head.

"It was nice seeing you, Beatty. Take care of yourself." Terra lazily waved, then let her heavy hand collapse onto her bed.

"It's OK. Get better, Terra. Everyone back at the station wishes you well." Beatty tipped his cap. "If I see Dana, I'll discuss it with him." Beatty turned and darted out of the room. Passing by the nurses' station, having ventured further down, he came upon the familiar face. "Detective Dana Deupree, how are you?"

Dana leaned against the wall, gazing at the big blue monster before him. "Well, I'll be—Officer Beatty Oedek." Dana pressed off the wall and shook Beatty's hand. "It's been a while. How have you been?" Dana smiled. "Looking sharp, Chief."

Beatty smiled as he returned Dana's firm handshake. "Good. I just stopped by to see how Terra was doing. I see Walter finally mustered up the courage to . . .?" He tilted his head as he motioned with his eyes, grinning.

"Yeah, that old dog still has a few tricks up his sleeves," Dana said with a laugh.

"Well, that's good. Walter needs to be happy." Beatty nodded a few times. "I saw your 'friends' Ellis and Elias nearby."

Dana sighed, rolling his eyes. "Yeah, ran them out of Terra's room to give Walter some time."

Beatty nodded. "Hmm, you know, Dana—" Beatty stopped abruptly. "Speak of the devil." Beatty motioned behind Dana with his head, and Dana could hear the clacking of Elias's shoes walking up behind him.

"Well, well, sticking your nose where it doesn't belong again, Deupree? I don't recall this being your case." Elias stopped behind Dana and shifted the toothpick in his mouth from side to side. Dana rolled his eyes again as he spun around to face Elias and spotted Ellis leisurely approaching.

"Oh, I'm sorry, Elias, I was merely doing your job. Then again, I suppose it's easy to get lost in your ego so easily. Seeing as how it says right here on this little wittle piece of white paper,"—Dana turned to point to the sheet next to a small whiteboard with *Mark Colley* written on it— "'Victims and Witnesses: Law enforcement is required *at all times to be present.'"* Dana turned back to face Elias. "Well, gee gosh golly willy wankers, Elias, it sure doesn't seem like you're doing your job. Oh, wait, let me guess. Did you have to go take a potty break and have your bitch Ellis hold it for you?"

"Yeah, yeah, really smooth there, Deupree, and where's your partner? He could be attacking an already frail victim, the fat fuck that he is. Smothering that poor girl to nothingness!" Elias made a sobbing gesture. "Wah, wah, I can't get a girlfriend, wah. His ex, Debbie—she's better off without him. Man, she's really tight—a real fine piece of meat, mmm, mmm! And don't even get me started about that ass of hers!" Elias grinned fiercely while Ellis sidestepped away from him as he glanced at Dana.

"Elias." Ellis shook his head, "I don't think that's—"

Elias turned to Ellis and snapped. "What, Ellis? Do you want some deadbeat insomniac fucker walking all over you for the rest of your goddamn law enforcement career? I don't care if he's first grade—that don't mean shit to me!"

Ellis mumbled something under his breath as he turned his head away.

"What was that? What did you say!"

Dana had already wound up before Elias turned to face him again. He sent him rushing to the cold hospital tile, his nose bloodied. "Don't bad-mouth someone who isn't here to defend himself. You attack my partner and friend. You attack me. Oh, and just so you know, Elias, Debbie died today, so I hope you feel mighty good about yourself right now."

Beatty stepped beside Dana. "Elias, I think you better leave. You're lucky Walter wasn't here. He would have squashed you like a small animal."

Ellis helped Elias to his feet as his partner cupped his nose with his hands; streaks of red slipped through his fingers. The two disappeared with Elias's never-ending commentary on how he would tell Brad. At last, an edge was removed. The tension was relieved.

Dana smiled. "My God, Beatty, that felt great."

Beatty laughed. "Well, it was great! I only wish Walter had been here to see it." Beatty then sighed. "Though you know he might *actually* drag this out and file a report on you, you know?"

Dana shrugged. "Eh, that's fine with me. I actually think Brad will give me a slap on the wrist then say, 'How about a drink?'"

"Well, let me know when you're leaving. I can stick around here until one of them comes back, or I can radio in a replacement. I have to make a stop upstairs to administration." Beatty patted Dana on the shoulder before readying himself to make his trip.

"Thanks, Beatty. Take care of yourself." Dana shook Beatty's hand and returned to leaning against the wall.

While waiting, he watched the TV that had become his newfound friend as time passed. The screen grew dark, and a professional, deep voice spoke from within the small black box: "Welcome to Middleton Hospital. We are a team of professionals led by one goal: offering the best care possible and getting you on the road to recovery." The box slowly faded into an orange-yellow flicker. The camera panned a campfire. A tall, thin man with a well-trimmed mustache sat upon a rock. The light reflected off his gray hair. He wore blue-gray scrubs with a matching lab coat. Sitting under the simulated starry night against a backdrop of pine trees, he clasped a stick with a white marshmallow on its end. He slowly brought his head up and looked towards the camera. "Here at Middleton Hospital, my staff and I will place you on the right track. We will put you and your family on the road to recovery. As we cherish our family and all cultures, we are all one when bringing you the best possible care."

The marshmallow ignited, and the scene slowly faded away. The narrator's voice echoed again: "Dr. Vir Jaymes, part of the elite staff leading modern medicine to a brighter future. Middleton Hospital—we care for you."

Dana shook his head and let out a sigh. The voices inside the room became quiet. He could sense someone coming. His gaze drifted to the man leaving the room—the same man he had seen on the television. He pressed himself further against the wall, head back. He heard a female voice again. *It sounds like she may be leaving*, he thought. Dana took a slight sidestep closer to the door.

"Li . . . lah," Dana heard Mark utter. "Meat, he's looking . . . coming after you." Silence, then Mark cleared his throat. "Please . . . be careful."

The door soon opened, and out came Lilah, who almost bumped into Dana, seemingly startled by his presence. Dana pretended to ignore her, though he caught her image in his peripheral vision. *Her . . . I've seen her before.* A few days ago, Dana thought back at the red light on the corner of Constance Avenue and Main Street. It all came back to him. *Lilah Dean.* He watched Lilah walk towards the elevators and then rush to find Walter. As he returned to Terra's room, he felt a tremendous pain run along his neck as he thought hard about Lilah. *What the hell is with this?* He brought his hand up to his cheek and ran it down his neckline but found no blood. The pain seemed to circulate in his neck but slowly subsided. He finally got a grip on himself as he approached Terra's room. Beads of sweat formed upon his brow, and he felt lightheaded.

He heard a distant echo, a deep hissing in his mind. *"She has marked you."*

Dana scanned his spinning environment. *Who—who, what? Marked me? What the hell?*

The deep voice spoke again: "*Lilith.*"

Dana slowly slid down against the wall with his head in his hands, wincing as the pain pulsed in his neck, waiting for the room to stop spinning, trying to make sense of the voices in his head, trying to make everything slow down.

Walter came out of Terra's room, closing the door behind him. "Dana, are you alright, buddy?" He crouched beside Dana, placing a hand on his shoulder.

"Yeah, Walt, just indigestion, I think, heh." Dana gave a faint grin.

The spinning stopped, as did the voices. It seemed his mind had woken up in a belligerent lobby where people were shouting at one another.

Walter helped Dana to his feet and offered him his shoulder. "Did you see Beatty?" Walter asked as he helped walk Dana past Mark's room.

"Yeah, he watched me deck, Elias, too." Dana gave a light chuckle.

"Whoa, what the hell happened?" Walter stopped and let Dana stand against the wall by the elevators.

"He was talking about you . . . and Debbie. So, I socked him. Pow! Right in the kisser." Dana looked up at Walter, smiling.

"Dammit, Dana, I would have wanted to film it." Walter shook his head.

"Nah, you'd have wanted to throw him down the stairs or out the window. I know you." Dana patted Walter's shoulder, "Besides, I'd rather you spend time with Terra."

Walter smiled. "You're a real kiss ass, you know that?"

"Ah, jeez," Dana said with a laugh. "You get me all fluttery when you talk like that." Dana scanned the room as they reached the elevator. "Call Beatty and let him know we're leaving." Dana stared at Walter and pushed the down button.

"What's the matter?"

"That Ward Estrada—you may get your chance to have him pick you out a new shirt." Dana's right eye and head twitched violently as he pushed the down button again.

"Damn, Dana, that actually looked kind of creepy, but then again, I look at your face and think, 'Better you look fuck ugly than me.'" Walter laughed as he brought out his cell phone.

"You're worse than a piece of shit that's clinging on for dear life and just won't drop off my ass, Walt." Dana chuckled. "Hurry up. Something, somewhere, will go down sometime soon. I can feel it."

"Are you sure it's just not in your pants? —Oh, hey, Beatty, Walter here. Dana said to let you know we're jetting. Right, yeah, he told me. Ah, damn, how I wish I'd been there. Yeah, he said you said that. Alright, yeah, you too, Beatty. Take it easy."

As the elevator arrived, a thought dinged in Dana's mind in time with the elevator's bell: *Lilah.*

9

IT WAS LATE EVENING. The sun had already descended under the horizon. The stars had bloomed in the twilight and were sparkling like diamonds. The moon had also risen above, offering a silver sliver of soft, majestic light to the world below. The only disturbance in the silence was the rustling of grass under Lynaly's feet as she approached the hill overlooking Middleton. She slowly sat upon the lone boulder, and a black shadow leaped out of the darkness, planting itself on her lap. She cradled the little beast.

Lynaly looked down at Sheila. The cat's eyes were clenched shut in pure pleasure as it purred. "You can sense it, can't you, my sweet?" she muttered.

A meow escaped the little beast's maw as it slowly opened its majestic golden eyes and gazed upward at its queen. A smile crept across Lynaly's face, and she continued to stroke Sheila's back. She looked down upon Middleton, waiting, patient as a fisherman.

"Soon, we will." Lynaly fixated on a location only known to her.

"*Do you think he knows yet?*" A disembodied male voice echoed in Lynaly's mind.

"Perhaps—because of that *flea*," she replied, annoyed. "It's of no importance, for he will become mine." Lynaly's grin glowed faintly under the moon's soft light. She picked up Sheila and looked her in the eyes. "Soon, we will have all the pieces. However, you will do another task for me." She stared deeper into Sheila's eyes. "This will be your last task. Complete it and come back to me. Soon, you'll be whole."

The cat gave a light bob of its head. Lynaly placed the beast back onto her lap, running her fingers down Sheila's back.

The golden eyes closed again, and the cat nodded. "Yes, *my queen, as you say.*" Lynaly grinned back in the night's pale light.

"Now then, I have matters to attend to elsewhere. Come find me when your task is completed," Lynaly said as she straightened her person and set off for town.

)

Deep in Middleton, far below Lynaly had perched, a ragged man sat alone in a barroom, contemplating. The bright orange neon sign in the large picture window displayed "Nomad's Motorcycle Club" to the world. Inside, groups of men and women drank and conversed while music loudly presented itself.

The Motorcycle Club was massive. The bottom half of the building's front wall was painted black, and rich oak extended to a sloped roof resembling a chopper's fuel tank. To one side of the room was "the motorcyclists' grave." Various dismantled motorcycle frames were stacked up to the "fuel tank." Near makeshift memorial markers, names of fallen cyclists and members who had frequented the club were etched on a piece of wood staked beside the bike. A front wheel was proudly displayed (it was often remarked that since the wheel was pointed skyward, those who had passed away could ride up towards the heavens).

The bar was the main attraction, with more than a hundred brews and all the liquor one needed to douse himself into drunken death and beyond. In an alcove near the front was a small arcade with a few classics: Pac-Man, Tetris, Galaga, and a few fighting games. Adjacent was a riding bull, ridden hard by a cute biker chick; her cue ball boyfriend slugged his friends in the arm as their eyes wandered. Behind the bar was a kitchen, where burgers and BBQ ribs were plentiful, and pulled pork sandwiches were done right. On the counters and tables sat bowls of beer nuts beside ashtrays. Tables and booths were plentiful, open to all shapes and sizes, while barstools were occupied with bodies whose heads were heavy.

Ward "Gigan" Estrada sat in a wooden chair, a glass on the table before him. He examined his bandaged hands, the red that had soaked through. Pus and plasma clouded the once white, pristine bandages. Ward couldn't tell if it was the pain he felt or if it was anger building up steadily. He flexed his hands and watched more ooze seep into the bandages. Ward slammed his fist down onto the table.

"Hey, Gigan, ya alright there, mac?"

Ward glared at the patron at the next table, who had turned around.

"Do I look alright? Huh?" Ward's bandages hid his burned face but not the anger that seethed like the flames that had scorched him.

"Easy, man. I just wanted to help. That's all." The man turned back around to tend to his bottle of cold brew.

Help? What exactly could you even do? Ward suddenly stopped in his train of thought. *That smug little bitch. I'll pay her back tenfold—no more waiting. Tonight's the night.*

Ward stood up. "Actually, yeah, there is something you can do, Eagle. Get your boys ready for a ride."

Eagle's left wingman turned back to Ward. "You mean, right now?"

Ward's bandaged eyebrows twitched, and in a sudden rush, he grabbed hold of the back of the man's head and, with a savage roar, brought down the mighty gavel of his own. The man instantly dropped to the ground, unconscious. Other patrons rushed to the man as Gigan glared at the scared Eagle. His lips curled, ready to scream at the man. His fists clenched. "Did I stutter? Get them and get outside—pronto!"

)

The night air was taking on shape, thick, with a sense of rising uneasiness, as there were cold and indifferent eyes elsewhere in Middleton. Beth stood atop Graves Diner, the wind slicing through her black robe, causing it to billow behind her like a funeral shroud. The sting of her last encounter with Lynaly hadn't faded, nor had the humiliation. She should have died that night; she would have if not for Shane. But tonight, there would be no mistakes, no saves, no intervention.

"*She's close,*" Amii whispered inside her mind, a serpentine hiss that slithered around Beth's thoughts, coiling tight around her resolve.

"*I know,*" Beth muttered, eyes narrowed as she scanned the empty streets below. The same sick hatred that burned every time she thought of the massacre churned inside her, molten and consuming.

The neon glow from the diner reflected faintly in a puddle on the cracked asphalt, and then there she was—Lynaly, strolling as if the night belonged to her.

Beth didn't hesitate. She pounced.

As she descended, the wind screamed in her ears, a blur of motion and fury. She hit the ground hard, knees bent to absorb the impact, and before Lynaly could turn, Beth struck. The silver dagger, enchanted with holy runes, slashed through the air. Lynaly barely twisted out of the way in time, the blade cutting a shallow line across her collarbone. Magenta blood welled, and for a fraction of a second, surprise flickered across her face.

"Oh? I see you've learned a trick or two." Lynaly smiled, and it was the kind of smile that spoke of ancient hunger and cruelty.

Beth answered with another strike, faster, more precise. This time, she connected, and the blade sunk into Lynaly's side, causing the witch to let out a growl of pain, a sound low and primal.

"YES!" Amii hissed, her excitement a jolt of electricity through Beth's veins. "*Do you feel it? The power? You could end her now!*"

Beth felt a wild, intoxicating rush that made her want to drive the blade deeper, to rip Lynaly apart piece by piece. She pressed harder, her other hand glowing a blue-white; Amii's magic fed into her body and fueled her rage. But Lynaly was not prey.

With a sneer, Lynaly grabbed Beth by the throat and slammed her into the brick wall of the alley behind the diner. The impact knocked the air from Beth's lungs, and light exploded behind her eyes. Still, she fought, stabbing again—but this time, Lynaly caught her wrist, squeezing until the bones ground together painfully.

"Did you really think you'd win?" Lynaly whispered, her voice almost tender, with her iron grip. She twisted Beth's arm cruelly in an unnatural direction, forcing the dagger from her fingers. It clattered to the ground.

"I—I'll kill you," Beth gasped, kicking out, but Lynaly barely flinched.

"No, darling. You won't." Lynaly leaned closer, her breath hot against Beth's ear. "Because you don't understand who . . . or what you're fighting. Not yet."

Beth struggled, but Lynaly was stronger—inhumanly so. The witch slammed her to the ground with bone-crushing force, pinning her beneath one knee.

"*Kill her now,*" Amii whispered, cold and insistent.

"I can't," Beth thought, despair threatening to choke her. "I—I'm losing."

"*Then give yourself to me.*" Amii's voice was seductive, a dark promise that made Beth's heart pound. "*Let me end her.*"

The temptation was there, a black hole threatening to pull her in. To surrender to that power, to the rage that burned so brightly. To give in and let Amii take over completely.

But then Shane's voice echoed faintly in her memory: "There are things you're unaware of."

A thread of doubt pulled taut inside her. And then there was him—*Brian.*

"No," Beth whispered, her resolve snapping into place. "Not like this."

"*Fool,*" Amii hissed, but there was something else there now—not anger, but almost . . . concern?

Lynaly's hand closed around Beth's throat again, and this time, there was no playing. Magenta fire danced along her arm, searing Beth's skin.

"Goodbye, little mouse," Lynaly whispered, eyes burning with triumph.

But before the killing blow could land, a blinding pulse of energy exploded from Beth—not Amii's power, but her desperate will to survive. It sent Lynaly staggering back, giving Beth just enough time to roll away and scramble to her feet.

Panting, bleeding, and broken, Beth stared at her enemy, and Lynaly looked truly angry for the first time since this charade. Then, it subsided to reason from within.

"Remember this, my dear. The third time will be the charm," Lynaly sneered, vanishing into the night, leaving Beth alone in the empty alley.

Beth collapsed to her knees, clutching her burned skin, trembling.

"*I could have saved you,*" Amii whispered, softer now, almost sad. "*All you had to do is just let me . . .*"

"No, not like that," Beth whispered, her voice hoarse. "I know what will happen if I were to depend on that power, and I . . . have already lost so much."

She felt Amii shift inside her, not with cold anger this time, but something warmer, something hesitant. "Rest now, child. I'll take care of you." The healing warmth of Amii's magic flowed through Beth's body, closing her wounds and easing her pain—but it was different this time. Gentler. It was as if, even just a little bit, Amii herself had changed.

)

Far away, beyond her senses, the Order was already moving. Watching through the crow's eye, Albedo scorned Beth's hesitation and Amii's weakness.

"Pah. They've lost their edge," he whispered to a cloaked figure beside him. "I suppose it can't be helped since they fell."

Albedo waved his hand, and a portal flickered to life.

"I suppose it's time we remind them who they work for."

The robed figure bowed and vanished through the portal, the magic disappearing behind him.

A look of disgust manifested on Albedo's face.

"Curse that damn man-child and that boy. How could we have let that one slip?"

Albedo paced around his chambers before stopping at the table with documents, photos, and other materials about multiple targets. He thought something was amiss, and it had been staring at him for so long.

"There's something there . . . and why does it feel like there's always another presence when he is around? Perhaps. . ."

An idea came to mind, and he acted upon it.

☽

The archives were a place of history for things much older than the world of man and were just as grand as any library you could find in the world. They were deep underground, hidden away from the other wings, where rituals, torture, and other typical chores were carried out.

Tonight, Albedo wagered he would strike gold with the amount of information he gathered. As he walked to the most exclusive areas within the Archives, he never would have imagined how wrong he was; it wouldn't be gold he struck, but something far more valuable. In the order of life and death, knowledge was power.

He found tomes dating back to the Old Days of the Order. A smile crept across his face—fond memories. Then he inspected the passages regarding the matter with Atreyu when he first became initiated—*Ah, yes, back when the leash was its tightest!* There, he saw it. Pages were missing. There was no record of the rituals carried out against Lilith, Samael, the parents, and . . .

"Wait," Albedo stopped, his eyes moving over the words and names. "Where's the boy?" He tried to remember the name of one familiar but struggled to do so.

"Master Albedo, can I assist you?" asked a white-robed woman, the Archivist.

"Hmm? Yes, do we have any other information for these records? Also, who was the last here to use this book? He asked, thumbing through the pages.

After a moment of thought, "I believe that's all there is now, and I think the last to use that tome was his Excellency, sir," she replied.

Albedo's stomach turned, and he hid his fear. Perplexed, his mind began running rampant with conspiracies and the thought of being watched by unseen eyes—a faint chill ran down his spine as the torches flickered at such a thought.

Had the Master committed a cover-up? Ah, but were there any other eyes watching? No, it's just the Archivist. Why were there missing records on the boy? What about Atreyu? Had he . . .

And then he began to settle; confidence returned, and he was himself again. Unnerved, he closed the tome and put it back. "Thank you, Archivist."

I suppose it's time to move things along. If my suspicions are correct, I need only give a little nudge, and that man-child will break. As he exited the Archives, a smile stretched wide.

)

The night had crept upon her, and Lilah hastened her step as she weaved through the silent streets. Somewhere in the night, a cat sang a forgotten tale. In the distance, the quiet rumbles of street bikes steadily grew louder. The sounds came from different directions and coalesced in the echoes that rolled towards her like an oncoming thunderstorm.

Lilah paused her mental attempts at conversation for a moment and took note of the intersection. Finding her bearings, she continued. The demon had been unresponsive since she left the hospital, and this was an item of concern for her. Strangely, he had become a source of comfort. His presence had become normal, and she felt comforted that his being there seemingly justified her recent questionable actions. *Justification is a good mortar when the walls of sanity begin to crack*, she thought.

The roar had grown so that it could no longer be ignored. It seemed to clamor through the buildings like a cyclopean horror recently awoken from a long slumber, dragging itself on its belly, gripping the structures around it, unleashing its cries of anguish into the still air.

Mullin had been candid with her since she learned to establish safe communication. Lilah knew drastic dives into herself were dangerous, so she always kept herself on the verge when she wanted to talk. While he could possess her, she realized he could never take complete control as their deal had been made externally, or so it was told, forever embodied in the deck of cards. He could certainly not force her out of her own body because he only existed apart from it.

Behind Lilah, the thunder of eight motorcycles rounded the corner two blocks back. They fanned out and positioned themselves across the lanes on Constance. The lead bike seemed to scream suddenly, its exhaust drowning out its companions. It started its journey toward the lone figure draped in black walking down the street. Lilah snapped out of her attempts to find Mullin and spun on her heels. Before her, there stretched a blend of loud and bright. A crackling yell echoed from the chaos, and the lights and sounds intensified. The scene resembled the mouth of Hell breaking open and releasing a roar as lone embers from its blazing belly leaped out at her, threatening to scorch her with a touch.

She recoiled in sheer terror before turning and breaking into a full sprint. Her jerky motions loosened her glasses from her face, and before they could finish their trip, she ripped them off, slowing down only slightly to ram them deep into her purse.

The beast clambered up behind her and then beside her as if mocking her futile escape attempt. She could vaguely remember her coach's words from her track-and-field days. *You can outrun the devil if you try!* She clenched her eyes shut and redoubled her efforts. Her black skirt kicked up and down as her legs made their last attempt at liberty.

Two motorcycles rode ahead of the leader before swinging onto the sidewalk, just past the alleyway she was making her break for. Lilah came to a complete stop, her path now obstructed by two gruff leather-adorned men. Her attention shot from side to side, and she began to back into the alleyway, not daring to turn her attention from her stalkers. One by one, engines fell silent, but the sound of bootheels on the pavement chased the silence away. The footsteps stopped at the beginning of the alleyway, save for one pair.

The figure of a giant of a man stepped into focus. Through the glare of the headlamps, she could make out tufts of singed hair set against pink and red—almost wax-like—skin. Around his face ran strips of gauze covering his nose and ears. Across his face was the grin of a kid who had just received the one present he'd wished for all year. Lilah reached into her purse but froze as the figure opened its mouth and began to talk.

"Ah," said the low, raspy voice. "I was hoping for a repeat of this trick!"

)

Outside the Wagon Wheel Motel, Dana and Walter sat in the car, surveying the case of a possible suspect in a prior murder investigation. The chilly night had set in. Walter handed Dana a small package containing a spork and napkin. The motel was a shoddy establishment. How it was still considered up to code was beyond Dana. He rubbed his eyes while Walter arranged packages of duck sauce, soy sauce, and plum sauce on the dashboard.

The giant wagon wheel in front of the entrance was worn, weathered, and splintered, possibly infested with termites. The vermilion neon sign illuminated vacancy, and a white billboard projected the silhouettes of letters spelling out feasible rates per hour, night, and week. The ruddy brick building offered no sign of the "comfortable stay" promised on the billboard. Dana stared at the magenta door, which was numbered four.

"Alrighty, let's dig in!" Walter smiled with glee as he lifted the lid. Steam poured out from the container as he scanned the almond chicken and chicken fried rice, salivating. "Man, I swear, Charlie makes the best Chinese take-out in town. This never gets old. I love it!" Walter took a huge sporkful of chicken fried rice, and pieces clung to his chin and lips.

"Christ, Walt, what kind of food don't you love?" Dana looked over to his left at his famished, gluttonous partner, grinning. "I mean, it's like you're a bottomless pit."

Walter chuckled as he swallowed. "Ah, you're just jealous." He choked for a second, coughing on a renegade rice kernel.

Dana raised an eyebrow, "Jealous of your eating habits? Please." Dana smirked as he shook his head, diving into his piping-hot order of General Tso's chicken.

Walter spoke with a mouthful. "Nah, you're jealous because I will have a Missus Conway again." Walter paused for a moment. "Plus, Debbie was quite the bed shaker; rest her soul. Damn, she was a hell of a sack rocker."

Dana set his spork down and looked at Walter. "Walter, I am happy for you, but don't try to be a twisted, sadistic sex fiend. I don't want to know about your bedside manners." He rolled his eyes.

"Gets you every time!" Walter laughed

Dana suddenly heard stuttering in the night. He rolled down his window, and the night revealed a monstrous bellow not far from their location. "Hey, Walt, listen." Dana nudged his partner, who grunted as he continued to pick at the remains of his former meal. "Walter Conway!"

"W-what! What the hell?!" Walter jumped in his seat, hitting his head on the car's roof. "Gah, son of a bitch! Dad gone it, Dana!"

Dana cringed. "Eh, sorry, that's your bad."

Walter hissed in pain, rubbing his head. "Ah, goddamn it, what's so important you couldn't wait?"

Dana held up his finger. "Quiet! Listen . . . do you hear that?" He motioned out of the window.

"Hmm, yeah, it seems like a motorcycle brigade. The town's full of them. What's your point?"

Dana glared at Walter. "Remember your shirt? Hot coffee, big bad burned biker-mummy Meat? Ward Estrada? Ring any bells yet?"

Walter rolled his eyes. "I knew that."

Dana covered his face with his palm. "You sure did, Walt, you sure did." Dana sighed. "I got a bad feeling." He looked down the road, where the roar was coming from.

Walter closed the lid on his container. "Well, let's go check it out then."

Dana nodded as they tossed their rubbish into a plastic bag and lobbed it into the backseat. The monster's roar fell silent. An urgency overcame them.

"C'mon, Walt!"

Walter turned the key in the ignition and cranked the car into gear.

As they traveled through the city square blocks, the usual shapes of the night crept out here and there. Dana fixed his gaze further down the road as they passed through intersections, looking for hints. Then he saw a pair of headlights dim, like an eye closing shut.

"There, turn here!" Dana pointed down the road, and Walter quickly obliged.

As they neared the abandoned bikes, Walter slowed to a halt and dimmed his car's lights. A few shadows could be seen in the nearest alleyway, one looming high above the others. "It's him." Dana got out of the car fast, not even bothering to close the door, with Walter straggling behind.

As they stealthily approached the alleyway along a brick wall, Dana motioned at Walter to stay put. He scurried across the entrance, catching a glimpse of a group of men led by Ward Estrada. The wolves were cornering their provoked prey. Dana pressed his back against the wall, and both detectives took peeks to assess the situation. Then Dana held his index finger to his lips.

☽

Two bikers dashed towards the goth girl Dana had seen in the hospital, but her hands were quicker. In a blur, she whipped five cards off the top of a deck and held them before her, not bothering to examine them first. The effect was immediate. The cards flashed a bright orange-yellow, and the two men went flying. They landed at the giant's feet as crumpled messes with steam rolling off their leather clothing, their hair a new shade of white.

Two more bikers tore down the alleyway, and Lilah again worked her magic. This time, a spray of electricity sent sparks arcing from every metallic surface. The air filled with the acrid smell of ozone, and the two dropped to the ground mid-flight, convulsing.

A series of pants and quick gasps running down the alleyway toward them caused the cautious duo to duck behind a neighboring dumpster. Two bikers rushed past them. One's helmet resembled an eagle's head, while the other resembled a goat's.

"Pah! Cowards," Meat uttered.

They both jumped on their choppers and tore off with a rip-roar of whelps into the night. Dana watched as their taillights disappeared into the thick forest of city buildings. *I can't say I blame them. Their friends are getting deep-fried and barbecued by a little goth girl.* Dana withheld a grin as he looked back down the alley while Walter watched for unsuspected interruptions.

Lilah stumbled backward; her strength seemed to be fading. *They haven't laid a finger on her. How is it that she's weakened?*

She stepped back further into the alleyway, wincing. She looked at the hand she'd pulled, and Dana noted the despair on her face.

Tucking the hand back into the deck, she began to shuffle.

"Blondie, you're up!" Meat announced. A new challenger stepped forth from behind him.

He was young, at least for the crowd he associated with. Despite the spectacle before him, he seemed remarkably confident. He tapped a baseball bat stained with reddish-brown blotches against his shoulder as he made his way over the bodies of fallen comrades toward the girl. With each step, the smile on his face grew, becoming ever more sadistic. Beads of sweat welled upon his forehead, some of which got caught in a single lock of hair hanging down from his full head of curly blond hair.

Lilah continued to step back while her hands worked at the stack of cards. She stumbled over an empty pop can and planted herself against the dumpster at the end of the alleyway.

Walter stared at Dana from the opposite side of the dumpster and whispered, "We're going to do something, right? We can't just let her get squashed like an egg."

Dana raised an eyebrow at Walter, breaking his gaze away from the scene. "I think the word you're looking for is a *bug*, Walt. Squashed like a bug."

Walter blinked. "They both break."

Dana pursed his lips. "Yeah, they do. You have a valid point. I'll allow it."

The blond biker continued his slow approach like a creeping terror. His hair appeared gray in the shadows, and he almost looked like the appropriate age for being in a biker gang. He opened his mouth as if to declare something important. Lilah wasn't interested, and with a quick motion—a new set of cards was in her hand—the boy was stifled as his hair and clothes burst into flames. He attempted a scream but was silenced by the fire and smoke, filling his mouth and burning his vocal cords. He dropped to the ground, occasional shudders running through his body. A jolt ran through Lilah, and she dropped to her knees, her arms and legs going limp. The deck of cards landed in a neat pile before her. Her chin fell to her chest. On the pavement before her atop the heap, facing up, was a single card: a two of hearts.

Get up! Get up, damn it! Dana gritted his teeth as he watched.

"Well, well, just as I suspected. All out of ammo." The monstrous, scarred biker made his way down the alley towards Lilah, stepping on and over bodies. "I heard the stories from those stupid brothers. They talked without a single act of violence. However, they won't be able to drive their car for a while. They told me all about how, after you torched me, you dropped to the ground in pain. I figured that you couldn't just keep doing your little trick. That it took something out of you every time."

Dana and Walter stared at each other and nodded, slowly readying their guns as they inched toward the warring pair. Dana cringed as Ward's boot planted itself on the fingers of the blond bastard's outstretched hand. The bones crunched like dried twigs beneath a car tire, gently echoing against the walls and down the alleyway.

"It didn't take a genius to realize who you were. After seeing your email and messenger images, which were of some stupid vampire chick, we realized you were into that whole 'dark spirit of the night' thing. Silly vampire goth girls—you probably use those pictures for everything. Then we merely watched the school, waiting for someone like you to leave. Poor Blondie here was the one who tailed you to the hospital." He motioned casually over his shoulder to the burned body.

Mullin's voice bellowed in her head: "LILAH, YOU STUPID GIRL! IT'S IN EACH CARD, NOT IN THE HAND COMBINATIONS! NOW, PULL!" Lilah returned to reality and realized the giant was standing directly over her. She looked down at the deck of cards on the pavement.

"NOW!"

She mustered her strength and moved her right hand enough to drop sloppily on the deck.

The biker reached down, grabbed a handful of Lilah's hair, lifted her to her feet, and then off the ground until she was at eye level with him. His sour breath reeked of smoke, beer, and tuna left out in the sun for two weeks too long. The girl winced, both in pain and from the stench. Her limp body helplessly rocked back and forth in the giant's grasp.

"Oh, I forgot to introduce myself. I am Gigan. I am the man whose life you ruined back at that stupid poker game." His left hand reached behind him, and a huge hunting knife was slid out of his pocket. Each point of the serrated edge gleamed like a wolf's tooth in the streetlight's glow. "Now, it's your life that will be ruined!"

The point of the blade came to rest just under Lilah's rib cage. With a bit of pressure, it made its way through two layers of fabric and one layer of skin. She tried to struggle and managed to let loose a scream as steel worked its way past muscle and into organs. She twisted in an upward motion, and her cry was abruptly stopped by the blood rushing into her punctured right lung. She hacked and coughed as red worked its way up to and then out of her mouth. Gigan pulled the blade out; thick dark blood poured out of the wound and formed a horrible parody of a waterfall as it split into two streams, one that ran down to the edge of her skirt and one that ran down her leg before splattering on the pavement at two distinct points. He cocked his head sideways and put a gauze-covered remnant of an ear to her face. "What's that? I'm sorry. I didn't catch your name, little girl."

Lilah's eyes shot open, now glowing a dull green. "It's Mullin."

Dana and Walter stopped in their tracks. "What the hell!"

Walter's jaw dropped. Dana scratched his head, but inside, a sick sense of relief came over him, and he was unaware of the slight grin that sprawled across his face.

Warm blood sprayed out of Lilah's mouth with each syllable of the name, speckling Gigan's face with red droplets. The voice was not that of a girl, let alone anything of this world. Her right hand revealed a card tucked between two fingers: a thirteen of spades. "Nice to meet you."

Walter and Dana stared at the root of everything that had happened as of late. It is you!

Gigan dropped her and took two steps back, a look of genuine shock and terror claiming his face. He raised his arms to cover his head, but the effort was for naught. A blindingly white stream of electricity erupted from the tiny card and shot into his chest, sending the giant biker two feet in the air and crashing back down to the ground next to the blond. The green glow faded from Lilah's eyes, and after a moment of confusion, she began to hack wildly, clearing her throat and lungs of blood. After she'd settled a bit, she checked her person, her fingers probing the hole in her clothes, but the knife wound was gone. Still coughing, though lightly now, she knelt and grabbed her glasses; one lens was smudged with red. She put them back in their rightful place across the bridge of her nose before carefully collecting all the cards off the cool pavement.

"YOU LITTLE BITCH!"

Lilah shot up, but it was too late. Gigan was up and moving at her with the speed of a demon. In his hand was the bat. She clenched her eyes shut in anticipation. Her arms came up to her head, and she knelt as instinct gripped her in a futile attempt at protection. The biker roared angrily and gleefully as he brought the baseball bat over his head for the perfect arc.

"Now, Walt!" Dana yelled.

The magnificent duo fired their standard-issue Middleton Police Department Glock 22s. The consecutive series of shots pierced Ward's back, filling it with pockmarks. The beast jerked violently, his arms flailing. The thunderous snaps and cracks died down to silence.

After a moment, Lilah slowly opened her eyes, bewildered, as the bloodied giant collapsed before her, dead.

Dana ran towards Lilah. "Are you alright?"

Lilah stared at Dana hesitantly. "Y-yes, I'm fine." Dana offered a hand to help her, but she refused with a glare, collecting the last of her cards and putting on her glasses.

Walter walked over and checked Ward "Gigan" Estrada for a pulse, digging through the thick mesh of bandages around the base of his neck, then joined Dana and Lilah. "So,

Dana, how do you want to explain this?" Walter holstered his gun and pulled his long brown coat over it.

There's no way we could arrest her. She'd probably rip Walt and me to shreds. C'mon. . .think of something.

Dana followed suit, having thought of a plan. "Let's say we witnessed the local bike gang having a civil war and attacking civilians. They resisted, and the threat had to be neutralized."

Dana looked down at Lilah. "I know what you did." He stared hard at her, through her glasses, into her dark-brown eyes. "Get out of here, and don't let me catch you doing anything of this sort again. If I catch wind of another incident, I'll happily expose you for what you are."

Lilah packaged her cards neatly and placed them into the depths of her purse. She stood and checked Dana over. "So, you'd prefer to cause mass hysteria among people who cannot comprehend what is . . . currently unknown? I doubt the public would be so accepting, let alone believe you over little old me . . ." She smirked. "But don't worry, Detective, you have my word."

Dana stood baffled and in awe as he watched her return to the night.

"Well, she's got you there."

Dana smacked Walter upside the head. "Shut up and get a hold of dispatch."

Ho boy, this is going to go over really well. Dana ran his fingers through his hair as Walter got on his cell phone. *She has a hell of a lot of spunk.* Dana smirked, and his gaze scanned the felled bikers that littered the alley.

A short time later, red, white, and blue lights waltzed down the street and situated themselves at the end of the alleyway.

An officer came strolling towards them, adjusting his cap and fixing the badge on his shirt.

"Hey, Walt, look at this—it seems we got a rookie in our presence." Dana chuckled as Walter spun around and squinted at the fresh new face.

"Well, well, you sure got the short straw, champ. What's your name?" Walter stood with his head tilted, hands on his hips, and a big grin spread across his face.

The rookie seemed fresh out of the academy, his eyes darting to and fro, then stopping on Gigan's hulking, bloody corpse.

Dana grinned. "Is this your first time on a scene, Officer . . .?"

"Uh, oh right, Officer Forge—Ed Forge. Pleased to meet you, Detectives Conway and Deupree."

"Aware of who we are? My, my, have been doing our homework, haven't we?" Dana smirked at the newbie, who nodded.

"Yes, sir, I hope to help the force greatly. I've heard about plenty of the cases you've worked, gentlemen." Valentine paused for a moment before continuing. "You're not like those assholes, Elias and Ellis." Silence fell upon the trio. Dana's gaze drifted over to Walter, who matched it—both then looked at the rookie. Forge twitched in the silence. "Uh, I mean . . ."

Dana slapped the kid on the back while Walter put his arm around him. "Now you're speaking our language, Forge! Welcome aboard!" Officer Forge visibly sighed with relief. "Now then, let's get you going. If you don't mind, grab a camera and take photos. We'll mill around here." Dana patted Forge on the shoulder, and he obediently rushed off.

Other officers blocked off the far end of the alleyway with police tape. Dana turned around and looked around at the scattered remnants of the baseball bat Estrada had dropped.

He knelt, removing white latex gloves from his pocket and stretching them over his hands. He noted the red-brown stains on the remnants—dried blood. *Mark Colley was beaten with a baseball bat.* He examined the errand boy and uncovered the remains of a wallet in one pocket. Inside, he found a warped student ID. His name was Johnny Birka, a senior at Middleton High. He turned the boy's shattered, scorched hand over, revealing a crushed spade insignia ring on his finger. In Johnny's other pocket was a partially melted metal wiring spool and a box cutter that adhered to the leather pouch he wore around his waist. *What do we have here? Interesting . . .*

Walter had his findings—a custom-made .45 revolver complete with a number ten and spade in its handle.

"Hey, Dana, check this out."

Dana shuffled carefully to the corpse Walt was crouched over. "Does this look pretty familiar to you?"

"Well, I'll be. I see us a possibility." He grinned at Walter, who rolled his eyes in response.

"You're taking me to get some breakfast after this hell of an adventure, buddy." Walter patted him on the arm.

Dana curled his lips upward. "Seems fair. Let's get Forge and the others down here to clean up. Then we'll hit the town. What do you say to that?"

"That sounds delightful. When do we start?" The two began to stroll down the alleyway.

"Does this kind of remind you of not so long ago?"

Walter stopped as he pondered Dana's question. "Yeah, now that you mention it. It sure does have the feel, except for two things." Walter resumed walking, and they ducked under the police tape.

"What's that?" Dana inquired.

"I don't have a doughnut and coffee." Walter smiled as Dana shook his head.

"You're a machine, Walt, a real machine."

"Call me the grinder," Walter said with a chuckle. "Or the pit, your choice."

Dozens of vehicles were parked erratically on the street and sidewalks, and law enforcement personnel and gawkers littered them.

Dana shrugged. "Either way, let's get the boys down there."

What a night. At least that's over with. I suppose it can't get any worse now.

)

Somewhere else and later in the night, a thin fog crept along the empty streets of Middleton, curling around the town's worn edges like fingers reluctant to let go as the moon shone brightly. A train blared its horn while the clock on the lone sentinel struck the hour. A slight gust of wind kicked up leaves that tumbled along the pavement.

Beth moved quickly through the shadows, her gaze locked on a lone figure in the distance: Lynaly. The same sick hatred that had festered within her since the massacre now blazed like a furnace. She was ready. This time, she wouldn't fail.

"*She's right there,*" Amii whispered, her voice both sweet and chilling. "*If we strike now, and it'll be over.*" Beth didn't respond, but her grip tightened around the silver dagger. She could feel Amii's dark excitement coursing through her veins, fueling her courage and sharpening her rage. This was what she had been waiting for: retribution.

Lynaly stood alone beneath a flickering streetlamp, unaware of the predator stalking her—or so Beth believed.

As she lunged forward, dagger raised, Lynaly turned at the last moment, her magenta eyes sparkling, and a twisted smile spread across her lips. "Again? You never learn, do you?" Lynaly sneered, her voice a velvety mockery. "I told you, the third time . . ."

Beth struck, her blade slicing through the air with lethal precision. For a moment, she thought she had her. But Lynaly sidestepped, catching Beth's wrist mid-swing with inhuman speed.

"Not this time," Beth growled, channeling Amii's power as her free hand ignited with searing blue-white energy.

The blast sent Lynaly skidding back, singed but unbroken. Beth advanced, fueled by fury, grief, and the insatiable hunger for revenge that Amii instilled in her.

"YES," Amii hissed, her presence intensifying. "FINISH HER."

Beth charged, ready to deliver the killing blow.

"THAT'S ENOUGH!"

An unseen but undeniable force slammed into Beth, knocking her back into a pile of trash bags. Her dagger clattered across the damp pavement, spinning before resting beneath the streetlamp.

"What the—" Beth scrambled to her feet, ready to strike again until she saw him.

Shane stood between her and Lynaly, hands raised not in defense but in command. Something about him felt different—the air around him seemed to pulse with restrained energy, sending a spike of confusion and rage through her.

"Get out of the way," Beth snarled, her eyes glowing with Amii's unnatural light. "The bitch dies tonight."

"No," Shane said, calm but firm. "Not like this. Not yet."

Lynaly, observing with detached curiosity, raised an eyebrow but refrained from attacking. She had become . . . entertained.

"You don't understand," Beth spat, stepping forward. "She's the one who killed them all! She deserves—"

"Do not speak to me about all those deaths. Trust me, I know what she did," Shane interrupted, his voice sharper now. "I *was there*. But you won't survive this fight without losing yourself completely."

"You don't know anything about me," Beth retorted, but even she detected the tremor of doubt in her voice.

"I know more than you think . . . and about Amii."

Beth froze. The world seemed to tilt around her. She suddenly felt dizzy, her breath catching in her throat. Instinctively, she reached inward for Amii's power, expecting the usual surge of strength—but for the first time, it faltered, slipping through her fingers like sand.

"You . . . what?"

"I've known for some time," Shane admitted, his gaze steady and unwavering. "I can see her. And I know what she is." He turned his attention to Lynaly. "And I know you . . . Lilith."

"Impossible," Amii whispered, her voice tight with something dangerously close to fear.

"How?" asked a genuinely shocked Lynaly.

"In time . . . but not now," Shane replied suddenly, speaking to the air around them as an invisible power gathered. "I'll see you around . . . Lilly."

In an instant, Beth and Shane were transported elsewhere, leaving Lynaly to stare at the space where they had been—a mix of amusement and curiosity flickering in her magenta eyes.

She turned toward the streetlamp, narrowing her gaze as she spotted a silver dagger lying abandoned on the pavement. Slowly, she reached for it. But just as her fingers brushed the hilt, it vanished. Lynaly froze, blinking at the spot where the blade had been. A smile crept across her lips. "Well, this is interesting."

)

Shane collapsed onto the floor of an abandoned run-down apartment, gasping for breath. Moonlight cast a pale blue glow across the room. Beth looked around, trying to understand where she was, but soon, her concern for her friend took over as she noticed Shane's condition.

"Are you okay?" she asked.

He coughed up some blood and wiped his mouth with his sleeve. "I'm fine. It's nothing."

"Ah, young one. That was *quite* the display of power in such a short amount of time. Don't rush into using higher-tier spells; remember the cost."

Shane responded with another cough of blood and a thumbs-up.

"Who the hell are you?" Beth snapped, her panic gnawing at the growing rage inside her.

"He's a friend," Shane replied, panting.

The Man with the Red Right Hand stepped from the darkness as if he had always been part of it. The crimson glow in his hand contrasted starkly with the black of his robes. He gave a slight bow, his expression unreadable, yet his presence felt heavy, ancient, and knowing.

"Ah, *friend*, is it?" he said with a hint of amusement. "I thought you would refer to me as your 'business partner.'"

Shane sat down, still panting. "Do you think you could mend me?"

"My boy, you have the power to mend yourself," the Man with the Red Right Hand snapped. "Don't tell me you're growing lax in your training."

Shane whimpered like a discontented puppy, and the man remained unwilling to give in.

Beth leaned against the wall of the empty apartment, her breath shallow and her heart hammering. She could feel Amii shrinking inside her, recoiling from an emotion Beth had never sensed before—dread. And then . . . nothing.

Beth balled her hands into fists, her nails digging painfully into her skin. "What is all this?" Her voice wavered despite her best efforts to steady it.

"For you?" the Man with the Red Right Hand stepped forward, his crimson glove catching the dim light. "The truth." His gaze gleamed with a mix of amusement and pity. "Your dear Amii? She was designed to subjugate you, to leash you, and to use you as a weapon against Lynaly . . . who is possessed by Lilith."

"*Lies*," Amii hissed from within Beth, but her voice lacked its usual venom. It was thin and uncertain.

"No, that can't be—" Beth's breath wheezed as cold panic crept into her chest. She sensed Amii's presence flicker and felt her struggling against something unseen. But this wasn't rage or defiance; it was fear. Beth could hear her whispering, pleading, repeatedly muttering "no."

Shane stirred, his voice hoarse yet steady. "If you want to be angry—if you want revenge for what happened to you and everyone else—don't look at her." He gestured weakly at the space where Lynaly had once stood. "Look at them."

The Man with the Red Right Hand exhaled as if discussing something mundane. "The ritual—the one you witnessed that slaughtered almost everyone at your high school? It was never meant to spare you. It was a safeguard, a guardian of sorts. Designed to massacre everything in its path, including the summoner." His smile was small, yet terrible. "So you see, it wasn't Lynaly's or Lilith's fault. That was the work of the Order—protecting their own interests." He tilted his head slightly as though recalling a distant memory. "You were all just collateral damage, fuel for something far greater than you ever realized."

Beth's knees buckled as the world swayed around her. She clutched her chest, desperate to feel something real and solid, but it felt like trying to grasp smoke. The agony of loss, the blistering rage, and the all-consuming hunger for vengeance—had they ever truly belonged to her? Or had they always belonged to Amii?

Then, doubt crept in.

Beth couldn't speak; she felt paralyzed. She wanted to lash out, to scream, to fight, but she could only stand there, trembling. Deep within her, Amii curled in on herself, smaller than ever. There were no sharp whispers, no burning demands—just a flicker of something cold and fragile. Almost . . . human.

Shane stepped closer, wiping blood on his sleeve. "You can keep fighting her and die again," he said, his tone quieter now, more measured, "or you can help me—help us—put things right."

Beth felt the tremor within her; the space she shared with Amii was shifting. For the first time, the entity inside her wasn't calling for blood or twisting her grief into rage.

"A *pawn*," Amii murmured, her voice raw and unraveling in real-time. "No*thing . . . but a pawn.*" She didn't push back. She didn't claw at Beth's mind or flood her thoughts with hatred. Instead, she wept. "*This wasn't supposed to happen,*" Amii whispered, her voice breaking. Beth almost mistook it for her own thoughts. "*I wasn't supposed to care. I wasn't promised . . . this.*"

Memories began to surface, not just Beth's—but theirs. A name long forgotten over time, a home long abandoned, and a cycle of love, loss, and vengeance so endless that the being who called herself Amii had long since forgotten what it meant to be anything but wrath. Then there was Brian—his laughter, warmth, and how Beth had clung to him, needing him. Amii—Amii—did not resist this connection. She did not push Beth toward violence or pull her deeper into hate.

Then came a whisper, "*I remember.*"

Beth squeezed her eyes shut, nails digging into her arms. *Brian!* The name felt like a plea, an anchor in the storm. For the first time, Amii did not try to steer her away; she simply listened as Beth wept.

Shane knelt beside her, placing a steady hand on her shoulder. "Take your time," he said softly. "But know we're not done yet."

Still, the embers flickered in the storm, refusing to die.

10

A FEW HOURS HAD passed, bringing with it a cold wind that slithered through the west side of Middleton's alleyways, rattling loose signs and carrying the distant wail of sirens. The small city seemed to grumble as something darker stirred beneath its surface.

Shane paced near the rooftop's edge under the dim glow of a flickering streetlamp, forcing himself to steady his breath. His limbs still ached from the teleportation, exhaustion weighing heavily on him, but the moment of respite was slipping away.

Beth sat against the crumbling brick wall of the abandoned apartment building, her arms wrapped tightly around herself. The confrontation with Lynaly had unsettled her, but the truth behind Amii had struck an even deeper wound. She hadn't spoken much since, lost in the tempest of her thoughts.

The Man with the Red Right Hand stood apart, peering out over the city with quiet contemplation. His crimson hand pulsed with latent energy, a reminder that he could break the silence at any moment, but he let it linger.

"You don't have long," the Man with the Red Right Hand finally said. "Albedo and Atreyu are no fools. They will send something soon."

Shane rubbed his temple, frustration boiling just beneath the surface. "Yeah, yeah. We just need a moment to—"

A sharp whistle tore through the night, ushering in their attack.

Dark figures materialized from the alleyways below, moving in perfect synchronization. Cloaked in the Order's regalia, their blades gleamed under the streetlights as they ascended toward the rooftop with swift, deadly intent.

Shane barely dodged as a silver blade slashed through the space where his throat had been. He rolled aside, regaining his footing, his energy sluggish but sparking to life.

Beth shot to her feet, instinct taking over. One of the assassins lunged at her, dagger poised for her ribs. She twisted, barely evading, but her counterattack was clumsy—a flickering fireball formed in her palm, then fizzled before she could hurl it.

The Man with the Red Right Hand sighed heavily, observing the struggle unfold. "Children."

He raised his crimson hand and snapped his fingers.

The three nearest hunters utterly vanished to nothingness.

Beth and Shane froze as reality seemed to engulf them, leaving only an eerie void that closed in on itself. The remaining attackers hesitated, their movements betraying their unease.

"Sloppy," the Man with the Red Right Hand commented. "Very sloppy."

Beth clenched her teeth, refusing to be coddled. *I won't be a burden.*

"Amii," she murmured. "*I need you.*"

For the first time, Amii did not resist. A slow, consuming warmth flooded through Beth. This time, it wasn't a raging fire eager to consume, but a steady, burning resolve. The air around her shimmered as controlled energy pulsed from her core, igniting her fingertips with blue-white flames.

"*Much better,*" Amii whispered.

Beth's next strike was precise. She stepped into the attack, flames licked the edge of her blade as she severed through one of the Order's hunters. He crumpled before he could even scream.

Shane blasted another attacker with a burst of raw energy, his movements still rough but becoming more precise. They were learning. And they were still standing.

A crow watched from the shadows above, perched on the rusted edge of a fire escape. Its black eyes gleamed unnaturally.

)

Far from Middleton, Albedo exhaled sharply. *There you are.*

The connection formed in an instant. His mind reached for Beth's—searching, prying, seeking to latch onto the chaotic force within her. But . . . something lashed back.

The force struck like jagged glass, shredding through his intrusion. A shriek—not Beth's, but *Amii's*—rippled through the link, filled with rage, pain, and something far more dangerous. Ah. Recognition.

Albedo recoiled. *Impossible.*

Beth's body tensed, panting. Amii's voice, usually so cold and composed, seethed. **"I know you."**

Albedo staggered back from his viewing crystal. The glass cracked under the force of his own disbelief.

"You shouldn't be able to," he whispered. A flicker of panic, something ancient that, stirred in his bones. Then, fury took over. He slammed his fist into the crystal, shattering it. "She's been compromised," he snarled. "Kill her. Kill them both!"

☽

Back in Middleton, the street fell eerily silent. The last of the hunters lay motionless. Beth's chest heaved as the fire in her hands dimmed, and Shane wiped blood from his temple.

The Man with the Red Right Hand exhaled softly. "Well, now you've done it."

A second wave approached—stronger, faster, and more refined.

Beth and Shane fell into step beside each other. Beth's flames burned brighter, not out of rage, but with purpose.

Amii's voice was no longer a separate entity whispering venom. "*We fight together.*"

Shane glanced at Beth, saw the newfound resolve in her eyes, and nodded.

The Man with the Red Right Hand smirked faintly. "Good." He turned, stepping back into the darkness. "I leave the rest to you."

Beth barely had time to process that before the next wave was upon them. This time, she did not hesitate. And this time, she did not burn alone.

As the bodies of the second wave lay crumpled on the street, rooftop, strewn across a mailbox, cars, and through buildings, there was no respite. The air had barely settled from the second wave when the third emerged.

They didn't rush. They didn't fumble. The way they moved—the eerie quiet in their approach—sent a chill through Beth's spine.

Then he stepped forward. They called him Bjorn, and with his towering figure and predator's stillness, his smirk barely hid a quiet amusement.

"I was expecting more," he mused, his voice smooth yet edged with iron. "They said you had potential. All I see is wasted effort."

Before Shane could react, Bjorn was on him. A brutal strike to the ribs sent Shane crashing into a parked car, the metal frame crumpling under the impact. Beth lunged. Bjorn caught her wrist mid-swing. His grip was vice-like.

"Stay down," he said flatly, then threw her across the street.

Bjorn exhaled, bored. "This is what Albedo was worried about? These children? Pah!"

His foot pressed against Shane's chest, pinning him down. Then the temperature dropped. The shadows stretched unnaturally, blending into each other like ink in water.

Bjorn turned his head slightly. "And you must be—"

Dark hands erupted from the void. They latched onto his wrists, ankles, neck—pulling in opposite directions. The mountain of a man barely had time to react before he was wrenched apart—the unmovable object was gone.

The remaining hunters hesitated, a fatal mistake, as the Man with the Red Right Hand hardly lifted a finger.

They popped—torn into confetti—shredded into fluttering specks of black and red that scattered into nothingness.

He tilted his head, watching the remnants fall. "Funny," he mused. Then, with a slow snap of his fingers—everything was undone.

Shane groaned. "You really could've done that sooner."

The Man with the Red Right Hand offered an amused smile. "But then you wouldn't learn, would you?"

His ember gaze flicked upward to the crow still watching from the rooftops. The bird tensed, its beady black eyes fixed on him, caught between flight and fate.

The Man with the Red Right Hand exhaled, his voice dripping with quiet menace. "There's going to be one hell of a reunion."

With a flick of his red fingers, an unseen force yanked the crow from its perch to his right hand. It flailed midair, screeching as its body convulsed unnaturally, twisting and splitting—its inky feathers scattering into the night. Then, silence.

Where there had once been a single crow, two ravens now perched in the Man with the Red Right Hand's outstretched palm, each with a red eye on either the left or right side. Their sleek bodies pulsed with a strange, unearthly energy. Their eyes gleamed not with simple avian intelligence, but with something more profound—and bound.

A gentle smile spread across his face. "Ah, yes." It felt like a spark of brilliance or perhaps a timeless joke. "Huginn and Muninn. You are both in my service now." The ravens cawed in unison, their voices unsettling in the stillness. The Man with the Red Right Hand released them lazily, watching as they soared into the sky, their wings slicing through the darkness.

"Find Albedo," he murmured, his voice soft but firm. And somewhere, through the shattered vision of his former spy, Albedo finally understood fear.

11

DANA STOOD AGAINST THE vanilla-brick wall of Grave's Diner, smoking a cigarette. He took a deep breath and recalled the night: Lilah, Estrada, the cards, everything. He scanned the early-morning streets, which were beginning to stir. A few people were reading the newspaper on a bus bench near him. On the front page, in bold print "Local Motorcycle Club to Blame for String of Bizarre Deaths." Dana took another puff of his cigarette, noting the portraits of the deceased—Ward "Gigan" Estrada, Johnny "Blondie" Birka, and others.

One of the readers took note of Dana's gaze and gave a wave. Dana nodded and snuffed out his cigarette in the outdoor ashtray. He returned to the sparsely occupied diner and quickly spotted his round partner in crime.

He strolled down the aisle until he stood behind Walter. "You know, from this side, you look like a big ol' bear." Dana grinned as Walter slowly turned around.

Walter snarled. "Oh, to hell with you, Dana."

Dana chuckled as he removed his coat and placed it on the hanger. "Yeah, yeah." Dana scooted inside the booth. "So, what are we having this morning?"

"Well,"—Walter yawned— "I don't know about you, but I am going to have a big breakfast."

Dana raised an eyebrow. "When don't you have a big breakfast?"

Walter glared. "When don't you have a big breakfast," he replied mockingly. "What are you, my wife? Jesus."

Dana held up a hand. "Whoa, whoa, easy there, big guy. Don't go getting your tighty-whities in a knot."

Walter smiled. "Nah, I'm not. I'm just making you feel guilty. Plus, the doctor said I could have a splurge every now and then." He held his index finger up. Also, they're not tighty-whities. Thank you, good sir."

"As long as you're not going commando, I could care less." Dana laughed.

An attractive young waitress soon came over. "Hello, boys. My name is Mona, and I will be your waitress this morning."

Dana and Walter gave Mona a slight look-over, then looked at each other and giggled. The waves in her russet hair bounced when she shifted even slightly. She batted her cobalt eyes at Dana, suddenly recognizing him. "Oh, you boys are the ones who uncovered the crazy stuff that happened with those biker guys, right?"

Dana smiled slightly. "Yes, ma'am, we sure are."

"Oh, well, then, I'll have to take extra special care of you!" Mona flashed a smile that could warm any heart.

Walter smiled back. "Well, dear, could I trouble you for a brew of Mikey's coffee?"

Mona nodded. "And for you, sir?"

Dana took another gander at the menu. "Hmm, I'll have a Coke with a slice of lemon if you'd be so kind."

Mona smiled again. "OK, I'll get those right in for you."

"Ho boy, I think she's going to expect something," Walter said when she was out of earshot. "I can almost smell it." He shook his head.

"That's probably the eggs, pancakes, and sausage you're smelling." Dana scratched his head.

"Mmm, nothing like a good breakfast to get the day going."

Dana sighed. "Yeah, well, I'm still not too happy about last night."

"I know, but you gotta say . . . all the evidence was there."

Dana shook his head disapprovingly. "I know, Walt, but really, we just got lucky—that's all. I just . . . it all leaves a bad taste in my mouth."

Walter sighed. "Well, at least we know who the girl is."

"Yeah . . ." Dana became lost in thought. *Will she do it again, though? With what she's capable of, I wonder if she has any connection to . . . her.*

Soon enough, Mona returned with a steaming hot cup of coffee and a Coke with a slice of lemon hanging on the side of the glass's lip. Dana noticed Walter glance at the lemon's placement and grin. "Well, here you go, boys. Now then, can I take your orders?" She popped her hip to the right and stood at the ready with her pen and notepad.

Dana motioned at Walter to go first. Walter grunted. "Alrighty then. I'll take four eggs, six strips of bacon, four sausage links . . . hmm, two half-dollar pancakes, and a side of hash browns." Mona scribbled frantically to keep up with the big bear's demands while Dana sat with his head in his hand, watching, grinning.

Dana let Mona regain her composure before taking a deep breath and unleashing his flurry of an order. "I'll have three eggs, eight strips of bacon, a large side of hash browns, a small stack of pancakes, and six sausage links."

Walter stared at Dana, wide-eyed, "Damn, Dana, and here I thought I was getting a lot too."

Dana grinned as Mona brushed strands of hair from her face and finished writing. "OK," she said and smiled again at the duo. "I'll get these in right away."

"Thank you, dear."

Walter leaned across the table and swatted Dana's arm. "And here you are, dogging me for what I order."

Dana laughed. "Ah, Walt, you know I'll give you some of that."

Walter smiled. "You're a sly bastard."

The smirk quickly left Dana's face, and he stared past Walter. The face pressed against the window wore a malevolent grin. A rush of recognition coursed throughout Dana. Sweat beaded profusely upon his brow. *It's her . . .*

Walter looked Dana over. "Dana? Hey, Dana? Are you alright?"

Dana continued to stare past Walter. The shade smiled in return with maniacal glee. As she peered into his soul, he could hear her words softly echo in his mind. *"Surprised? Oh, how sweet."*

Dana scanned the restaurant briefly to see if anyone had noticed. Walter waved his hand before Dana's face and turned around but found nothing unusual. Walter bit his lip as he leaned over the table and slapped Dana in the face without result.

"What the hell is going on?" Walter mumbled.

Dana watched on in horror as the shade steadily moved inside the dinner. Little by little, people were devoured by a series of heinous, hideous, and demonic shadows scouring the room. Dana was frantic but paralyzed in the booth.

*"Oh, no, dear. I have something much more . . . worthwhile for **you** in store."* The wraith had approached Dana.

Golden eyes, almost catlike, fixated on him, scanned his person—poking, prodding, ah, such intrusive eyes! Black mist mixed with the blood of the victims, swirling around the wraith.

"W-what do you want with me!" Dana jerked about as he tried to writhe himself free from the inquisitive stare. The seductress halted.

"*What do I want with you? Ah, yes, well, I suppose you wouldn't remember. After all, it has been quite a long, long time since then . . .*" The shade sighed, running her fingers slowly up and down Dana's arm. "*Surely, you've had some dreams—visions of a lifelong past, perhaps even of when it all ended.*"

Dana's mind ran rampant, recalling a few dreams and visions but nothing involving anything like "smell." "I-I don't remember."

The shade drifted to Walter's side. A disgusted look befell her already darkened face. "*Ah, the other interloper. I see you are quite fond of him, aren't you?*" The black lips parted to reveal a vicious, twisted grin, and her gaze spoke of dire intent.

"Leave him out of this! It's me you want, isn't it? Leave him alone!" Dana watched on in horror as the banshee began systematically dismembering the captive Walter. The shadows then took on the form of razor-sharp teeth; a darkened maw formed from the nothingness, gaping wide, and devoured the pieces sliced as elegantly as deli meat.

"No, Walter! Oh, God, no!"

Then Dana heard Walter's voice resound in his mind. "Snap out of it, Dana! Wake the hell up, you son of a bitch!"

Dana opened his eyes to find Walter slapping his face again. "Jesus Christ, Walt! What the fuck are you doing?"

"It's about time! I thought I was going to have to pistol-whip you next." Walter exhaled loudly as he wiped his brow.

Dana scanned the diner. Everything was intact, and all its inhabitants were fine. He then looked back at Walter and wiped the sweat that had poured from his pores off his face with a napkin. "I . . . I had the strangest daydream. Everyone here, even you, got . . . eaten alive." Dana looked down at the table.

Walter stared at the grief-stricken Dana. "Well, it did seem like you were a zombie . . . or something—creepy, really."

Dana shook his head. "I don't know, Walt . . . just strange."

Mona soon came by with plates full of breakfast. "Here you go, boys, enjoy." She flashed her bright smile before wandering off out of sight.

"Alright, well, after all that, I'm famished." Walter grabbed his fork and began digging away.

Dana looked his breakfast over, his appetite having faded. *It couldn't have been real. It was just a dream.* He told himself this repeatedly, trying to believe it was all a fantasy.

Walter looked up at Dana. "Are you going to eat, or are you going to go back into your wonderland again?" Dana gave Walter a fierce glare in return.

Walter chuckled and wolfed down a few forkfuls of hash browns.

"You're an ass, Walt. You know that?" Dana gathered his fork and began chipping away at his full plate.

"You know you're a fan of my love," Walter mumbled as he chewed.

Dana cracked a grin.

Several moments later, after both breakfasts had been demolished, Dana and Walter sat rubbing their bellies as though they were crystal balls. "Ah, man, I am stuffed." Walter sighed with contentment.

While Dana relished everything being fine, a familiar voice echoed in his mind. *"It's only a matter of time now, my dear . . ."* Dana glanced straight to where he had seen the wraith before but found nothing but the warm golden glow of the sun pouring in.

Mona dropped off the bill. "I trust you boys had a good time?" The magnificent duo nodded. "Great! So, could I get your autograph?"

They smiled at one another, and Walter cleared his throat. "Well, I suppose."

Mona's expression then became serious. "I meant for breakfast. Will this be on your Visa, Mr. Conway?"

Walter frowned and glanced over at a laughing Dana. "Wait a second. C'mon, Dana, I thought you were going to cover this."

"I got it, Walt, don't worry." Dana reached for his wallet and pulled out two one-hundred-dollar bills for Mona. "Pay off our tab too, sweetheart, and keep the change. Oh, and this is for your troubles." Dana and Walter scribbled on a napkin and gave it to Mona, who beamed.

"Oh, why thank you so much, Mr. Deupree!" Mona then skipped off to the back room, where kitchen staff were bellowing to one another.

Dana looked over at Walter. "Well . . . think it's about that time?"

Walter looked at his watch. "Yeah, maybe get there a little early so we can get some paperwork done."

Dana nodded. "Alright, let's hit it."

As they walked to the parking lot, Dana stared at where the wraith once stood and sighed. *Maybe everything is getting to me. It must have been my imagination or the lack of sleep. Who knows anymore?*

)

Amid the debacle with the bikers, Lilah had somehow forgotten to study for her finals. She figured, however, that it could all be chalked up to overwhelming grief at the loss of two classmates. As if sensing his parental calling, Lilah's father had spent most of his time at home talking with her and caring for her as best he knew how. Lilah guessed he believed seeing her "friends" die might shake her out of her gloomy and eccentric way of life. *How wrong he is*, she thought, as a small smile lit across her face.

She shrugged her shoulders at such thoughts; she'd seen death, and it didn't faze her; instead, it reaffirmed her belief that the other side existed. She figured this was part of why she felt so trivial in dealing it out, though she also thought the demon contributed to that part of the job.

She'd been uncomfortable thinking that Mullin could control her like a marionette. Still, after the scuffle with the bikers, she realized that the demon had no intention of letting anything bad happen to her. Hell, he had saved her life. As she sat on her bed, incense burning again, with the lights off and candles alight, casting fleeting shadows across the walls, she contemplated such things. She found herself torn between her life as a typical high school goth girl and the person she was turning into.

She felt that one day she would find herself on a broomstick, a black cat on her lap, flying across the night sky, cackling like a mad old woman from some long-forgotten fairy tale. Such thoughts amused Lilah. She knew that in the most classic context, she was basically what was defined as a witch. She fits most of the criteria anyway—well, aside from having done the deed with the devil. Perhaps there were some truths to those ancient tales of witchcraft, truths ensconced in the propaganda of the old church. Lilah had never bothered nor cared enough to take time out of her routine to research her unique situation. It wasn't something she'd been forced into, and she knew enough about it from firsthand experience that she doubted there was any amount of reading that could offer more insight.

Down the hall, in the living room, was her little brother, his mind-melting to the tune of that month's hottest new video game, something about cars and guns, like most. Her dad scurried about in the kitchen, whipping up something that smelled and undoubtedly tasted delicious. Lilah hoped for spaghetti, her favorite and her dad's specialty.

In her lap sat the book. On the inside of the cover was a message written by another hand:

To my dearest and only granddaughter.

Love, Grandpa.

Underneath it was a new line just added by the bright red pen on the bed beside Lilah: *I miss you.*

She wiped a tear from her cheek and closed her eyes. She took a deep breath and started to shut off all the sounds that ran through her mind, seeking again to find silence and her center.

A soft knock on her door, and her father's hushed, rough tone drifted in, but it seemed miles away. Gunshots from her brother's video game dulled to soft drumbeats until they were inaudible. Silence found its way to every corner of her being, and she stood on a ledge.

From the depths of the darkness came a deep, low voice. *"It seems we have a problem. The one detective, Dana, something's not . . . right . . . with him."*

Yeah, what about him?

"He has the taint of a demon about him, a mark—and I fear it does not bode well for you or me," Mullin spoke forebodingly.

Lilah pondered. *So, there's another one of you here?*

Mullin paused, then laughed. *"My dear, there are plenty like me. We make deals with mortals for power, knowledge, magic, or stupid parlor tricks. Whatever the reason, the contract is . . . negotiated. We make a pact and abide by it. You should know that part after all."* Lilah could sense a hint of a grin. But the slight enthusiasm in Mullin's voice faded fast. *"This one, though, she's ancient—she predates me. As far as I can remember, at least from the legends of the long past, she should not be free to walk about your realm as she's so doing now."*

So, what, who cares? I'm tired of all this fighting. Nothing gets solved; life goes on. So why get involved?

The phantom growled. *"Because, you stupid little wretch, if I can sense her, and she has already marked that man, then it's only a matter of time. I don't know her intentions, but she's out roaming—willy-nilly, as you humans say—and she will jeopardize your life and, in turn, mine. If you die before the term of our contract is up, I die, just as much as if I perish, you're coming along for the ride. So, it's best to be proactive and snuff her out of existence before she comes for us."*

Lilah thought for a moment. *So why can't you just talk to her and make sure that it doesn't come to hurt us?*

"STUPID GIRL! HAVE YOU NOT LISTENED? IT DOESN'T WORK LIKE THAT! WITH US, IT'S KILL OR BE KILLED!" The

roar jerked Lilah's still body so violently that she almost fell off her bed.

Her consciousness took two steps back from the chasm in which the demon had come to dwell. However, she soon felt the tug and stepped forward into place. The demon was pulling at her, all of Mullin's knowledge and power enticing her. She allowed a half-crazed smile at the thought of completely giving in, but that wasn't her style.

Lilah contemplated the demon's words. For such a base creature, he was wrought with inner complexities. She supposed that relying on instinct was the ultimate solution to all the problems brought on by their conversation. In a few words, he had peeled back the layers of darkness that shrouded his existence and purpose and shed light on the nature of their unique partnership. Lilah supposed this could be equated to a used car salesperson coming clean.

Alone, the cards simply represented the bond constructed by her pact with the demon. Each card represented a different layer of the deal, and the split of twenty-six cards in her blood and twenty-six in his represented equality. It wasn't within the cards that the power laid, though. The real power was in the strength of the bond, which was why Lilah felt the shift in her being whenever she used the cards to draw power.

A quick glance into her mind would have given the average person the impression that Lilah was just another youth at odds with herself. Belying her exterior appearance of self-confidence was a conflict of voices within. Control alternated between personas at slight urgings. The girl was there, sure of her actions but unsure of her motives. The darkness was also there, a force of pure compulsion—an immortal being that had already existed for an eternity now bound to mortal flesh. This creature knew full well the futility of contemplation. Ultimately, all things could be boiled down to instinct, which was the demon's nature.

Now, he guided the girl, promises of power and satisfaction on his tongue; he whispered to her very being. He didn't wish to control her absolutely, nor could he due to the nature of their deal, but they both knew now that each held the means to the other's end.

During this realization, Lilah reminded herself of the events that had led to her situation. The memories had been scattered to the corners of her mind. She remembered her dad's florid face as he rather loudly voiced his opposition to the trip; the bus to Branson, losing her college funds in the poker tournament, leaning against the brick wall with the knife in her hand, the weight of her life set against the blade; the darkness closing in as the warm crimson flowed out from her wrist; the shadowy creature's eyes staring into her soul as he made his offer, and she accepted; waking up from the darkness safe and sound in her bed, the deck of cards clutched tightly in her hand.

Lilah closed her eyes against the tiny influx of memories, then opened them, allowing two little tears to roll down her cheeks. Her mind was clear. *Alright, so what do we do?*

)

A low rumble bounced about inside the car. Walter patted his stomach, groaning in discomfort. He slightly shifted himself in the driver's seat.

Dana turned to Walter, catching a glimpse of his sneak attack. "Walt, don't you fucking dare . . ." His voice trailed off as he heard Walter's passing gas. He attempted to roll down the window in time, but his efforts were in vain, as he'd already caught a whiff of his partner's infamous stench.

Walter laughed hysterically. "What's the matter, Dana?"

"You're a real asshole. I mean, do you really want to make me transfer?" Dana shook his head as he finished rolling his window down.

"Ah, you'll be fine. I mean, it's not like you've never been enticed by 'the smell.'"

Dana muttered and grinned, shaking his head. He stared at the world as it moved past him—buildings, lampposts, street signs, and people waltzing to the early morning commuting tune. He thought back briefly on the diner. *What the hell was that all about? 'A life long past'?* He rubbed his eyes and caught sight of his reflection in the window. The dark circles under his eyes were more visible, the redness in his eyes increasing.

"Are you alright there, Dana? You don't look so well. Maybe something you ate?"

Dana shook his head. "I'm fine . . . just tired."

He ran his palm over his face and felt beads of cold sweat on his fingertips. His body began to get hotter and hotter. His mind raced. Finally, all of the world's light began to dim. The warm golden rays of the sun became cold and black—cold, black fingers of nothingness. Dana scanned the newfound world only to find the shell of his former partner deteriorating fast before his eyes.

His eyes widened in horror and shock. "What the hell is going on?" The car swerved violently.

The melting corpse disintegrated into ash, and the steering wheel was now in the hands of a phantom. The world began degenerating—dark, jagged rocks jutted upwards from the ground. The dark clouds—resembling question marks and other irregular shapes—with their malevolent gaze seemingly mocked the spectacle below. The streets cracked and rumbled beneath the car as it ventured on its unknown path. Before long, the earth threw the vehicle into the air and stopped inside the second floor of a three-story building.

After several moments, Dana awoke in the decaying world. He unbuckled himself from his seat and managed to writhe out of the car amid the debris. A metal rod protruded upwards through the driver's seat, where Walter had been. All that remained of the man was a sparse pile of ashes.

Dana spoke quietly to himself. "Walt, what is going on?"

He peered down at the sidewalks below. Pieces of debris continued to fall and break away. Dana stepped back and maneuvered himself over loose rubble to find a doorway that opened to a stairwell that led only up to the roof.

"Well, I guess I can't be too picky now." Dana sighed as he climbed the stairs that seemed to stretch on eternally.

Am I dead? Is it the end of the world?

Finally reaching the top, he saw a blazing inferno raging in a brazier, and various torturing devices were strewn about. A woman in a white dress with her head hung low was about to be crucified on a heavy dogwood cross. Straw and wood were scattered beneath her feet. A group of men donned in Crusader garb waited attentively, indistinctly poised for the execution. One man wielded an ornate wrought-iron cross that glowed orange and sizzled, while others gripped brilliant silver swords; the hilt resembled a holy cross that shined absurdly in the dead air that swirled around.

"What the hell is going on here? Who the fuck are you people? Where the hell am I?" Dana panted hysterically as his eyes fell upon the dead world that began to morph into the landscape of ancient Northern Europe—a tower stood high in the heavens. The ground was lost amid white puffs of soft cotton billowing by.

The phantoms all turned to face Dana; life was long absent from their eyes, skin pale.

The prisoner smiled underneath the mess of her hair. "Do you remember, my love, the last day of my life?"

Dana took a step back from the spectacle. He rubbed his eyes hard, hoping he was dreaming of such madness. His eyes slowly opened to the long-lost shadow of a world again as if looking at a picture from within the frame. The phantoms nailed the woman's hands and feet to the cross. One of the ghouls mumbled in a foreign tongue, yet Dana recognized it. Another raised the glowing iron cross and seared the heretic's stomach.

She did not struggle, weep, or make a sound. She only gazed at Dana beneath her mangy, matted, long black hair. One ghoul lit a torch using the brazier and then tossed it at the feet of the prisoner, igniting a hungry inferno. The flames erupted into a frenzy, rapidly consuming their fill, fighting over the pickings.

"Sire, as you have commanded, we have dealt with the heretic." A Crusader's raspy voice echoed through the air. Dana realized the sound was directed at him.

Dana scanned the men and then, finally, the woman. "Heretic? What are you talking about? I don't know any of you."

The woman's head fell towards the flames, her dirty hair dangling over her face like an overgrown vine.

"Lord Samael, you gave this woman up—a traitorous and blasphemous witch! One who has spat in the face of God practiced dark and foul magics, killed several of our men, and betrayed you. Her fate is to be carried out as ordered and as written by the bishop—her remains are to be separated. Her hellbound soul is never to reach the glory and everlasting grace that is He."

As the Crusader spoke, so did the woman.

"You damned me. You betrayed *our* love. You . . . you had me banished to the nether!"

Dana took a step back as the phantoms vanished, along with the inferno. Then, the shrieking banshee forcefully broke from her bounds. She came closer, floating. Finally, she flipped her head back, and a few strands of hair swayed onto her face—clear, pale, beautiful. A woman scorned. "You forsook me! You set me to be cast away into the abyss for eternity! Now, *my love*, I have returned, and all those you've come to cherish will know the pain—the pain *you* put me through!"

Dana raised his hands in defense, shaking his head. "I-I don't know what the hell you're talking about, lady. You must have me confused with somebody else. My name is Dana, Dana Deupree. Not this . . . Samael! I don't know what—" His voice was cut off as a vicious wind knocked him back towards the tower's ledge.

The banshee hissed at the unseen trickster who had caused the gust. "There is no excuse. Your soul knows the truth—it is what I want." The seductive wraith was now apparent.

Dana clenched his fist, still dazed. "You—it's you! You're the one who's been stalking me! You're why Debbie's dead and why Terra is in the hospital!"

The shade smiled with glee. "I told you, my dear—just a glimpse of what I can do." Slowly, the darkness drew closer. "Now, come to me. I forgive you, my dear, sweet . . . Dana. You can finally be with me forever. You'll never come to know age, never know death. You'll never know loneliness as those around you fail, desert, or leave you to die as Lord Samael did. Come to me, my love."

The soothing gaze and siren's voice entranced him. Closer, the seductress intruded, almost within arm's reach. Again, another vicious gust of wind came, sending Dana partially over the ledge. The wraith shrieked at the interference. Dana grunted as he hit the side of the tower hard. He gazed down into absolute darkness, to the absent ground. Dana tried to reach up, but the invisible geist returned, sending him into the abyss. Dana didn't scream; he welcomed the darkness as it fast approached.

However, a surprise awaited him.

"Dana, Jesus Christ, you're alive!" Walter laughed as he leaned back against the toilet seat.

Dana looked around to see that he was in his house and the shower. He looked over at Walter. "I hope to God you didn't take a shit . . ."

Walter chuckled. "Well, at least you still got your sense of humor. What the hell happened to you? You were fine one minute; the next, you rolled out of the car and ran down the street like a madman. Like you were hypnotized or something." Walter glanced down at his watch. "I mean, hell, it's almost been a full day."

Dana squinted as he rubbed the back of his head. "Really? God, I feel like I've been slapped around a bit."

"Yeah, well. You wouldn't answer me. So, I slugged you in the chops a few times."

Dana rolled his eyes. "When don't I answer you?"

Walter grunted. "Valid point, ya bastard." Then he sighed. "Well, let me call downtown back, tell them the situation and see what's up." He stood up and readjusted himself. "Do you need to go to the hospital?"

Dana shook his head, "Nah, I'll be fine."

Walter scratched his head. "Alright, well, why don't you take a shower? It could do you some good."

Dana sat up. "Yeah, wouldn't be too bad."

"I'll be out in the car. Your phone's on the counter—didn't want it to get wet."

Dana leaned forward in the tub. "Thanks, Walt!" he said as his partner left the room. He pressed his back against the tub, his head against the tile.

What the hell? It was all too real. He stood and discarded his clothes on the floor before removing his necklace and placing it on the counter beside his gun. He stood in the shower, letting the hot water run over his face and body. *I know her . . . but from where?*

Several moments passed. Dana retrieved his towel and dried off. He felt a lingering, familiar presence as he walked into his bedroom. Still feeling the eerie, uneasy sense of being watched, he dressed and started to walk back towards the bathroom, cutting by his bed and disturbing the salt circle. Suddenly, his fears came true. The light drained, and the room plunged into pitch-black. Slowly, a form manifested before Dana in the inkiness. The curves, the long, jet-black hair, the pale skin, the bright emerald eyes. "Lynaly."

The shade stood before him, smiling. "So . . . you didn't forget."

Dana stared sharply at the shade as it materialized before his eyes. Lynaly gazed back with a half-grin on her face. Dana gulped. "It's been you all along, hasn't it?"

Lynaly kept her smile on Dana. "It's been far too long." She began to pace around the bedroom. "Although, *you* don't quite remember, of course—you couldn't. But *he* would."

Dumbfounded, Dana threw his arms up. "What the hell are you talking about?"

Lynaly continued to pace, occasionally flashing her emerald gaze at Dana. "Before you existed a man. Your 'past life,' if you will." Lynaly sighed. "His name was Samael." She turned around and faced Dana, glaring fiercely. "He betrayed me. He gave me up to the Council of Six, and I was labeled a 'heathen,' 'wretch,' 'whore.' I was sent to spend an eternity in the nether for 'betraying' God." Lynaly stared hard into Dana's bright blue eyes as she sauntered towards him. She stopped just before where he stood. "When, in fact, the betrayer . . . was you." She paused. "You had infiltrated their numbers, but despite your rank, they eventually understood your true intentions, along with mine. They also discovered the resurrection ritual and how you had played a part in it. So, all the work that we had done was destroyed." She giggled, "Oh yes, the betrayer betrayed! The priests and cultists split your soul into three fragments. I came into possession of one piece through one of their guardians, another from this body's boyfriend, who was the living reincarnate but was killed by one of their lot, and the last . . . the last piece that has evaded me for so long"—she smiled— "is you."

Dana hesitatingly replied, "I have to say that is some pretty messed up shit, lady. It's all a bit much to take in.

Her lips formed a grin. "Ah yes, you always had such a humorous way of . . . coping."

"So, who are you really?"

Her eyes met Dana's. "Lilith."

Dana's ears began to ring, sharp and loud. He took a step back. His head ached in the perfect balance of excruciating pain and absolute pressure. The room spun about in a kaleidoscopic way, reality slowly slipping and, with it, his senses. *I can't . . . I-I, ah!* Dana grunted, struggling to maintain his balance. *She'll surely kill me.*

Dana felt as if he'd been stripped of his body and thrown to the sidelines. The sleeper had at long last awakened. Dana's lips moved but not of their own will. "Lily, my love."

Lynaly stared pleasantly. "Sam—Samael? Is it you?"

"I ask you, please, heed my words." The voice sighed. "I did not betray you. Your brother, Atreyu, had planned it all along. I am so sorry I wasn't able to tell you. I was captured and split into 'the three' long before they came for you. Atreyu—he, he took on my form and pitted us against one another. I wasn't able to save myself, let alone you." Dana's body became weak, and he collapsed to his knees.

Lynaly reached down and grabbed the false Dana by the throat. "Liar! You will not dare to speak of *him*. Do not lie to me to save your pathetic hide!" She raised her choking prey high into the air.

"I-I know you will not believe m-me. However, you must know this: there were two rings." Dana struggled for another breath of air. "One for you, that I had specially made, and one . . . one for if I should pass. It would bind me to you and allow the ritual." Lynaly slowly lowered him to his feet. "Your brother, he still possesses it. Surely, you remember—you must!"

Lynaly's vise grip on the possessed Dana loosened slightly, but she quickly, joltingly, hoisted him back into the air, enraged. "No, no, no, you're just toying with my emotions—playing with my heart again! I shall teach you not to fiddle with love as a plaything, my dear Samael!" Lynaly flung him to the ceiling, and his body lay within the indentation. One by one, the many strands of her black hair became sinister vines and ropes that imprisoned his whole being. She levitated parallel to him, gradually siphoning his life force. Lynaly grinned malevolently, fixating upon his ice-cold blue eyes with her now raging magenta gaze.

"All you warrant is a slow, painful death. Darkness comes, and with it, Death's last caress."

This ... it cannot end like this. Dammit, Walt, where the hell are you!

)

Lilah made her way down the quiet streets, gliding smoothly, with a purpose—with the air of a person who'd grown up in the town and knew every nook and cranny of her surroundings. Aside from random passersby, the world was a silent, solemn testament to the ingenuity of humanity. Vehicles and buildings were obstacles whose presence was only revealed by the artificial light generated by tall, narrow sentinels of public service. It was this world that the girl had been born unto, and it was in this world that she was indeed at peace. She wore the camouflage of a veteran of such a life, and in the dark gaps between the streetlights, her garments were rendered next to invisible. Her pale skin clashed with the darkness, her face a floating parody of a human visage.

The town had dumped her into a residential corner. Diminutive, dim houses lined both sides of the road. Cars were scattered on the curbs here and there, some practically taking up an entire lane of the small two-lane road. Streetlights gave way to sidewalk lamps far more spaced apart than Lilah was used to. She took a deep breath and began her journey into the new territory. With each step, the clopping of her boots reverberated back at her, giving her the eerie feeling of being followed.

Overhead, billowing white clouds raced across the sky, and occasionally, the wind blew the leaves and branches littering people's yards. In the darkness of the night and the yellow hue of the occasional light source, the trees appeared sickly abominations with gray appendages lashing out and attempting to reach for some form of salvation. The grass weaved to the same rhythm as Lilah's hair. Occasionally, Lilah would make out a small form while racing down the sidewalk ahead of her. At times, it would disappear entirely in the shadows, only to return a few minutes later, always keeping its distance from her. A cat, she assumed—probably a black one. She glanced at it, running into the bushes of a lone house with one light on—one light that seemed to be flickering intermittently.

"We're here."

Lilah wasn't too surprised to see it was this house Mullin had directed her to.

"I can't exactly guarantee our safety once inside, but do remember: it's them or us."

Lilah nodded. This wasn't the time to back down. Besides, she did owe that detective for saving her life. Now was her chance to repay society. This thought brought a genuine grin, and she liked it.

12

WHERE AM I? AM I *dead? Is this . . . is this my Hell? It must be. Cold, it's so cold.* Swirls of crimson mixed with the streaks of gray that engulfed Dana. Slowly, his vision faded to black. It was a sea of complete nothingness. He heard nothing, and the strain on his chest was gone. An icy chill coursed up and down his body; his teeth chattered. With this new sensation, he felt as though he were in the palm of death itself. His arms and legs swirled in a circular motion in an instinctive attempt at escape. An effort he wagered would prevent him from slipping further into the abysmal sable sea.

He rubbed his eyes as his legs continued kicking against the nothingness. He knew (or at least believed) that if he were to stop, it would mean certain death—that is if he was indeed not so already. Curiosity often nipped at him with a dare, egging him to let go. With so much darkness around, he couldn't tell if his eyes were open or not. He rubbed them again. Nothingness.

He looked up. High, so high up above, alone in the dark—like him—was a single star that sparkled and radiated brilliantly. It was out of reach, yet he could feel its soft glow. One by one, more stars began to ignite, and the light began to shift the darkness into the glow of the night. The moon smiled upon him, the stars its fingers.

It seemed to reach down to save him from the peril. He reached for his old friend, only to slip underwater. He sank—lifeless but awake—and as he sank, he looked down into the ever-absolving darkness that was now below him. He stared hard, and as he did, two bright-emerald eyes slowly opened in the dark and peered back. He could note their fine details—so beautiful, such fantastic eyes—but these were eyes of betrayal, pain, torture, anger, and . . . love. Oh, they were such familiar eyes! He swore he could feel a soft hand caressing his face, a loving touch as he gazed upon them. He closed his eyes, and his body melted into the vast sea of blackness.

He awoke later to find himself alone on a group of cargo crates forming a makeshift island. The sun had ascended enough to check for any warnings of trouble while the moon watched high above. He propped himself up, hacking water from his lungs. On his lap sat a small, ornate mirror. *This. I've seen this before, but where?*

He felt nothing as he stared into the mirror, and the image peered back. It was as if the reflection spoke of what he meant to himself, his life, and those around him. Slowly, a grin sprawled ear to ear on the reflection's face. *Look at me, look at you. I am nothing. You are nothing.* The image began to laugh maniacally. Dana clutched the mirror tightly before hurling it into the calm sea.

The sea raged in retaliation—crimson waves boiled with tremendous anger that sloshed and beat down on his small sanctuary and last beacon of sanity. One by one, the crates broke off and were forced under. He climbed inside the top of the sole survivor.

The moon and the setting sun began to swirl towards one another in a frenzy. Below him, shadows frantically clung to one another like hellish fiends—hungry, snapping their maws at the box, licking their sadistically misshapen lips in the hopes of having him as their sweet, delicious meal. He clung to the edges of the crate with all his might, fearing he'd be flung into the now putrid, malformed sea.

"What do you want from me!" He shouted to the hostile world. "What is it that you want so damn bad, huh?"

The moon and sun collided and spun into a gold, gray, and black kaleidoscope. On the horizon floated a familiar pair of enormous emerald eyes. The sea, now violet, formed a pair of perfect lips that stretched to a smile.

He heard a woman's voice echo.

"Just you and all that you never gave me."

As if the world had shifted on its side, the sea rushed towards the illusory lips; the eyes seemed fixated on swallowing him whole. He stumbled for balance in the crate. Out of the corner of his eye, he caught a glimpse of a star stretching out its hand for him, but it was all in vain.

Walter! He clenched his eyes shut, bracing for the onslaught.

When the certain doom never came, Dana found himself on his bed. The shadows were still, and the world was quiet. He scrambled to his feet and ran to each window, checking to ensure he was actually back in reality. After having affirmed this, he plopped down on the left side of the bed, sighing with relief. *What's with this crazy shit?*

He rubbed his eyes and face, noting they were soaked. "What the hell?" He patted himself down in a panic and found his person soaked. "Maybe I just slipped in the shower or something . . ."

Dana heard a noise from outside as he attempted logic and rational reasoning. Twisted laughter became louder with each moment. He ran frantically to the windows. Assorted beady eyes began popping up, one by one, in pairs, and then by the dozens. He took a step back, collapsing onto the floor. "What the fuck is going on!" Even more, eyes manifested—this time with faces—horrid and terrible faces, deformed, twisted visages of the darkness. They all shook and jerked violently, contorting and morphing into new beasts of the shadows. "This can't be real." He shook his head. "It can't be!"

The voices began to chant in unison. "Dana. (Let us in.) Dana. (Dana). Let us in!"

Dana's heart raced; sweat built upon his forehead. His body began to heat under extreme pressure. Whether prompted by survival instinct or his training, he didn't know, but he got up and raced down the hall, searching for his gun. A small, holy light emanated above it, offering him solace. He grabbed the gun and the ammunition next to it. The front door began to rattle and shake. Moans and groans populated his stoop in the hopes of successfully breaching. He ran to the door, making sure it was locked, and then started to barricade it and the windows with furniture. He stood poised with his gun raised, knowing it was only a matter of time before the door gave in. He wagered a look outside to assess the situation—or was it curiosity that prompted him? *What the fuck is this? What the hell are those . . . things?*

A voice thundered across the darkness, and his home shook violently. "HIDING WON'T SAVE YOU!"

A familiar man stood among the amassed creatures of shadow, their beady golden eyes resembling a cat's. He'd been a vicious giant—a man without barriers to getting what he wanted. Here and now, he was still a giant, although decrepit—a charred, undead tyrant: the former Ward "Gigan" Estrada. He tore through the shadows, ripping the creatures to shreds in bloodlust, all just to get to Dana's front door.

Shuffling, lopsided, close behind the massive meat bag was a disfigured man.

The John Doe, Dana thought.

His face was completely gone. Only his hollowed skull and what was left of his dangling tongue remained. His arm was in shreds, and he dripped fiery blood that scorched the ground, setting the darkness ablaze.

To the sides of Gigan were his ushers of death—the boys Gary and Henry—who set others ablaze, laughing maniacally, their faces twisted into hellish, sadistic grins that spread ear to ear. Blue arches of light would sporadically jump to each young man, causing nightmarish creatures to explode or be engulfed in a hellish inferno. "What the hell? H-how can they be here?" Dana stared out the window in confusion.

Gigan caught a glimpse of his executioner and rushed for the window, snarling, rampant. Dana only took a few steps back to see a putrid green inferno engulf the giant.

A familiar female spoke aloud outside his door: "Not this time."

One by one, the creatures of darkness were fended off. Shrieks and cries came and went. Eventually, when it seemed the night was wholly abolished, Dana slowly opened it. On his porch stood the last person he'd expected. Slowly, she turned around, her long black hair waving gently in the twisted breeze of death and destruction. Her face was evident in the night. There she was, standing on his doorstep, smirking. Her dark-brown eyes emanated a dull, frosty green that shone brilliantly in the pale moonlight.

"It can't be. Lilah?"

)

Lilah crossed the lawn as calmly as she possibly could. Glass, along with the crumpled figure of the overweight detective, littered the grass and sidewalk with a beat-up sedan with a big dent in the passenger door. By her guess, he had been tossed out of where the large front window had once been. She noted his disgusting, pure aura, one that she could hear Mullin growl at. Lilah gave little further attention to the scene. She knew her true destiny lay beyond the threshold. She reached forward to try the doorknob. Immediately, the door swung in, having not been properly shut.

The entranceway was dark save for the fluorescent light from the kitchen. Lilah turned through the living room to the long, ominous hallway lit by wavering light. Her attention turned to the door at the end, where she could make out strange utterances, otherworldly voices, and the sounds of a human struggle. A peculiar pressure emanated from the room, and each step down the hallway was more challenging than the last. Lilah could feel Mullin's power begin to swell up within her, and instinctually, she opened her purse and withdrew the deck of cards. They fluttered out of her hand and began to dance about her in erratic orbits. They reacted to each movement she made and failed to stray as she continued down the hall.

Mullin's rage came to a head when Lilah was only several feet from the dark portal of Dana's bedroom. He worked his way through her psyche and beyond her wide-rimmed glasses; her eyes began to change, glowing a sickly green. She paused at the doorway, and in the last moments before the storm that was coming, she slid the purse off her shoulder and set it down in the hall. The cards fluttered and twirled around her furiously; sweat began to bead upon her forehead.

)

Lynaly studied Dana's limp body, feeling the life within weakening steadily—it wouldn't be much longer now. She reached out and caressed his face, rubbing the stubbled cheek. A sense of sadness overwhelmed her being. *What if he's right? What if this has been all for naught? What if I've been misguided if I was freed just to be a pawn in Atreyu's grand scheme?* Lynaly closed her eyes, and the memory of her "dear" brother's voice echoed within, mocking her, stirring the anger and hatred flowing throughout her veins. She clenched her fists and pushed away the weak thoughts, for she had a mission to complete—her task and no one else's, as it wouldn't be long until she could possess it. Her skin tingled, sensing a presence.

Outside, a slight grin formed on a man's face in the darkness, illuminated only by the yellow glow of the spectating streetlamp.

The shadow lurked behind her in wait. Lynaly opened her eyes, which had now burned crimson with anger. Slowly, she turned towards the putrid emerald pair that peered back at her.

"Well, well," said Lynaly in a low tone. "If it isn't Mullin and his little puppet." She cocked her hip to the side, taunting.

Mullin's hate swelled, and he let loose a ravenous shriek. Lilah's body arced towards Lynaly, the tips of her toes dragging across the carpet, the flurry of cards sputtering about her. Dana dropped from the ceiling onto his bed, freed of his bonds.

Lynaly and Lilah grappled, grasping at each other. Lynaly wrapped a hand around Lilah's throat, driving her into the wall. The two spun; this time, it was Lynaly's turn to hit the wall. They took turns planting each other into the walls before crashing through the ceiling.

The two wrangled as they shot high into the starry night, the full moon spotlighting the main event. They arced further into the twilight depths, shadowy figures bobbing and weaving in the darkness.

Below, housing gave way to industry and business. Streetlights created the illusion of a cracked earth steadily sinking back into the primal, molten world from which it had come. The occasional farmhouse with illuminated windows on the horizon created the illusion of an extended background.

)

Walter had come to his senses and finally found his footing. He leaned against the passenger side door of his car and looked up to see the two entities spiraling and colliding in small bursts of light. *I didn't know it was the Fourth of July*, he thought, confused. Walter clung to his car; only moments ago, the world was still spinning fast from his last adventure. He reached up and felt the back of his head, noting a warm patch. "Ah, that son of a bitch." He recalled being tossed around Dana's bedroom and bouncing off his bed before being sent flying out the front window and getting reacquainted with his car's door.

Walter glared back up at the lights bursting across the aerial battlefield.

His gaze fell to Dana's house. Most of it lay in ruins. He stumbled and struggled to walk straight as he approached the house. "Dana! Goddamn it, Dana!" His vision still wasn't focused. He wandered inside through the maze of debris littering the living room and hallway that led to Dana's bedroom. Taking a moment to support himself against the hallway wall, he felt warmth rush through his right leg. He looked down at the stain building upon his pant leg. Walter's brow furrowed. "You have got to be kidding me." He sighed heavily as he pressed on towards the wrecked bedroom. Walter called out again for a response from Dana but was greeted with only silence. He pushed his way over several boards that blocked the entranceway. Poking his head in, Walter found his partner lying on the bed covered in debris. With a surge of might, he plowed his way to Dana. He checked for a pulse. "Dana! Dammit, Dana, I'm not giving you mouth-to-mouth, you hear me!"

Dana raised his left hand. "I wouldn't want your lips near me anyway."

Walter let a chuckle escape in relief. "Let's get you out of here. Can you get up?"

"Yeah, yeah, I think so," Dana said with a grunt and slowly sat up. He looked up at Walter standing before him, his eyes wide. "Jesus, Walt, what the hell happened to you?"

"Ah, yeah, well about that . . . funny story." Walter sighed again. "Bed's soft, by the way." He pointed as Dana looked back at it. "Anyway, can we save the 'warm and touching reunion' for later. I'm not going to have a house fall on me."

He motioned at Dana to move with haste and helped him stand, propping one arm around his neck.

The rest gave way as they left the house, roaring as it swallowed itself whole and leaving only an ashen haze that wafted into the night sky. The two watched the house collapse. "Ah, I told you that the contractor was shady."

Dana looked over at Walt with a smile. "Ha, yeah, guess I should have known better."

They stared into the glistening night sky, watching a rampant, spiraling light stream fall into Middleton's midst. "This is not going to end well, Walt. We gotta do something." Dana squinted in pain as he tried to hold himself up.

"I'm not going to lie—I have no fucking clue what to do. That . . . *thing* could have easily tossed me to China. This is not in our capable hands." Walter stared at the light while Dana slowly looked at him.

"Well, fuck it. Let's go. C'mon, maybe we can catch up!" Dana hobbled to the car and got in the passenger side.

Walter sighed as he glanced down at his right leg. Then, he also hobbled to the car.

Dana had rolled down the window, sticking his head out, following the witches wrestling in the now bewitched hour.

Dana turned to Walter as his partner got in the car and sped off without looking at him. His lips curled with displeasure. "You think you could drive any worse? I mean, really. We aren't kids anymore. Besides, I think if I were going to take out a mailbox, I'd use a goddamn baseball bat and not my head!"

Walter spat out the window as he rolled it down. "Then keep your ass inside, glued to the seat! And stop complaining because you drive like a twat anyway."

They drove downtown, laughing hysterically at everything that was unfolding.

13

♠

LIGHTS FLICKERED AND WAVERED in homes far below. The earth was embroidered with twinkling white gold. They had been airborne for some time, hurling their weight, exchanging blows. Together, they tumbled across the blackness, burning bright with each strike. Hints of murky crimson and malevolent green intertwined. Finally, Lynaly pushed down on Lilah with a force that sent the two crashing into an unsuspecting concrete monster. Glass shattered and littered the hospital lobby.

In contrast, concrete and other debris flooded the entrance. Hospital personnel scattered and retreated. Lilah burst back with an attack, sending Lynaly through several concrete columns. The ceiling gave way, collapsing atop Lynaly. Lilah halted, waiting for a sign of the next strike. A small laugh escaped the rubble before a shock wave sent debris everywhere. Lilah covered her face, and Lynaly quickly appeared behind her and sent her through the hole in the ceiling Lilah had intended for Lynaly.

The two spiraled down the hallways, once again exchanging blows. Lynaly grabbed a hospital gurney and attempted to smash it against Lilah, only to hit it against a wall. Lilah dodged Lynaly's attacks gracefully and with form, further antagonizing Lynaly. With precision, Lilah then caught sight of an IV pole and coaxed Lynaly to just the right spot. A full-fledged swing sent Lynaly tumbling through the air. With incredible dexterity, she stopped herself in midair and flew back at Lilah. Having obtained an IV pole of her own, she struck with a series of blows, crushing Lilah into the floor.

Lynaly knelt and grabbed the motionless Lilah by the hair, and tossed her down the hallway, knocking over hospital personnel, gurneys, and monitors. Lilah came to a halt as she smashed into an elevator, whose bell gave a dull ding. She gathered herself and lunged back towards Lynaly, her cards fluttering around her person. Lynaly snapped the IV pole with ease and threw it down the hall. Lilah placed her hand before her. The cards formed a shield that deflected the debris away. The two grappled again, head for head, knee for knee, fist for fist. It seemed almost like a perfect match. Finally, they separated for a moment, staring each other down. Blood and sweat beaded upon their faces and dripped from their chins. Anger continued to swell.

"*She's just toying with us!*" Mullin snarled.

Lynaly grinned fiercely, and with a swift upward motion of her hand, she sent an unseen force to sweep Lilah off her feet and soar up through the ceiling.

Dr. Jaymes recoiled from his desk, nearly falling over as the girl crashed through his floor. "Oh, my goodness!" He watched in horror as Lilah flew into the ceiling with Lynaly in close pursuit.

They burst through the bed formerly occupied by Gary Only. Blue-white sparks scattered and danced about the room while lights flickered, gasping for life. Concrete crumbled; nothing was unturned, nothing unscathed. Lynaly focused, and a reddish aura built up in her right hand. She glanced up quickly and swung upwards, her feet landing square in Lilah's jaw, sending her crashing straight to the roof. The red aura diminished from her right hand. Lynaly stood over the fallen Lilah on the rooftop. Rolling away, Lilah sprung up with a somersault kick that caught Lynaly off guard and followed up with fists to Lynaly's gut and face. Finally, Lynaly caught Lilah's hands and bent them inwards, squeezing with tremendous force.

Lynaly laughed hysterically. "I'm sure you know by now that you don't stand a chance—not in Hell, and certainly"—her eyes burned more brilliantly, and Lilah could feel the raw power radiating from her— "not here!"

In an eruption of indescribable energy, Lilah suddenly felt as if Lynaly's skin were a seething flame slowly enveloping her.

Breaking free of the grasp, Lilah attempted to kick her captor, only to be backhanded and sent soaring in a wild spiral. She burned brightly in the night sky, arcing towards downtown Middleton, where the stone sentinel watched over the city. Its powerful hands, however, could not protect its face from its fate. Lilah streamlined as she crashed into the mighty titan and then to the ground. The battered girl picked herself up as glass and metallic shrapnel began to fall like a bizarre hellish rain about her in slow motion.

Beyond the spectacle and far above Lilah's head in the crisp night sky, her dark attacker skirted towards her. While select cards deflected anything harmful, Lilah raised her hand, and the remaining cards began orbiting her arm, unleashing volley after volley of alternating streams of fire and crackling electricity at her assailant. A few bursts connected with the figure, but it was barely enough to buy Lilah and Mullin time to catch their breaths and contemplate a new strategy.

Mullin worked quickly to repair Lilah's body from any damage, weaving his green energy through her wounds, stopping any bleeding, and closing gashes and cuts. Lilith, Mullin had called her. At least, that's what Lilah thought he had growled menacingly.

The thought lasted only a second as her demonic opponent smashed into her, driving them through the rest of the structure, utterly devastating it. They crashed against the grassy lawn, kicking and screaming, and rolled their hands over their heads into the middle of Main Street. Lilah found herself on her stomach. She proceeded to pick herself up off the ground as the putrid green light emanating from within mended the scratches and cuts. She caught a brief glimpse of a car further down the street, but before she could react, a cold, firm hand grasped a large chunk of her hair and dragged her onto her feet.

）

Walter and Dana had seen the falling star collide with the giant stone-time-lord. "Holy shit!" Walter swerved around the debris that rained from the heavens. Dana clung to the dashboard as the car swayed, still nauseated from his earlier conflicts.

"Walt . . ." Dana tried to maintain control of his stomach. "Oomph, don't . . . make me sp—mmph, spew." Walter continued to dodge debris. "Well, I, ugh, can't—fuck, I'm trying!" Several near misses later, they arrived in the town square.

)

Lynaly stared blankly at the prisoner within her ironclad grip. Raising her to eye level, she peered into the ravenous green eyes. The girl's glasses were long lost amid the grand bout. "What hope do you have?" Lynaly snarled in Lilah's face. "Do you really believe you have what it takes to kill me?" Lilah closed her eyes for a split second. "You were a fool to interfere, let alone challenge me." Lynaly's grip on Lilah's hair tightened, jerking her up more. "Now, I will teach you"—she threw Lilah into the air with tremendous force— "TO LEARN YOUR PLACE!" A resounding echo flooded the town square.

Lynaly had concentrated her life force into a single attack. Blood poured down her right arm and pooled in her hand—a small, bright magenta spark ignited into an inferno. The flames twitched and danced, biting, hungry. With the magnificence and beauty she held within her hand, Lynaly shot through the air to Lilah. Fire wrangled and tamed, with blood its fuel. She struck Lilah in the stomach, followed by fists to her face, and finished with a kick that sent her rolling back to the cold, dark earth.

The star burned brightly as it fell. The cool of blue-black flickered with green as a magenta consumed it wholly. The lightning struck the ground several yards from where Dana and Walter watched in awe. Dust billowed, pipes ruptured, and gas lines were severed. Car alarms wailed in unison in the mocking destruction.

Lynaly waited up high, for she knew it wasn't over yet. She peered long and hard into the blackness, waiting for the smoke to subside.

Below the street lay retribution in waiting. Bone and sinew snapped painfully back into place, each repair sending the cards that danced about Lilah into a momentary frenzy. After a few painful moments, she dragged her now adequately functioning body back to its feet and looked up high to her nemesis. She saw the smirk sprawling across Lynaly's lips. With nimble precision and elegance, she leaped through the air to meet with the terror in the sky. A flurry of cards followed the streak of green in hot pursuit.

Despite its rich New England background in the subject, Middleton could never have anticipated the wrath of two hellfire-infused and incredibly agitated witches.

Lilah began unleashing her own attacks, which resulted in the cracking of bone, the gushing of blood, and the feeling of adrenaline. She filled the gap between her and Lynaly with card-driven bursts of magic, letting her opponent have no respite. As the shorter one raged, the taller one's shrieks of glee grew.

Finally, Lynaly stopped and floated before her, battered and broken, laughing hysterically. "Is that all you can muster? Because if that's it"—Lynaly spread her arms out, stretching her hands— "THEN YOU ARE TRULY MISTAKEN, MY DEAR!"

Lynaly's earrings glowed softly and then ignited into a bright ruby. Her necklace glowed as fiercely, levitating off her chest. She then hunched over and groaned in pain before screaming in agony as blood spurted from her back. She clawed at her arms as bones popped and jerked their way out of her back—wings, transparent and dripping with blood. They flapped violently in the pale moonlight. She pulled her head back, her eyes fierce with rage; tears of blood streamed down her cheeks.

Lilah stretched out her hand, and the flurry of cards surrounding her assumed their standard orbit, with a handful breaking the pattern and beginning a new orbit around her arm. One by one, they took turns dancing before the palm of her hand and launching an alternating stream of electrical and fiery destruction towards Lilah's winged opponent, who had resumed her maniacal assault. A tango of destruction played out high above the collapsing town. The flashing crackle of blue-white energy exchanged with the blows and the resounding thunder that followed was felt far below by two distinct figures who struggled to keep up with the midair chaos.

)

Walter cocked his head to the side, raising an eyebrow. "Ya know, this almost reminds me of spring break."

Dana slowly turned his head to Walter. "Really? How does a city being destroyed remind you of spring break?"

Walter pointed. "That."

Dana turned back as the two girls continued to pounce on one another. He sighed, shaking his head. "Sometimes, Walt, I don't know about you."

Walter folded his arms, smiling. They watched as Lilah rolled to her back and, with a timed kick, freed herself from Lynaly. She wrapped her hands around Lynaly's neck and hurled her into a series of street lamps, then dashed through the air towards the limp body, sending forth a series of relentless assaults. Lynaly plummeted to earth and crashed deep below the city streets. Silence finally settled. Lilah floated on high, watching, waiting. Dana and Walter also watched and waited, wondering if it was over.

Moments passed, and still, there was no sign of Lynaly. Then, a low rumble shook the city from deep within its bowels. Buildings collapsed and were swallowed by the earth wholly.

Walter clung to Dana as they stumbled and fell to their backs. Dana slapped the round weight that lay atop him. "Walt, get off me! I can't breathe!"

"I-I c-can't m-move!" Walter gasped before finally rolling off Dana.

One by one, maintenance hole covers burst into the air, crashing into various establishments and vehicles. Sewage spouted and flowed onto the streets. Hydrants popped and flew in multiple directions. The concrete of the sidewalks and streets formed jagged ridges, jutting upwards into makeshift, ravenous, razor-sharp teeth—a scream resounded from where Lynaly had been sent crashing—a shrill cry for vengeance.

A familiar magenta consumed the darkness within the gaping hole. The inferno raged and lashed wildly, and in an unimaginable rush, Lynaly erupted from the hellish prison, her sights fixed on Lilah. Lynaly lashed out viciously, mercilessly at Lilah's face. Flame consumed her hands, and each contact seared Lilah's person. With a mighty somersault kick in midair, Lynaly sent Lilah to the ground in a blazing roar. Flames encircled the area where Lilah landed. She struggled to return to her feet while noting a black figure charging right for her, shape-shifting from a small cat to a full-sized panther, which leaped through the flame circle for her throat. She wrangled with the beast briefly before tossing its lifeless body into one of the surrounding buildings.

"No, Sheila!" Lynaly clenched her fists and then bellowed towards Lilah. "You meddlesome insect! I will see you charred from the inside out!" Lynaly dove with great speed towards Lilah.

Walter and Dana watched as Lynaly began to burn clearer and brighter in the starry night, her entire being engulfed in a somber-magenta inferno. The town square lit up as if it were the day.

)

High above, on the skeletal remains of a half-constructed medical office building, Atreyu watched the battle unfold with a serene, calculating smile.

"Check," he whispered to himself, eyes gleaming. "Just a little more."

He had counted on Mullin being too weak to defeat Lilith—A pawn played to its final square, sacrificed without hesitation. Although he was pleased with the byproduct of the demon's timing by ridding him of Albedo, a wounded Lilith would have been a perfect slow-moving target for Beth to finish off. But there was something he hadn't counted on—Shane. The Order proved its incompetence, *Putting those two damn detectives over getting that brat.* He frowned. Shane had stopped Beth earlier and held her out of reach, removing her from the board—for now, and whether she was incapacitated or dead didn't matter; both were malleable in ways, and he knew he could exploit their joint memory of their high school another time. Still,

Atreyu sighed as though inconvenienced. "There's always a deviation," he muttered. "No matter. That's why there are plans for plans!"

)

During her descent, Lynaly caught a glimpse of a lone, dark-garbed figure standing on the rooftop of a nearby building directly under the moon. Atreyu had been watching, waiting. The realization hit her with a chilling clarity. She had slowed her assault. Everything had been put into place—finding Samael, this little witch and her demon Mullin, Beth, everything so far . . . all to draw her out and weaken her.

"You . . ." she whispered. "You son of a bitch. This was your game all along."

Lilah braced for the impact. She clenched her eyes shut, and the image of her opponent's swift approach burned into her retinas. Inside, Mullin cringed as well, his fury now shifting towards acceptance of defeat. The moment stretched on, but the death strike never came. Lilah ventured a peek from the corner of her eye and witnessed that her opponent's immense presence had begun to waver. The sadistic expression of glee was gone, and Lilah thought she could now see a vague hint of sadness in the rival demon's eyes. Mullin amassed his power within her, and the world around Lilah seemed to slow down.

"*We've got one more shot at winning this, one last opportunity—so make it count!*"

Lilah started to question the entity within but stifled herself immediately. She realized that time had become the single most crucial factor. She raised an outstretched hand before her in the gesture that had become instinctual over the past ten minutes. Like clockwork, the cards began their orbit around her arm, and one broke the pattern to settle before her extended palm. The corner of the card was decorated with an ominous black thirteen; its distinct medieval style set it apart from its flock. Lilah drew in two lungsful of air and calmed her mind, focusing the wills of her personalities into her hand and then into the card that hovered before it. Her body cringed instinctively as it prepared for the familiar but soon-to-be more volatile result of her actions.

"NOW!" Mullin roared within. The force of their combined wills snapped within her like an overextended bowstring. The power rushed down her arm and jumped to the Black Thirteen. The card, a magnifying agent, amplified the energy a hundredfold, and the explosion of blue, red, and orange flame engulfed the world before her.

The flames stifled Lilith's cries of anguish, sending her like a rag-doll into a two-story red-brick building with a large sign proclaiming, "Marie's Delicatessen, the greatest sandwich shop in a fifteen-mile radius." The explosion and resulting shock wave brought the vintage building crumbling down on the semi-human projectile that was Lynaly.

He gestured in kind with a smirk and turned to leave but paused. His eyes moved over to an anomaly he noticed.

"What is that?" Something shimmered in the distance at the edge of his vision. A distortion in the air, subtle but undeniable. Yes, it was a ripple of magic. He had seen this before, but where? He frowned. His gaze shifted to the rooftop across the way, where he saw him—the Man with the Red Right Hand.

Atreyu's breath caught for just a moment. Recognition flared like a dormant ember. "No . . . You . . ." Atreyu whispered. He smiled faintly beneath his wooden mask, though his heart thundered with sudden doubt. Then he realized this was not his game alone for the first time in years.

The Man with the Red Right Hand stood silently, watching, shielding Dana and Walter with invisible wards. A cold, terrible understanding passed between them as their eyes met—a long-forgotten familiarity that struck Atreyu like a physical blow.

For one moment, Atreyu saw something he hadn't seen in years: tears. One rolled slowly from his right eye, trailing down his cheek. He reached up and wiped it, gazing at it, perplexed. But before he could speak and fully grasp the flood of memories threatening to surface, the Man with the Red Right Hand was gone. And so was Atreyu. Both were alone, and both would quietly weep on their time.

A silent, bitter civil war that would reach its inevitable climax, but that would be for another time.

)

Lilah stood looking at the spectacle and resulting wreckage for an untold amount of time, straining to stay upright in her haggard body. At the same time, the demon slipped weakly back into her subconscious, forcing the girl to rely on everyday old human will once more. The corners of her vision began to darken, and she slumped down to her knees, all feeling draining itself. Exhaustion struggled for her will and slowly began to overwhelm her ravaged frame.

Sweat and blood poured down her forehead, taking what remained of her white makeup in long, oily streaks. Filth and debris tangled in her gnarled, matted hair and dripped off her chin, staining her clothes in odd shades of gray and white.

"Damn, did I . . ." Her chin slumped down to her chest, and her eyes closed. As the world grew dark and distant around her, Lilah fancied she could hear the distant sounds of screaming and emergency sirens as the rest of the world woke up.

)

In a surge of raw emotion, Walter withdrew his gun and fired it in the air. "Ah, ah, ah, ah, ah, ah!"

Dana looked over at his disgruntled partner. "Walt. Walter! WALTER JAMESON CONWAY!"

Walter stopped and looked at a glaring Dana, whose hands were on his hips. "What?"

"What the hell was that all about?"

Walter glanced down to the ground and back up at Dana, grinning. "I saw it in a movie. You know—Point Break?" Dana shook his head, bringing his palm to his face. "What? Have you never fired your gun while going 'Ah'?"

Dana sighed and slowly approached Lilah, who had crumpled onto the ground. "No, Walt, I haven't fired my gun while going 'Ah.'"

Walter shook his head, sighing to himself. "Well, that's a shame. Really. I mean, you're missing out." He followed his partner.

)

Lilith had all but vanished from Downtown Middleton. She had retreated deep underneath the now-ruined deli shop and was saved by someone she had not expected. Shane carried the exhausted young woman away in secret, using the shadows, far away from the warzone. She had heard the boy say something about it "being the least he could do," but the words were jumbled and became a series of incoherent, mumbled mess.

Now, she came to rest in a dilapidated house on Middleton's outskirts. The young woman who had become a passenger to the entity known as Lilith, Lynaly, had awakened to the familiar friend sitting across from her . . . and then there was Beth.

)

A gentle clatter of debris shifted above the constant prodding. A small black puff of fur poked its head out. Bright golden eyes surveyed the area slowly, watching, waiting. Chaos, complete and utter chaos, surrounded the little creature that stirred under the weight of tons upon tons. Firefighters, police officers, and local power and gas companies scrambled about. Civilians gazed in awe at the sheer spectacle of their beloved town lying in ruins. It was as if an atomic bomb had exploded in the town square. Cars were strewn about in pieces, halves, and wholes. Buildings were crumpled against the earth that once helped them stand upright. The metal was twisted and still glowed. Water continued to spew up from the town's depths. The little black puff of fur wriggled more, freeing a leg, then her torso, until finally, she stretched out into the chaotic turmoil that had befallen Middleton. Sheila licked her paw. She glanced over at the ruins of Marie's Deli and let out a meow.

"Well, look at that."

Sheila gazed up towards a familiar man who had crouched down before her. "Hey, there, pretty girl." Sheila retracted her ears slightly, sniffing Walter momentarily, then cocked her head at him.

Walter turned back towards Dana. "Look! It's that girl's cat I found—you know, from the other day?" Dana trotted over. "See? Look—" Walter and Dana stared at the empty, cracked sidewalk. "What the—? She was right here."

Dana shifted. "Walt, I think the commotion's finally hit ya." They looked at the ruined sandwich shop. Walter wiped his eye while Dana patted him on the back. "Don't worry, Walt. I'm sure it'll be even better next time around."

Walter looked at Dana with a teary-eyed glance, then roared with laughter. "Had ya going, didn't I?"

Dana shook his head. "You never cease to amaze me, Walt."

The brilliant duo retreated to the old brown sedan. Dana lit a cigarette and stared out the passenger window at the ruins of Marie's. A blanket covered Lilah, who lay unconscious in the backseat, hidden from the rest of the world. Dana glanced back, making sure she was undisturbed.

Thoughts escaped from his now clear mind, and he sighed aloud. *Lynaly . . . Lily.*

It was Walter's turn to give him a pat on the back. "Don't worry, Dana. Next time, I'm sure it'll be better."

Dana shook his head, grinning. "You're an ass. A Grade A asshole." Walter put the car into gear and sputtered away from the chaos. "But ya know what? You're right, Walt."

As the car meandered through the hectic streets of Middleton, Dana couldn't shake the unsettling feeling that it wasn't over.

As the vehicle passed the last stop sign out of the town square, something black caught his eye. As it vanished, he looked ahead, for his eyes were set on tomorrow's future.

EPILOGUE
The Middleton Daily Post

Middleton Remembers "The Cataclysm"
by Mark Sinclair

It has been more than a year since the devastating event that rocked the very foundation of Middleton. City officials released a statement shortly after the event: "Faulty gas, underground electrical lines, and an outdated sewer system resulted in a bizarre cataclysmic event in our peaceful town. Rest assured, we are getting all the aid we can and will be diligent in our beloved town's reconstruction."

The total amount of damages is still unknown but has already been estimated to be billions of dollars. Just months before the destruction of the town square, a catastrophe had already transpired with the dam on the outskirts of Middleton. Whether or not the events were a means to gather money to help renovate and update the town remains shrouded in conspiracy.

Officials, however, state that every step in meeting with insurance, state, and federal regulations is being achieved, and, according to Mayor Chet Bennington, "any rumors and conspiracy theories that point to such acts are sheer fiction and are to be dismissed."

Since the disaster, Middleton has prioritized avoiding such calamities. Prototype technologies are being implemented to monitor, survey, and warn of impending events, including natural disasters, terrorism, and other natural and unnatural incidents. These safety technologies will also be implemented and given to major metropolitan areas nationwide.

The project will also secure Middleton as a prime location for the Broadband for America Project, which has long been delayed due to the lack of government funding.

The catastrophe has also created a surge of jobs, causing the unemployment rate in the area to drop from 5% to unmeasurable numbers. Citizens have jumped on the bandwagon of rebuilding Middleton, and most have a bright and positive outlook on the town's future.

"It has taken some time, but we are the shining, prime example of what community is—where we are all one, regardless of status, race, or religion. We've restored our humble town to its former glory and made Middleton even better than we thought possible," remarked Mayor Bennington.

On a different note, the mayor presented Detective Lieutenants Dana Deupree and Walter Conway the Key to the City in honor of their dedication, enthusiasm, and honorable work in solving the mysterious cases of crime that swept through the city shortly before the catastrophe and in stifling the civil unrest that was beginning to brew at the Nomad's Motorcycle Club, led by Ward "Gigan" Estrada.

Numerous arrests were made after a probing investigation was launched into the Motorcycle Club. The arrested group members were the Dirty Dozen, the Torch Bearers, and the Trinity Avengers. Many cold cases were solved as a result. Detectives Deupree and Conway had closed in on the gang's actions and were staked out at a local motel. Witnessing a brutal attack on an unnamed civilian, Detectives Conway and Deupree sprang into action. According to their official statement, Estrada turned his gaze from the civilian to them and charged at them with a deadly weapon. When Estrada disregarded their warnings, the detectives shot to wound. However, Estrada was on a cocktail of medications and was relentless in his assault, leaving the detectives no choice but to neutralize the threat.

Estrada had been hospitalized before the accident for third-degree burns over 100% of his body as a result of a freak accident at a poker party. It is unknown if he was driven into madness as a result of his condition. After the death of Estrada, the detectives were able to piece together the bizarre deaths of several Middleton citizens. New initiates of the Trinity Avengers had partaken in cruel, unusual initiations that had baffled police officials.

"These guys are great. They really go the extra mile and do their damnedest to ensure they get the job done right," Captain Bradley Branigan of Middleton Police stated. The cases are now closed.

The Middleton Police Department said its goodbyes to Captain Branigan shortly after Branigan retired from his duties. Officer Beatty Oedek has replaced him. The MPD also celebrated the promotions of Detectives Conway and Deupree, who now head the combined Homicide and Criminal Response Division, as well as the marriage of Officer Terra Branigan to Detective Lieutenant Walter Conway. The outdoor wedding occurred at Branigan's estate on October 13, 2010.

"I got to say, it'll be strange to call Walter my son-in-law, but hell, at least I know I got one hell of a guy to protect my Terra and the town," Branigan commented.

Detective Lieutenant Dana Deupree was offered a liaison position in City and Civil Matters in City Hall but declined, stating, "Walter and I, we're bound at the hip. Take one of us away, and then everything falls apart. I honestly couldn't have a better partner. Besides, I'd like to think that my job is on the street, not in a big cushy chair."

Middleton continues to recover and rebuild itself to be stronger than it ever was. These catastrophic events have brought one town closer than one could have been believed.

MARIE'S DELICATESSEN, THE VAULT, CELEBRATES GRAND REOPENING!

By Bill Pogorzelski

Marie's Delicatessen celebrates its grand reopening as The Vault this Wednesday. Last year's events destroyed the establishment famed for its gourmet sandwiches, rich atmosphere, and friendly service.

"I can't believe I'm finally opening its doors back up! It's been hard to serve people in our makeshift center," owner Marie Champagne commented.

Marie's Delicatessen won numerous awards, including Best Sandwich in a Fifteen-Mile Radius and the Greater New Boston Area Award for Superb Service and Sandwiches. They were inducted into the Sandwich Crafters Order, a first in Middleton's history.

The former bank vault, for which the building was named, was the only artifact retrieved from the debris. Due to structural damage from the sewer and gas line breaks, the vault plummeted underground. A salvage crew found a toothpick lodged in the locking mechanism. The vault was successfully reinstalled after the foundation was assured to be safe. The new Vault features an eat-in area upstairs, overlooking the streets of Middleton, and new items are on the menu.

"I'll be hosting a wine tasting and offering free samples of beer and other freebies!" Marie exclaimed. She invites everyone to come to the celebration and try something new or old. See the *Middleton Daily Post* on-site to vote for the Best Sandwich Shop 2011.

MISSING PERSONS

Billie-Jean Jackson: Age: 36 **Sex:** Female **Race:** African American **Height:** 5' 9" **Weight:** 145 lbs. **Hair/Eye Color:** Black/Hazel

Description: Last seen driving towards Providence in a white '92 Chevrolet Impala. Highway Patrol found the car abandoned on the side of the road with the driver's door open.

Charles "Chuck Star" Puckett: Age: 63 **Sex:** Male **Race:** Caucasian **Height:** 6' 2" **Weight:** 215 lbs. **Hair/Eye Color:** Black/Blue

Description: Last seen on I-95 heading southbound, Mr. Star was in route to Atlantic City. Mr. Star's red '89 Ford F-150 was found wrapped around a tree on a desolate, undisclosed dirt road.

Lynaly Sargent: Age: 19 **Sex:** Female **Race:** Caucasian **Height:** 5' 10" **Weight:** 132 lbs. **Hair/Eye Color:** Blonde/Brown

Description: Last seen in town with Detective Lieutenants Dana Deupree and Walter Conway. It was stated she returned home after the detectives found her lost cat.

On the eve of the Cataclysm of Middleton, her family home, where she was staying, was found in ruins. There were no bodies found.

Sargent's uncle and aunt's location is currently unknown. Before moving to Middleton, her parents were slain in their home in Mason, Ohio, during a breaking and entering.

An investigation is still ongoing into the matter of the parent's homicide.

DEATHS

Vacationing Canadians Die in Bizarre Accident

By Michael Sanchirico

What was supposed to be a holiday trip to the States for the four friends turned into a disaster. All four died in a motor vehicle accident on September 9, 2011, on their way home.

Investigators claim the driver, Nicolas Voki, had apparently tried to maintain control of the vehicle when a woodland creature suddenly ran onto the road and struck the side of their rental car. The car flipped violently before crashing into the highway median. Voki and Ydi died on the scene. Costello and Rocco survived the crash. The two were rushed to New Boston Metro Area Hospital, where, later that night, they died due to unknown complications. Their bodies will be returned to their families for burial in Canada.

This is the 73rd report of a woodland creature causing an accident between Massachusetts and Virginia in the past 5 months.

A new interstate monitoring program is being implemented hastily, but in the meantime, law enforcement officials are asking drivers to travel cautiously and to help one another. Dial 9-1-1 if you witness or are the first on the scene of an accident.

The Return of Sheila

DANA FLIPPED THROUGH THE newspaper, jumping from article to article. The sun was high, the air mild, and the sky's pale blue stretched on and on. Sparse clouds floated on high, some dissipating in high noon's glare.

He sighed as he rested his head against the tree trunk in his backyard. Birds chirped and sang, which was a much different tune than explosions. Electric sparks, crimson entwined with pitch-black and putrid green—it all seemed like a dream to him. However, he knew better, for he had lived that dream. He closed his eyes, and everything flashed before them again. One thought kept pressing, urging, nudging him frequently.

Lynaly . . . Lilly. . .

He heard a meow nearby and opened his eyes. A black cat slowly wandered into his yard and crept up to him. Dana put down the newspaper to pat the little black puff of fur. "Well, hello there. I wonder who you belong to." The cat purred as it climbed onto Dana's lap, absorbing her newfound friend's attention. Dana picked up the animal and looked her in the eyes. An eerie sense of familiarity settled inside him, and the cat smiled at his acknowledgment.

"Sheila, where are you?"

Dana snapped his vision to the outcry behind him. He could hear tufts of grass being pressed down, the sound coming closer with each step.

"Oh, there you are, my love."

A little ginger-haired girl appeared in pigtails, torn blue jean overalls, and a tattered orange shirt. She looked to be no older than ten.

"Hey, mister, thanks for finding Sheila!" The girl's big blue eyes beamed with happiness.

"Huh, oh, she's yours?" Dana sighed with relief.

The little girl nodded enthusiastically. "Yep!" Then, there was a long pause. "Well, she's my neighbor's, but I'm just watching her for now. Her house got smashed up pretty good."

Dread returned to Dana like a sack of potatoes hitting him in the face. He swallowed hard, trying to keep cool. "Oh—I see. W-who's your friend?"

The little girl put her index finger on her lips as she thought aloud. "Hum, I can't quite remember her first name, but she's really nice and really, really, really pretty. I think it was Lyn—or something. Can I get Sheila back? I'm sure she's hungry."

Dana nodded and started to hand Sheila up to the little girl. "Well, here you go. Take good care of her."

At that moment, he caught a glimpse of magenta in the cat's eyes. These weren't the persecuting, vengeful eyes that wanted him dead. No, these were sad, brokenhearted. And they were angry, but not at him. Dana received the message and gave Sheila a pat on the head.

I know . . .

The little girl hugged Sheila tightly before trotting off back through the yard. In his mind, he caught sight of a sadistic and malevolent grin under a wooden mask. It wasn't hers. No, this was the grin of someone capable of something far worse.

INTERLOPERS

THE LIGHT OF THE day had already been extinguished. Elsewhere, plans had been set into motion, the turning of the gears of archaic proportions, the ushering of the liaison of destruction. Death was busy—unusually busy. The dilapidated old warehouse in the shipyard was well-lit for this time of the night. The moon bled above yellowed city lights. The stars cried—icy streaks in the abysmal sheet of darkness—in unison with the celestial act that had unfolded below.

Inside the vast shell of a building, windows were boarded up. Debris and trash littered the ground. Assorted holes punctured the roof, allowing a peek of the motion within. A man was busy, occupied with the latest set of interlopers.

The stifling cold had long wrapped around the interloper's body, constricting him like an invisible serpent. He awoke and found himself bound to the wall, stretched limb to limb on a makeshift cross made of scraps of metal and wood. His mouth was stuffed with sweaty rags soaked in God knows what. He was soaking wet but couldn't tell whether it was from blood, sweat, or water. Before him stood a vague shadow of a man, head tilted to the side, peering back with a set of raging, bright-red eyes. The interloper's gaze shifted sluggishly around the room, searching for answers from this . . . intruder. Behind the vengeful wraith lay the twisted and mangled body of a man bathing in a pool of crimson.

The shade spoke deeply, with assurance. "There is no one else here, just us. Well, except for your partner, but I wouldn't exactly be counting on any backup." The silhouette shrugged. "You know how it is—collateral damage."

The interloper's head refused to budge, causing his body to jerk with fear; his nose caught the hint of gasoline. The shade materialized at last. The raging redness of his eyes settled to a cold, deep blue, and his face settled into ease and peace.

The now seemingly gentle man spoke, waving his hand over his hostage's face. "Calm yourself."

A cloud of serenity came over the prisoner. A wooden tribal mask fell to the floor with a light thud, like a drop of rain on the surface of a pond. Long black hair, matted, and mangy. A face of torment and pain—of scars and wounds, past, present, and future. A traitor.

"I tire of your persistent meddling," said the man to his prisoner. "No longer will you be following anyone around, sticking your bothersome nose in matters far beyond what your pathetic, frail mind can comprehend!" He turned to face his victim. "Oh, no." He grinned fiercely, then burst into a gleeful, sinister laugh. "NOT ANYMORE!" He closed his eyes and sniffed the air. "Some big plans are unfurling now, but you already know that, and there is NOTHING, nothing, you or anyone can do about it." He grasped the man's throat and peered deep into the frightened green eyes. "Any last words . . . *Detective?*"

The man shook violently, trying to writhe himself free, grunting with empty pleas. The vagabond leaned towards the grunting man and whispered, "I'll be sure to say hello to them for you, but don't worry—*they* won't be too far behind."

The nomad plunged the blade into the man's gut with a grin and a wink. The starving knife's teeth clawed and pulled at the man's insides. While carving the hapless fool, he jerked the knife—over to the right, then, at last, at a downward angle. The man coughed for a moment, choking on his blood. He let loose a low mutter and groan, following with his gaze the rush of blood that crudely cascaded down onto the floor. As the savage nomad turned to walk away from his latest kill and lit a match, a whisper caught his mind's ear.

"No matter how many times you keep telling yourself you won't, you will die. She still lives, and this time, she will see to it. Oh yes, it will be all the sweeter—your death."

The match slowly fell to the ground, igniting a stew of blood, gasoline, and waste.

"Yes, this time, the real traitor will be betrayed."

The flames rushed with hunger up the base of the cross, devouring the man's feet, legs, and torso.

"Killing the "fodder," as you say, will only fuel the fire that awaits you in Hell! "

The voice trailed off into maniacal laughter as the husk of the man on the cross was engulfed in flames.

The unnerved wanderer picked up his mask and placed it over his face. His chin and lips were still exposed, splatters of blood speckling them. He grinned to himself and closed his eyes, inhaling deep the air that began to rage hellishly behind him.

Atreyu licked his lips. "Hmm, well, I can't wait to see her . . . try."

THE END
. . . for now.

The Lost Chapter

Author's Commentary: This was originally to take place shortly after Lilah faces off against 'Meat,' but we decided to cut it. I also thought it could be something of an off-screen scene. In any case, we wanted to include it. Please, enjoy the deleted scene.

— RJM / AJD

THE NIGHT
6♠6♣6♦

A FEW DAYS HAD passed since the tragedy that befell the Illicit Nomad's Motorcycle Club.

"Eagle" sighed heavily and drained a frosty mug of beer. He set it down on the counter with a dull thud.

Goddamn it. What was I thinking? What the hell was that shit? And that girl . . . Gigan, Krueger, Blondie—all of them dead.

His eyes drifted to the eagle helmet beside him. He rubbed the wings along its sides with trembling fingers. Gigan had given it to him years ago, when Eagle had been promoted for recruiting an obscene number of members in his first year.

He signaled the bartender, who filled his mug to the brim, foam spilling over the lip. All around him, classic rock blared in honor of the fallen. Beer glasses clinked in toast. Some played pool. Some laughed too loudly. Others sat alone, like him, drowning grief in alcohol.

Keggar, the barkeep, glanced over his shoulder while mixing drinks. "You gonna be alright there, Eagle?"

Eagle nodded without conviction. "Yeah, Keggar. Just . . . you know." He dug into his pocket and pulled out a small black box. When he opened it, a delicate tune spilled into the air. A tiny platinum bike spun on its back wheel, keeping time with the music.

He hummed softly along. Inside the lid was an inscription:

To Eagle,
A great member, a great rider, and a great friend.
Always respect the road and your biker brethren.
—Ward 'Gigan' Estrada, INMC Middleton, MA Chapter Leader

Eagle wound the box again, then set it beside his drink.

The lights flickered. He barely noticed—this old bar always had wiring problems. He never thought it might be a warning.

The massive iron doors burst open. A freezing gust swept through, killing the warmth inside. Chairs scraped as men stood, glaring at the intruder.

Eagle turned slowly. His face drained of color. His body shook. He felt like he was staring at death itself.

A girl stood framed in the doorway, pale and unblinking. Her eyes swept across the bar, locking with every set of eyes before fixing on him. Eagle's stomach turned.

One biker stomped forward. "What the hell do you think you're doing here, girly?"

"N—no, don't!" Eagle yelped.

Poker cards fluttered around the girl, glowing with a dull green light. She smirked, her eyes igniting with sickly verdant fire. Her arm rose, cocked and ready like a gun.

"Get her!" someone bellowed.

A single burst of green energy erupted. The bar plunged into chaos.

Patrons grabbed guns, bottles, knives, even barstools. Others bolted for the exits. But the cards absorbed every attack, snapping back into formation like soldiers. One biker was flung across a table, lifeless. Another froze midair before collapsing like a puppet with its strings cut.

She advanced with a cruel grace, spinning as if she waltzed to her own ballad of destruction.

Three bikers rushed her in unison. A fourth crept up from behind with a machete. Lilah already knew the outcome. She laughed silently at their foolishness.

In one fluid motion, she arched back, caught the brute behind her, and hurled him into the bartender. Skull met wall with a wet crunch. Blood splattered in a scarlet spray.

She seized the machete, twirling past the remaining three, opening their bellies with one swift stroke. Guts spilled onto the floor. With a flick of her fingers, three bursts of green energy hurled them screaming into the rafters, where they hung like grotesque trophies.

A female biker squared off, feet dancing in martial rhythm. She spun, launching roundhouse kicks. Lilah deflected them with ease, mocking her with inhuman laughter. The biker lunged with a knife. Lilah backhanded her clear across the room, through the front window. She dangled from the shattered frame like a broken doll.

Gunfire erupted. Dozens of bullets clanged against the wall of swirling cards. Lilah moved through the storm untouched. Blood sprayed. Screams choked out. Glass shattered and beer mingled with the gore on the floor.

And then there was only one left.

Eagle.

He ducked behind the bar, yanked free his twin .45 Magnums, and drew a shuddering breath. *If this is it . . . it's now or never.*

He sprang up, guns aimed—only to find the girl gone. Cold air whispered through the room.

"I–it was all Gigan's idea," Eagle stammered. "I didn't want to go! I didn't want any part of it! He made me! I was just—"

"You were what? Just following orders? Being a good comrade? A good friend?" Her voice echoed from everywhere and nowhere. She emerged from the rafters, eyes blazing. "You hunted me like cheap game and tried to kill me. You are just as much to blame. Now you'll pay for it."

Eagle stumbled backward. "Just let me go, please! I never wanted this!"

"You should have thought of that before."

He edged toward the kitchen door. Slowly, it creaked open. The girl stood waiting, shaking her head.

He tripped over bodies, scrambling for the front. Again, she appeared—smiling, wagging a finger.

"AHHHH!" He fired wildly. The cards snapped into place, blocking every shot.

He dove for cover behind the bar, but searing pain tore through his back. His vision blurred. Warmth flooded down his spine.

In the cracked mirror near the kitchen, he saw the eagle helmet buried in his back, wings jutting grotesquely from the wound.

He wheezed a laugh, blood bubbling on his lips. He fired a final shot, nicking her cheek. A thin red line ran down her face.

"Got . . . y-you . . . bitch."

He collapsed.

The girl loomed over him, cards coalescing into a neat deck in her hand. She planted her boot on his chest, grinning.

"And then there were none."

She stomped. The helmet drove deep into his chest. His dying screech cut off. The music box sputtered, then fell silent.

The lights flickered again. The wind howled through broken glass and splintered wood.

She stepped through the wreckage, boots crunching glass. Outside, the neon sign sputtered before settling into new words:

No . . . More.

Crimson stained the dirt as the girl vanished into the black.

Acknowledgements

Thanks to my friends and family for your ongoing support.

I want to thank the members of Morphine (rest in peace, Mark Sandman and Billy Conway) for their incredible music. We truly appreciate it. Thanks also to Buckethead and many others for their amazing tunes. A special shoutout to Ghost, Priest, Magna Carta Cartel, Avatar, Volbeat, Gojira, Gothminister, and Night Club. Much love to you all!

Blizzard Entertainment for *World of Warcraft* and my *World of Warcraft* friends on the US server Aegwynn and in the Horde Guild, Revolt: you're all demoted to "Village Bicycle." To my friends in the guild Reboot on US-Illidan: please post more dank memes.

With love,

Sincados

Finally, to *you*, our lovely readers.

See you next time. . .

About the Authors

Robert J. McCartney is the author behind *This is Bob* and the ongoing **Willborne Saga**, which includes *Requiem for Lilith* and *Lilah's Guide to Hoyle*. He writes strange and human stories that explore identity, autonomy, and the will to defy fate—often wrapped in dark humor, dream logic, or emotional gut punches.

He lives in Tennessee with his wife, their two children, and an ever-growing backlog of games. When he's not writing or working under his independent label, A.B.Normal Publishing and Media Group, he's probably logged into *World of Warcraft* or plotting the next chapter in his ever-expanding universe.

He also writes an ongoing web series called *The Diary of the Wasteland Bear God.* To read more about Robert's worlds—or to reach out—visit www.abnormalpublishing.com.

Albert J. Debusschere III resides in MI. He likes to write, make and play music, and ponder about society and the nature of the universe.